REFLECTIONS

IN A

DRAGON'S EYE

BALTIMORE PD REFLECTIONS SERIES

#1

Bradley Harper

&

Lydia Galehouse

First edition 2023

ISBN hardcover: 978-1-915221-08-7
ISBN paperback: 978-1-915221-09-4
ISBN e-book: 978-1-915221-10-0

PAPILLON DU PÈRE
PUBLISHING
www.papillon-du-pere.com

iii

Dedications

Bradley Harper

To my mother, who taught me the two most important lessons in my life: that I was worth fighting for—and to love the written word.

Lydia Galehouse

This book is dedicated to Pat Dupuis, who told me about the bookmakers and helped me believe I could be one of them.

Acknowledgment

To Lieutenant (Ret.) Mark Bergin, a wonderful writer and former police officer, who tried his best to help us portray a cop's life in a major US city.

Any residual errors are despite his best efforts.

Contents

REFLECTIONS IN A DRAGON'S EYE

Come not between the dragon, and his wrath.

William Shakespeare, *King Lear*

Who's to say that dreams and nightmares aren't as real as the here and now?

John Lennon

Chapter One

Dec. 31, Monday, 2013 to Jan 1, Tuesday, 2014

K yle Owen "KO" Bannon could remember a time when his hands were faster but not when they'd been warm. The phone's screen lit up. Digits started counting the prepaid minutes, and KO held his breath.

Rrrr-rrrrrr ...

Rrrr-rrrrrr ...

"C'mon, c'mon ..."

Rrrr—"Hello, Amy Sellers."

"Amy—"

There was a click. He thought he'd heard a child laugh in the background.

KO flexed his cold fingers and jabbed the redial. As the wind tore down the street like an icy knife, he hunched against the brick wall of the World Trade Center of Baltimore, tried to clench his teeth without biting his tongue. Shivers racked him from head to toe like a demon trying to get out. Had to concentrate. Had to get this done.

Rrrr-rrrrrr...

"Hello. If this is ..."

"Amy, I just want to call and say Happy New Year 'cause I—"

"Leave us alone, Dad."

Click.

KO remembered another time, a time when he'd come home from training and she'd come running to the door yelling, "Daddy, Daddy!" and they'd pretend to box. After she'd "knock him out," she'd lean over and tap him on the nose with her forefinger three times and say, "I. Love. You." One word with each tap.

Another time.

The wind cut deeper while KO clutched the phone between his hands. The shelter wouldn't let him in drunk, but the whiskey's promise to make the phone call easier was too strong to resist. Now its warmth was gone and the cold, like the dark, was getting stronger, and he wondered if he'd make it to sunrise.

He needed to find a place, fast. A dumpster maybe? He thought of the climb. He could barely move from the cold, and it wasn't even midnight.

KO turned his phone off and stuck it deep into the pocket of the old, lined trench coat, down past crumpled pages of newspaper that served as extra lining. He took three attempts to button his pocket. Couldn't risk losing the phone. With her number on the phone, the police would know who to call if ...

KO stomped his feet as he walked toward the docks. *Can't waste time thinking like that. Not yet.*

There had to be some place he could spend the night. He'd found his social security check in his P.O. Box earlier that day, so he'd gotten new gloves and a burger—blessing the one-dollar menu for a cheap day's worth of calories and a place to recharge his phone. There was still some money left, and tonight was New Year's Eve. Another year nearly over and good riddance, though there wasn't much to hope for in the next.

The Four Roses whiskey he'd bought for the occasion was raw and burned his throat, but it was cheap. Enough of it would warm you up—a bit more would knock you out. Two birds, one stone. He lifted the bottle for his traditional salute.

"Here's to you, Howard ..." A long, slow swig. "Y'greedy bastard."

He slid down the wall until he was sitting on cold asphalt. He squinted at a flashing sign across the street. Well, one part was flashing anyway. O ... C ... PEN? He gave up, and darkness overcame him.

***

Marty had only one thing on his mind, and she was wearing his coat.

"But Marty, we were having so much fun at the club ..."

"It was fun, Carly. It's always fun with you. But tonight's special. It's New Year's Eve. You really want to spend New Year's Eve at work?"

The stink of cheap perfume and sweat followed them out of the club, but Marty hardly noticed. He watched Carly spin and laugh, her sharp heels leaving tracks in the fallen snow. She was skinny but had a dancer's grace. Two years at Juilliard on a scholarship, she'd said. She might have been better off taking a cosmetics course, he thought, given how much rouge she was wearing.

Marty had never had a dancer before, but she was perfect: the right height, hair color, bust. It was almost a new year, and he liked its promising start.

Eventually she skipped back. "You gonna get me in trouble tonight, Marty?" she asked.

"Babe, what fun would it be if I didn't? I'm a rebel. I play by no one's rules but my own."

She took his arm and laughed. "Some rebel you are, Marty," she teased as she grabbed his tie and pulled him close for a kiss. "You're the only guy I know who comes to the club wearing a tie." She released him as their lips reluctantly parted. "So where're we goin', rebel? You finally gonna take me to your special place you been teasin' me about?"

Marty smiled. He was freezing his ears off, but it paid to act the gentleman, so he dropped his hat on her head for good measure, grinning at how it made her look small.

"Tonight's the night, Carly: You and I will be watching the fireworks from the best seat in the house. But pick up the pace. I've got champagne on ice waiting for us."

"Champagne? *Real* champagne?"

"A classy New Year start for my classy lady. None of that fake sparkling stuff."

He teased her curls, then clutched her arm and staggered a little. To anyone watching, they were just another couple looking for a hideaway for that midnight kiss.

Distant music clamored in a frantic drone. Along the dock, yachts bobbed softly on the icy black water. Out in the Baltimore harbor, a few were cruising, waiting for the midnight show. Cabin lights beamed brightly as figures moved back and forth before windows, all too distant, too distracted, to care for the dark of the dock.

The cold, damp air felt like a cold hand on the back of his neck, and while the girl laughed and swept her arms about in joy, Marty kept his face buried in the collar of his cardigan as a few other couples passed in the opposite direction. He wished she wouldn't draw so much attention to them. Someone might remember.

"Right down here, babe. Five ... six ... That one right up ahead's my boat. We'll ring in the New Year in style."

"The one with the carved lady snake in front?"

"That's the one."

"Based on an ex-girlfriend?" Carly said, laughing.

Marty smiled tightly as he gave her a hand up over the gunwale. He drew the other hand across his bottom lip as Carly strode like a dream across the yacht's polished deck. He'd spent the day getting the wood boards to gleam and didn't regret the sight.

"Marty, this is just lovely."

"I call her *Lamia*. It's ... mythological."

"Poetic, huh?"

It was, if you knew anything about mythology. Marty winked at the snake woman before shooing Carly along.

"Hurry up and get inside, babe."

***

A few minutes later, Carly sat in the saloon and sipped a drink Marty had made her before he went below "to prepare the cabin." She felt a little claustrophobic in the close-heated confines after the cold of the harbor air, so she took off Marty's jacket, then eyed the champagne in the bucket of ice on the bar. Cristal. That was expensive, and she liked expensive. Growing up in a double-wide on government cheese and food stamps, she'd had few tastes of it. Dancing was a step up. Sometimes you got drinks out of it, and you certainly got better than food stamps.

Carly frowned as she noticed a thinness to the Scotch. She'd watched Marty mix it himself, all smiles. Letting her eyes roam, she spotted a honey-brown shine in a decanter hiding in the recesses of the bar.

Maybe he was all charm, but sometimes a girl had to look out for herself. She wobbled toward the decanter and frowned, catching herself on the counter.

She was pouring out a glass when her vision began to blur.

"Wasn't even the good stuff," she muttered. She threw back half the glass in one go before she carefully hid the decanter back in its place of honor.

The boat rocked and she felt her head sway twice as much.

Shit. What have I got myself into?

Just then, footsteps thudded on the stairs from the cabin. Marty. His smile had gone crooked. He was dusting his hands the way certain people do when they're pleased with their work.

"Everything a'right, babe?"

Carly let her hand hide the color of her drink and pretended to be looking at the stars. "Lovely," she said.

"You really are."

Carly fought a smile. No sea legs, that was it. Had to be. Why did she always think she couldn't have nice things? Everything about Marty was nice.

"How's your drink?"

"Yummy!" Emboldened, Carly stuck out her bottom lip. "When do we drink the champagne?" she asked. "I've never had Cristal."

"You mean a fine girl like you has never had quality champagne?"

"Finnegan won't stock it at the club. The usual customers are a beer and pretzel kinda crowd."

By now, Marty was back at the bar, slicing a lime for his gin and tonic. The bar knife snagged a little, not quite sharp. "No champagne until midnight, my lady," he said. He spun the knife for show. "Good things shouldn't be rushed. Won't be long."

Again, Carly felt her head start to tilt. The twist in her gut wouldn't leave her alone. She made herself stop looking at that smile and looked back at the stars. She had to think. She'd had Valium slipped into her drink once before. You learned to watch for drugs while working in a bar.

But, no, he'd mixed it right in front of her, hadn't he? And why? It wasn't like she hadn't already ...

Shit.

She told herself to breathe, then carefully set the drink down and headed for the door in the slow, precise way she knew how to do when she was trying to look sober. She aimed for the deck but let herself sway on her bad sea legs. *Can't let him know I know.*

"Where you headed, babe?"

"We'll see the fireworks better outside," she managed without slurring.

She turned on what she hoped was her own charming smile and hung in the doorway 'til he picked up another lime—then she sprang down the deck for the gangplank.

She never made it.

***

The parties out on the water rolled on.

"Damn," said Marty, sucking bloody teeth marks on one hand.

He staggered to his feet as he did so, still clutching the bar knife. He backed into the shadows, looked for movement at the dock, at the water. His breathing was rough, but it was the only sound.

"Damn," he said again, turning the knife, "Friggin' thing can hardly slice a lime."

Now he'd have to clean the deck again.

***

Ten ... nine ... eight ...

As the hands of the clock swung upward, the countdown began and all along the East Coast strangers huddled together in the cold or with family at home to watch the inevitable passing of another worn-out year.

Seven ... six ... five ... four ...

Glasses were filled and passed around. Couples clasped hands and chanted together.

Three ... two ... one ...

Happy New Year! Happy New Year!

"Should old acquaintance be forgot ...?"

In Baltimore, KO was dreaming when thunder rolled like God descending. Lightning flashed many colored. A storm spread over the city and the stars began to fall.

He woke, startled by the blaze of lights and boom of explosions. Cheers carried across the water from private boats. KO lumbered upright, then staggered forward, trying to hear something despite them, something nearer. There'd been ... a splash?

The sky roared again. How could there be thunder and snow? His feet were unsteady on the ice-slicked dock. The world tilted right, then left. His vision was elastic, now stretching, now contracting, right along with his stomach. And the sky—it was all the wrong colors.

KO staggered onward. Then the world turned completely upside down as his foot hit black ice and he fell hard. KO knew how to fall on the forgiving flex of a boxing ring but not the hard, frozen wooden planks of the dock. Red pain burst into the back of his skull, but he'd taken a beating before and wasn't about to cry from a few bruises. Flat on his back, he opened his eyes again.

Above him, the face of a longhaired thing ... a half-woman, half-serpent bared its fangs in the flashing lights from the sky, looking like something emerging from the depths of Hell. Then it began to rain, a rushing dark torrent gushing out on either side of the creature like blood-tinged wings.

KO flipped onto his stomach to flee—

Beneath the serpent's mouth, a pale woman floated in the dark mirror of the harbor, eyes staring but unseeing, mouth frozen in a silent scream as she sank out of sight.

KO's scream wasn't silent, but it was lost in the boom of the fireworks' finale ringing in the New Year. Even Marty didn't hear him as he hosed down the mess on *Lamia*'s deck.

Chapter Two

Jan 1

His name was Mankiller, a name far back in the legends of the Cherokee people. Anyone else and it might have been a joke, but his carved face and coffee-brown eyes didn't encourage jokes. Neither did his reputation. So to everyone in the office he was Sergeant William Mankiller, or just Sergeant.

Except—

"Hey, *Jefe?*"

Detective Maria Esperanza Ruiz, recently promoted from Patrol to Detective in Robbery/Homicide, offered the file again. It was thick and held together with a heavy metal clip. She had to practically stick it under his nose to get his attention.

Mankiller blinked and squinted at it, then at her. "What's this?"

"The report update you wanted: the North Bay Area anyway. I'm working on the South after New Year. I think it'll be another week, no more than that. I'm having trouble deciding on a few of the girls, but I'm sure there are more that match the profile."

The detective unclasped his fingers and took the folder like it was the fiftieth of the day, which it was. He let out a low whistle at the weight. "A couple of these missing persons files go back three years, Ruiz."

"These missing girls look like clones of each other," said Ruiz. "Pretty blonde Barbie dolls, right down to height and boob size." She shook her head. "Girls with jobs. Friends but no boyfriends. All suddenly disappearing without a trace. No goodbye message to anyone, not even their mothers. Bills unpaid. Someone is making that happen; they've either got a basement full of missing girls, or we've got a serial killer with a very precise taste in women."

"And after three years, it's looking bleak, Ruiz," Mankiller admitted. "I'm not arguing with you, but until bodies turn up we can't call it murder."

Ruiz said nothing, tired of a world that saw women as targets. The string of missing women was her first assigned case as a detective, and the file would only grow thicker as she continued to comb the missing person files.

Mankiller flipped the folder open and scanned her typed notes. "As always, you don't disappoint."

Ruiz was the youngest in the homicide division and was determined to show she deserved to be there. Like Mankiller, she'd had to fight for respect coming up through the force, made somewhat easier by her street smarts. She knew she was good, whatever the *Anglos* thought.

Her sergeant let out another low whistle. "Excellent work." He flipped the file shut and handed it back. "You'll be part of the investigation if a body shows up."

"Thanks, Boss."

"You did the work; you should get some credit. Besides, you're the people person." He looked around the office. Lights had gone dark over other desks and cubicles. They stood in a halogen halo. "Speaking of people, where is everyone?"

"Doing what most folks do after midnight on New Year's Day."

"Then what are you doing here?"

"Pete wanted me to make sure you got out of here. You going straight home?"

"What else?"

"No late-night partying?"

Mankiller evened a stack of files and stood to shut down his computer. He waved a dismissive hand as he grabbed his coat and hat. "Nope."

When he looked at Ruiz again, she gave him a slight smile. "You know, my mother's having a big party over at the house. It's probably just getting started. You could come. Dancing, drinking ...."

"No thanks, Detective." He rubbed his neck, stiff from hours at the desk. "I'll see you in the morning, Ruiz." He waved a calloused hand as he headed for the door.

Her smile sagged as she hugged the folder to her chest. "OK, Boss. You're missing out on some fine *Boricua* food. Your loss ..." she said as the door closed.

She turned to go, shivering at the thought of going into the cold, dark night. Alone.

Again.

Chapter Three

Jan 1, Tuesday, 1.00 a.m.

Officer Michael Richardson had been on the force for twelve years. A street cop and proud of it, he knew the people on his beat, and many knew him. He tried to be fair and took his job seriously, so when he saw KO stumbling down the street, obviously upset, he slowed down. Everyone on his beat knew KO as a local legend, and Richardson enjoyed listening to his stories about his glory days in the ring. He wasn't going to let the old boxer freeze to death on his watch.

He pulled alongside KO and rolled down the window when he noticed fresh blood trickling by his left eye.

"Hey, KO, what happened to you? You get back in the ring?"

KO turned, confused by the voice, and saw Officer Richardson.

"Officer," he said, slurring a little, "you gotta come with me! I-I saw a dragon kill a woman ... down in the harbor!"

"Uh ..." Another thing cops on this beat knew about KO was his fondness for drink. "A dragon, you say? Sorry, KO, but I think you need a magic sword to slay a dragon. I'm fresh out." More seriously, he added, "Did that dragon attack you? Looks like you got into some kind of scrape."

KO shook his head slowly. "I saw ... That is, I slipped and fell. That's when I saw the dragon."

"Uh-huh ... I see. How about I take you to the ER over at Hopkins and get you checked out? I think between the booze, the fall, and the cold, you're hurting."

"Ol' Sugar Ray did worse to my head for eight rounds, and I kept standing."

"I'm sure you did," the patrolman said patiently, "but you know, KO, the older we get, the better we were. My car's nice and warm, and so is the ER. Whaddya say? Courtesy of the Baltimore Police Department."

"But the dead lady ..."

"Will still be dead in the morning. I don't want you to be, too. Come on."

KO considered this. Warm sounded pretty good about now, and his head was hurting. He might not make it to dawn on his own.

"Yeah, a'right," KO said at last. "No way to start a new year, dying ..."

"Can't argue with that."

***

A rapid drug screen was negative. The blood alcohol level wasn't life-threatening, and the neurologic exam was normal enough given his intoxication, with pupils of his eyes equal size. A skull X-ray showed a poorly healed old nose fracture, but the skull was intact, and so the big-knuckled, skinny old black man was placed in a quiet corner of the ER to sleep it off. Turning him loose to freeze to death wasn't going to help him or anyone else.

***

By dawn's early light, the blur of Fort McHenry was coming into focus and so was KO, now sobered up from alcohol's fog but not fear's. The image of a bloody dragon with a woman's face looming over a pale body in the dark water remained crystal clear.

A young man in scrubs with short-cropped red hair and a clipboard stuck his head through the curtains. "Good morning, Mr. Bannon. How you feeling?"

KO rubbed his face as he took stock. "My head's a bit sore." He held up his hands, then noted the tremor he always got when it'd been too long since his last drink. "Got the shakes, too."

The man looked back over his shoulder at the people slowly filling up the ER after a vigorous greeting of a new year and checked his clipboard again.

"It says you've got a bottle of whiskey in your personal possessions, Mr. Bannon. That should fix you better than anything I've got here. Anything else?"

It wasn't the most professional advice, but KO had too much of a headache to be shocked. He squinted at the doctor's ID badge and noticed "INTERN" under his name. *Hasn't learned not to say what he's thinking*, he considered as he slid off the gurney. He didn't need a mirror to know what the doctor saw when he looked at him.

"No, Doc. Nothing else. Thanks."

He picked up his jacket and personals, then limped out of the hospital. The pain in his hip reminded him of his fall the night before, his slow progress marked by whiskey sloshing as he made his slow way to a bus stop. It was New Year's Day, and most offices were closed, so he had the bench to himself. He looked at his hands again, hands he had spent years training to be fast and strong but were now weak and shaking. Almost useless.

He could make them still again. It was so easy, the cure in the bottle in his coat pocket, just like the doctor said. He pulled it out and swirled the brown liquid inside, studying how the light reflected off it. He could almost hear it whispering to him, promising everything. Taking more.

He thought of Amy.

He opened it and breathed in the familiar fumes. That smell had been part of him for most of the past seven years. *Here I am, KO, it seemed to say. Your friend. Your lover. Your mother. A warm blanket on a cold night. Just let me in and the pain will go away.*

His hands shook more as the words in his head sang their familiar song. Somehow, it just didn't sing so sweetly this morning.

Maybe that dragon with the dead woman was a vision, he thought. *Maybe it's God trying to speak to me. Like he spoke to Moses at a burning bush. Maybe he's saying I got one last chance.*

His eyes fell on a storm drain in front of the bench. It sang a different song. If he followed that song, Amy might one day take his call. He just had to listen.

The bottle sang its chorus again.

"Nah," he said. "I'm full."

With trembling hands, KO poured the remaining whiskey into the dark drain below his feet, then limped over to a trash bin and put the empty bottle where it belonged.

He squinted through his headache up at the sky. He needed someplace to ride out the storm that had already started. His shaking hands would soon be joined by the rest of his body; the sweats were already beginning.

KO stuffed his hand into his pocket and fingered a small aluminum cross, then pulled it out and eyed the shelter address stamped on it, somewhere in Greek Town. The cross had been pressed into his palm a few days ago but now felt a lifetime away.

"You need help, my son," the priest, Father Tomas, had said, pressing a warm hand against his. "But the first step is up to you."

KO invested some change in a bagel and a bus ticket and, like so many on that bright new morning of a new year, set out on a new path.

***

Mankiller got the call around nine. He'd gone straight to bed but slept maybe four hours, the quiet of the empty bedroom louder than his ex-wife's snoring. Funny, it was five years since they "split the blanket" and he still wasn't used to sleeping alone, so the phone's summons as he sipped tepid coffee was almost welcome.

Almost.

"Feliz Navidad, Jefe."

"Wrong holiday, Ruiz."

"But I got a present for us. A floater. Young woman. You said if a girl who fit the profile turned up, I could handle it."

Mankiller put his mug down and gripped the phone harder. "You think she could be one of our missing girls?"

"Got it in one, *Jefe*. Short height, blonde hair, body type," she cleared her throat, "'ample boobs.'"

"Anything else?"

"Exotic dancer. Found her driver's license and eighty dollars tucked into her right boot. No phone. Name's Carlene Wyatt, age twenty-three. I called her boss this morning. He wasn't happy with me waking him up but said she left the club early with a john flashing a lot of bills."

"Must have been a lot to take her away on New Year's Eve. That's a big tip night."

Ruiz's voice lilted, mischievous. "Voice of experience, Boss?"

"I was plainclothes before they broke the unit up, Ruiz— emphasis on *clothes*. No one ever stuffed a fiver in my belt."

"With your sunny personality? It'd be a 'tenner' at least."

"Very funny, Ruiz."

She coughed.

"What do we know?" he asked, steering the conversation back to business.

"Got the call from Bailey. Some jogger out to honor her New Year's resolution saw the girl in the water."

"Drowned?"

"No, throat slashed. Bailey checked the ID, wants me to get her off his hands in case she's related to the file."

"We'll have to deal with it either way since it's going to our squad, and it's time you got a case of your own. I'll help, and if it turns out to be tied to our missing girls, this could be our big break."

"Anything else?"

He considered. "I'll come in to see what we can find out since I'll have to oversee it anyway. We'll need to talk to the manager again. Maybe surveillance video from the parking lot or inside the club will give us an ID of the john with the fat wallet. See you in an hour."

"Where, Boss?"

"At the morgue, not the office. If I walk in there, I won't get back out until this evening."

"Working stiffs *are* a bit more demanding than dead ones."

Mankiller let that pass without comment. "This'll be your first autopsy, right?"

"Yes, so?"

"So, I should probably be there anyway to teach you what questions to ask." And, Mankiller mused, perhaps be ready to continue if she had to run out of the room.

"As you wish, *Jefe*."

***

The morgue was busier than usual: there had been motor vehicle accidents, bar fights gone wrong, and a domestic dispute settled with gunfire on both sides. If Baltimoreans had a collective New Year's resolution, it was welcoming each New Year with twice the fervor of the last one.

Doctor Hamera kept up with it. Called "the Hammer" (behind her back), she was a five-foot-four, two-hundred-pound ball of energy. Ruiz wondered if it was nature or necessity, but either way the woman never seemed to tire. She bustled about her morgue any hour of the day in her fresh white lab coat, spectacles polished and always, *always* smiling.

She was also the best in the ME's office, and when a detective knew the autopsy could make or break the case, they'd say they wanted it "hammered."

She beamed at Mankiller and Ruiz as they met at reception. "Good morning, detectives, and which of my clients are you here to see, or did you come to wish me a Happy New Year?"

"As much as I enjoy your company, Doctor, only business would get me here today." Mankiller gave Ruiz a pointed nod. "The young woman who was found in the harbor might be tied to some missing girls we've been looking for."

Hamera looked satisfied. "So, you think the perp finally made a mistake and left behind something for us to work with?"

"Pure speculation for now," said Mankiller, "but she fits the profile of the girls we're looking for. What can you tell us?"

"Well, there are two homicides ahead of you." Hamera dramatically looked to her left and right. "But the detectives for those cases aren't here so ..." she made a flourish at the doorway, like she was inviting them into her home, "follow me."

In a long room down the hall, the autopsy tables were arrayed side by side along both walls. The whole place smelled of antiseptic, and in an uncanny way it made Ruiz think of the auto shop her father had owned, efficiently set up with adjacent bays for each vehicle. There the comparison stopped, of course. The bodies on these tables never ran again.

Dr. Hamera beckoned her assistants, then brought Mankiller and Ruiz to a table where a pale green sheet covered a female form. She pulled the sheet down to the collarbone. The pale visage underneath was rigid, and below the face were injuries that made even street-smart Ruiz stiffen.

The pathologist gave a shrug when she noticed. "It's not the worst I've seen today," she said. "The only visible injuries so far are in the neck. We're looking at multiple attempts to kill, based on these jagged edges. This tells me the attack wasn't a planned killing, or at least not a killing *as planned*. Otherwise, the killer would have had a better knife for the job."

Mankiller asked, "What do you estimate as the time of death?"

"Not long ago, less than a day for sure. Since she was found in the water, body temperature and rigor mortis are useless to me. I'll be more certain after I examine her stomach contents and analyze the vitreous humor from her right eye. Still, anything you learn of her movements beforehand will probably be more useful than what I'll be able to testify to in court."

Hamera beckoned the only other workers on the clock, the photographer and the *diener*, the German word for servant, a nod to Pathology's founding in Germany long ago. Stepping forward, he worked quickly with scalpel and scissors, opening the body in a large "Y" from the point of each shoulder and joining the cuts in the middle over the lower breastbone. As he finished the cut down to the pelvis, the smell of alcohol was evident in escaping vapor.

Ruiz's stomach lurched and she swallowed some bile but kept a poker face. Only the lessening of her normal color hinted at the effect the sights and smells of the morgue had on her.

The examination continued with professional efficiency. The diener worked quickly: the internal organs added little to the pursuit of the victim's killer, Hamera explained as they went. The stomach contents were unremarkable, save for a couple of mushrooms, perhaps the remains of a slice of pizza, she guessed.

Ruiz decided it would be some time before she'd have another slice.

Hamera remained beside the table as the work progressed, noting organ size and condition as each was removed and weighed. She called in the photographer, once the skullcap was removed, to document the absence of any acute brain injuries.

"Wait a minute," Hamera ordered after the last snapshot. She pointed to a small collection of blood beneath the scalp at the top of the forehead. "This is fresh. It must have happened around the time of her death. I don't see any pattern, so I doubt a weapon. Probably a fall."

The entire process took less than an hour. Once everything had been examined, Hamera nodded and what had once been a vibrant young woman was packed into a bag and placed into the cooler. The table was rinsed off and made ready for the next occupant.

Ruiz sighed and her stomach gradually unclenched. Mankiller and the doctor pretended not to notice.

"I can't add much more than what I showed you with the external," Hamera told Ruiz and Mankiller. "My preliminary report will list the cause of death as the severing of the right and left carotid arteries and jugular veins. Mechanism of death: exsanguination. Manner of death: homicide. Any questions?"

"None, Doc," Mankiller said. "Thanks for moving us up the line and for the explanation for the jagged edges. If she's one of our missing girls, a botched plan might explain why her body was found this time." He looked at Ruiz with a raised eyebrow, and she nodded.

"Got anything to ask?" asked Hamera.

"Not for you, Doctor," said Ruiz. "I guess I have my work cut out for me."

"You do what you do," Hamera said. "Unless you've got any more questions, I need to see to my other customers."

"It's a start, thanks," said Mankiller, but he didn't look happy.

His usual reaction to everything, Ruiz reminded herself.

***

Outside the morgue, the stink of antiseptic was weaker, and Mankiller blew his nose. He glanced at Ruiz, whose color was coming back quickly.

She did better than I did the first time, he considered and offered her the pack of pocket tissue.

"I don't have a cold."

"Gets the smell of antiseptic out," he explained. She took one, and he crushed his own tissue in both hands. His dark eyes flashed above his hawk's beak of a nose. "Anything new from the club manager? A description of the john, or a video?"

"I doubt we'll get anything more from the manager," Ruiz admitted. "He cussed her out for leaving early but didn't pay attention after that. They were too busy."

"Video then?"

"We're not looking at anything high quality, *Jefe*. The Gold Digger Club isn't what you'd call 'high-class' entertainment."

"Bad Yelp review?"

"Funny you should say that ..." Ruiz pulled a page from a folder and handed it over. "It's on Eutaw Street and has no parking lot. According to Yelp, the girls tend to be either 'too chubby' or 'too skinny' and the place is pretty rundown. Oh, I liked this one: 'Most of the performers are as desperate as the customers.' I bet our victim stood out compared to the other girls, which is probably why the perp chose her. You know the type—thinks he deserves the best."

"Most clubs open around seven. Bailey's the detective on duty then," Mankiller said. "I'll have him follow up at the club tonight."

"Sounds good, *Jefe*. I don't think he'll mind going to a strip club—in the line of duty."

"Show him the Yelp review and he might change his mind." Mankiller passed the page back. "I'll see what else I can put on his plate—we don't want him having too much fun at work."

***

Marty woke just before noon, so distracted and angry with himself that he poured a double portion of Scotch to calm his nerves. It was aged eighteen years and he didn't share it with just anyone. No one when he could help it.

Focusing on the rich, complex blend of smoke and peat was the closest he ever came to meditation. It allowed him to step back and review what went wrong the night before. He could analyze, learn, and improve for the next time.

Last night hadn't gone at all as planned. He'd panicked. No, he'd completely lost it. *Idiot. That's how you get caught.* What had he been thinking, shoving the girl's body over the side? The current would carry it away—but he hadn't done it right. Before, he'd always done it when he was out in the bay with weights attached, never in the harbor, and especially never at the mooring. The body would eventually wash up somewhere. The police would find it for sure, and they were much more persistent in looking for killers than missing girls.

Now he'd have to wait a couple of months before he could play again, and he needed to play again. Soon. The killing this time had been rushed and ... insufficient.

There were two magic moments that he craved the most: the look in their eyes when they knew they were going to die, and when they did. That sacred instant when they went from being a person to a thing, a limp piece of meat decaying from the moment their heart stopped ... Marty had no faith in God, but watching the light die in a person's eyes was a sacrament. In that brief moment, he was God, with the power of life or death—and he always chose death.

All that preparation wasted.

Marty ran the vacuum a second time just in case, nursing his hangover and grumbling at his idiocy. The cleaning ritual was calming. Vacuum. Wipe down. Disinfect. Everywhere the girl had been was suspect.

On the way back to his place near Camden Yards, Marty threw the vacuum bag into a dumpster, followed by the burner phone he'd lifted and wiped clean. He broke its SIM card in half further down the street and dropped it down a sewer grate.

Done. Clean.

Half an hour later, he tossed his keys into their bowl by the door at his condo and kicked back to watch a college bowl game. He cracked open a beer and grinned at a touchdown. At least this part of his routine was still on track.

"God bless America."

Chapter Four

9:00 a.m.

Father Tomas was far from his native Democratic Republic of Congo, but God's lost sheep were scattered to the four corners of this unhappy world and his search for them led to Baltimore. At five foot two and 115 pounds, Tomas's clergyman's garb made him look like a raven, fitting for Baltimore, but his thick prescription lenses were definitely owlish. Normally soft-spoken, he lit up with fire when speaking of God's mercy. He had witnessed that mercy in many lives, starting with his own—the ragged scars beneath his black shirt reminders of how far God's grace had healed him on the inside.

When KO appeared at the entrance to St. Roch's Men's Shelter, Father Tomas could have easily recited the man's life story, for it was the same as those filling the shelter's dormitory at night and soup kitchen by day. There were only so many variations on the theme: men without family—by tragedy or rejection—and lost. Some unexpected event had turned life into a downward spiral that drink or drugs accelerated. The result was a loss of self-respect, and the whole self soon after.

But there was something different about KO. Something promising about how this man looked him in the eye and told the priest he had once been a man of dignity and was determined to be so again. His face had been recently washed, his shoes neatly tied, and his jacket buttons properly lined up. Small things perhaps, unremarkable in most places, but these simple actions told the priest the man still remembered what it was like to be part of society.

A good sign. It was always easier to lead someone to a place they'd been to before.

Father Tomas also noted how the man took short steps, not shuffling, but never lunging, always keeping his feet centered beneath him, keeping his balance. When he learned the man had been a boxer, he understood why: here was a man always ready to dodge a blow—or take one if required. Surely life had landed him several.

Father Tomas could also tell by the shaking hands and the fine glisten of sweat on his forehead that the man was in the early stages of alcohol withdrawal. In many a case, a man would spend one night, then, racked by a brain screaming for the release of drink, return to the streets and their familiar pain.

Pain was an odd thing. Father Tomas had been as great a sinner as many of them. Worse than most, in fact. Alcohol had never been his weakness, but pain he understood. After a time, pain became your only true companion and defined how you saw yourself.

KO's darting eyes, shaking hands, and obvious distress were classic signs of the struggle Father Tomas had seen many face—and most fail—before. A counselor had once explained to him that alcohol was a depressant, so over time the brain made more chemicals to stimulate the brain to its natural balance. When the alcohol was removed, the stimulus was unchecked, and like a racecar without brakes, it would run at full speed until balance was regained.

KO was still in the early stages of this ordeal, with far worse yet to come. As with many who'd come before him, Father Tomas resolved to accompany the man on the journey.

If he had the will to complete it.

Father Tomas noticed KO holding a familiar aluminum cross in his right, trembling hand. "Are you Catholic, my son?"

The cross flashed between clumsy fingers as KO said, "No, Father, but I'm a sinner. That good enough?"

And, of course, it was. For every sheep seeking to return to the fold.

Father Tomas showed KO around as he led him to his office. "You are in good company here," he said, "but St. Roch's is more than a shelter from the cold. Tell me what you need, my son."

"I need to get sober, Father, and stay that way. Then I need a job. I need my life and family back." KO looked directly into the priest's eyes, a challenge. "Where do we begin?"

Tomas smiled, then sniffed sympathetically. "Perhaps we can begin with a shower and some clean clothes? As for a job, you can help around the shelter, once you are able. First, we must take care of you."

"Can you help me get sober?"

"Yes, if you have the will to endure it. You have a very painful trial before you, my son, and I cannot be with you every moment, but I will assign someone to stay with you when I am not. We will not leave you alone in your darkness— if you are truly ready to face it."

KO bowed his head, aware of the burden the small man had accepted without hesitation. "And after?"

"We have an AA meeting here every evening at five, before dinner. I'll speak to them about you joining them once you are ready."

"Will they take me, Father?" The question made KO feel small.

The priest reached into his pocket. "Of course. All are welcome who come with a humble heart and desire to regain control of their life. To start, take this." He pulled out a green poker chip.

KO eyed the offered chip suspiciously. "What's this for? A card game tonight?"

He placed the chip into KO's right palm. "No game and it's not a gamble, though you and I are playing for high stakes."

"What stakes?" KO turned the chip in his fingers. It was heavier than he expected.

"That's your sobriety chip," the priest explained. "Whenever you want a drink, hold onto this chip and remember your promise to God and yourself."

KO swallowed, his throat dry. This priest trusted him that much after only a few minutes? He searched the man's face, looking for any sign of rejection, but Tomas's expression was calm and open.

"I've never tried to stay sober before ... If I wasn't drunk, it was only because I ran out of money. Guess I didn't think I was worth the effort. You think I can do it, Father?"

"If you can't, you must promise to give the chip back before you break your word. Do you agree?"

KO weighed the chip, then curled rough fingers around it and nodded. "Father," he stuck out his other hand, "you've got a deal."

They shook on it. More warmth. KO thought he could get used to this. He wanted to try.

***

That night, KO felt like ants were crawling over him and got little, if any, sleep. The image of a floating woman glowing eerily amid fireworks reflecting off dark water appeared whenever he closed his eyes. He saw the lights of the flashing sign, too jumbled to make out. "*COPE* ...?" Maybe he needed to cope.

And then the dragon returned, vomiting blood, and KO sat bolt upright on his cot, heart pounding, before he rushed to the toilet to expel the burning bile.

Father Tomas had assigned another man, Gerry, in the bunk bed above him, to watch KO at night. When KO bolted from his bed, Gerry lay in his own bed for a few minutes until it was clear his charge wasn't coming straight back. He got up and stumbled from the dorm to the bathroom, finding the man collapsed on the floor. His arms were wrapped around the base of the toilet in a weak but desperate embrace.

"KO? You alright?"

"Not yet," KO managed to croak. "Help me back?"

Once he fell into bed, KO found the cross stashed under his pillow and clasped it tightly as he shivered.

What was this beast in his vision? A demon? A warning? He wanted a bottle more than he wanted another breath while fear whirled inside his chest like a trapped bird trying to break free. He needed something to take it away, and a bottle had always done it before. He pulled the green chip from under his pillow, held it tightly with the cross, talismans against the cruel thirst.

Not this time, he told himself. Not today.

"Help me become a better man," KO prayed, clasping his hands tightly.

Gerry patted his shoulder in support and murmured, "Amen."

"Show me how, Lord," KO pleaded. "Show me the path and give me the strength to walk it."

Chapter Five

Jan. 2, Wednesday

The next morning, Mankiller found Detective Bailey waiting for him in Mankiller's office. Pale, overweight, and dropping donut sprinkles on the floor, he made a grand gesture with his breakfast of bright carbs as his superior took his seat.

"Morning, Sergeant. I ever tell you you're the best boss I ever had?"

"You're in a fine mood this morning. I take it your trip to the strip club was ... revealing?"

"Good one," he mumbled, his mouth full of glazed pastry. "I think I've found my future third ex-wife. She's very upfront as to what she wants," he slurped some coffee, "and her front ain't too bad either. Hell, we even have the same taste in tattoos. Anytime you want to send me back, you know, 'undercover,' just say the word."

Mankiller looked at the moist donut fragments spreading across his desk with mounting despair as they flew from Bailey's mouth. "You actually do any work while you were there, Detective?"

Bailey wiped his mouth on his jacket sleeve, oblivious to Mankiller's glare. "Oh, yeah, that. Of course. Sorry, bad news there. The club's video is on a four-hour loop. If someone assaults one of the girls, the tape is copied onto a DVD and turned over to the police. Otherwise it's copied over again and again."

He dunked the last of his donut before continuing. "Your john was gone before the club closed around 2 a.m., so there's nothing with him on it."

Mankiller sighed. "OK, thanks for trying." He reached for his waste can and made a show of sweeping crumbs into it before looking up. "Anything else?"

"No, Sergeant," he said, winking as he rose. "I'll be sure to invite you to the wedding!"

Bailey nearly collided with Ruiz as she appeared at the door, bowing her in before striding out.

"What was that all about?" Ruiz asked, two folders in her arms.

Mankiller sighed. "Romance, I think." He placed the trash can back on the floor. "Bailey's visit to the club helped his social life, apparently. The investigation? Not so much. No video of the dancer's date. You got anything useful for me?"

She gnawed her lower lip. "Maybe. I went over the field reports from Central District since 10 p.m. New Year's Eve until 2 a.m. the following morning. I found one from a beat cop saying a drunk claimed to see a woman killed by a dragon down by the harbor."

"A dragon? That should keep the sketch artist busy."

"Yeah, I know. The cop didn't take him seriously either because the man said he'd fallen and hit his head. Between that and the booze, the uniform decided to take him to Hopkins for an eval and keep him from freezing to death. The drug screen and other exams were negative, so they let him sleep it off and then released him. No fixed address, just a name: Kyle Owen Bannon. I met him when I was still on the beat, and we all knew him as "KO." He struck me as a kind man. Sad though. He used to be a well-known prize fighter and now he's a homeless has-been."

Mankiller rubbed the back of his neck. Ten minutes into the day and a headache was already creeping up on him. "So, what's the punch line? Why are you telling me this?"

"Because we have a man who claims to have seen a dead woman at the right time in approximately the right area the dancer was killed. Want me to try to find KO and see what he remembers now? Right now, it's the only lead we got."

"I have to agree. I doubt we'll be arresting a dragon for the murder, but maybe, just maybe, he saw something that made it through his booze-soaked brain we can use, though God help us if we ever need to place him on the witness stand."

Ruiz slid one of her two folders on his desk. "Here's the addendum from the Hammer on the girl's autopsy."

Mankiller wagged his finger. "Rookie detectives haven't earned the right to call her that. Until I tell you otherwise, it's Doctor Hamera to you, got it?"

"Sorry, Boss. Doctor Hamera it is."

Mankiller fished an Excedrin out of his top desk drawer. Ruiz noted the bottle was the large economy size and nearly empty.

"Give me the executive summary," Mankiller said, "but I warn you, if you tell me dragon scales were found on the body, I'll take this whole bottle."

"There was no water in the lungs, *Jefe*, so the victim was dead before she hit the water. Preliminary blood tests show a blood alcohol level slightly above the legal limit for driving and something else—probably Valium. The exact level won't be available for a few days, but screening toxicology was strongly positive, so the final report should show high levels."

"Finally, something useful. Looks like our perp drugs his victims before doing whatever he usually does to them. We can't say what that is from this case as everything points to a rush job. If there's as much drug onboard as the good doctor thinks, then he doesn't give it to them in public to avoid drawing attention; only once he's in a secluded place where he's in control."

"Makes sense to me, Boss."

"That's why I make the big bucks, rookie," he said, almost smiling before his headache reminded him it was still there. "Good luck finding our dragon hunter. For the moment, he's all we got."

Ruiz nodded and left Mankiller alone with his building migraine.

"Probably a waste of time, arresting a dragon for homicide," he muttered once she'd gone.

Still, this "KO" was his only lead for now. He wouldn't take long to find. Drunks were predictable: they had favorite handout and crash sites and during the winter stayed close to a reliable source of warmth, so this has-been boxer wouldn't wander far ... Likely, he had nowhere left to go.

***

At St. Roch's Men's Shelter, KO was lying listless in bed—his stomach empty but the thought of food repulsive—when Father Tomas came by, blinking through his thick lenses.

"Good morning, my son. I hope you slept well?"

"Sorry, Father," KO said. He still stumbled over the title for a man nearly twenty years younger but nodded respectfully. "I ..." He tried to sit up, groaned weakly, and lay back down. "I saw something in the harbor on New Year's night, and it won't leave me alone." He paused. "Do you believe in visions, Father? That God talks to us directly?"

"I would not be a priest if I didn't." Father Tomas pointed to the sobriety poker chip KO clutched in his hand. "You might say I've bet everything on that belief."

"Good. Because I saw a dragon and a dead woman that night."

Father Tomas frowned. "You mean, in a vision, my son?"

"Maybe …" KO shuddered. "My mind tells me there ain't no dragons, not in Baltimore, anyway. But I saw something. Best I can figure out, God's offering me one last chance to get it right before some demon or dragon comes after me. I'm gonna take that chance. What happens after I do my part is up to Him."

Tomas knew that hallucinations were not uncommon when someone was weaning away from the poison they'd used to dull their pain. Tomas thought of it as the Devil trying to scare the sinner off the path to redemption.

"Now is not the time to speak of visions, my son, nor dragons. We must heal your body before we can explore your soul. Rest for now, as best you can. I will tell the cook to lay aside some food for you, whenever you feel ready to take it. Be sure to drink plenty of water in the meantime. We must flush the toxins out of your body so that you can return to the abundant life promised us all."

KO nodded and turned sleepily onto his side. "OK, Father. Day two. How long will this take?"

"Two to three more at least, my son, if you can take it. I'm afraid the worst is still to come. I'll have Gerry summon me when your crisis comes."

"Crisis? When will that be?"

Tomas touched the old fighter's shoulder softly. "You'll know."

***

Marty was usually the first one in the office, and today was no exception. He strode into the building with his hand bandaged from Carly's parting gift. The bite had started to throb within hours, and he'd had to go to an urgent care clinic to get it cleaned out, dressed, and shot with antibiotics. He'd taken the dull bar knife and slashed himself to hide the bite marks and blamed his injury on an accident as a New Year's party bartender. Given the number of alcohol-related accidents they'd already treated that day, his story didn't raise an eyebrow.

Bitch, he thought as he fumbled with his keys to enter the building. But then a vision of the look in her eyes beneath the fireworks' glare as her life left her came back and he felt a little better.

Almost worth it.

With his damaged hand in one pocket of his blazer, Marty turned on a smile at any ground staff he passed. He knew people acted twice as busy when he flashed his teeth, something between a grin and a snarl, which was why he did it.

Marty liked spending money, but he also liked making it— at least until he had enough to find a better life elsewhere. As usual, he'd arrived two hours before the markets opened to read the forecasts, looking for any news that might move the public toward one of the two poles of financial gravity: greed or fear.

His secretary Gladys—whom his father insisted on calling his "Executive Assistant"—set the paper down with his coffee, and Marty quickly scanned the story of a woman's body found in the harbor two miles from the dock. He let out a long slow breath when he read where the body had been found. The article said there were no suspects, and Marty smiled with less of a snarl this time. *Locked doors from now on*, he considered. *Cast off for good measure*. He'd have to make sure the girl couldn't run once he had her alone.

You live, you learn. Gladys shut the door, and Marty grinned at the page. *But first you gotta live.*

***

38

Around ten in the morning, Ruiz stuck her head into Mankiller's office to report.

"I told the beat cops to keep an eye out for KO. I looked him up on the internet and found out he once went up against Sugar Ray Leonard as a middleweight."

Mankiller looked up from his reading. "Being a boxer at that level makes him potentially dangerous, Ruiz. He got a record?"

"Nothing serious. Mostly just loitering, panhandling, and public intoxication. I doubt he'd kill our floater then report it."

"Some might, to avoid suspicion. What's that 'mostly' about?"

Ruiz checked her file. "About three years ago he got into a fight with three frat boys. He said they tried to steal money from a homeless woman ... Some sort of initiation, I think. Probably preparing them to be politicians. Anyway, he whipped their asses, and the frat boys wanted to press charges against him for assault but Louis Grange was his public defender. You remember Lou?"

Mankiller did. "What'd the old fox do this time?" he asked, smiling despite himself.

"Told the losers that everyone would read about how one old black man had taken on these three rich white boys and left them all flat on their backs—and their friends would never let them forget it. Anyway, KO spent the night in jail before being bailed out by a Mrs. Amy Sellers, his daughter, who lives here in Baltimore. He wound up doing one month's community service and six months' probation for disturbing the peace."

"Any witnesses to his act of chivalry?"

"Just the woman."

"Assuming she wasn't lying. Could've been threatened."

"You're such a cynic sometimes, *Jefe*."

"Frat boys do any time?"

Ruiz snorted. "Not a day. Their daddies could afford their own lawyers."

"So now you know why I'm a cynic. As the Romans would say: *res ipsa loquitor*. 'The thing speaks for itself.'"

"Ooh, I suppose if you're a philosopher *and* a cynic. That's fine."

"The cynics *were* philosophers, Ruiz." Mankiller shrugged. "The benefits of the GI Bill and a liberal arts education."

Ruiz shut the file with a little snap. "All right, Socrates, I'll give you that one. Still, he's our first lead."

"Then the sooner we find him, the sooner we can move on to someone sober. Let the beat cops worry about searching the streets."

Ruiz sighed. It was no secret Mankiller had a low opinion of drunks. She looked out the windows and noticed the dark clouds. "You know the weather guy says snow for the next few days," she said. "No one's gonna be driving, much less sleeping, out in this. KO might go to a shelter before the city shuts down."

"So checking the beat's a waste?"

"I've got a growing list of shelters. I can stay nice and warm calling them from here."

"Good idea. He may have taken the pledge long enough to sit out the storm. Let me know when you find him."

Ruiz smiled as she walked out. At least he'd said "when," not "if."

At her desk, Ruiz pulled out her contact list of shelters and struck gold on the third try.

The voice at the other end confirmed a Kyle Owen Bannon had been registered at the shelter since the day before, but he couldn't come to the phone at present. Would she like to talk with the director?

She would.

"Father Tomas," a soft voice said.

"Good morning, Father. My name is Detective Ruiz, with Robbery/Homicide. I'm looking for a Mr. Kyle Owen "KO" Bannon. I understand he's a resident at your shelter for the moment. Can I speak with him? The man who answered the phone said he was unavailable."

"He was correct in both instances, Detective. Mr. Bannon is here, but he will be unavailable for at least the next two to three days."

"Mr. Bannon may be a witness to a murder I'm investigating, and I really need to talk with him before any evidence is lost or destroyed."

There was silence on the other end for a moment, then a sigh. "I will have to take it on faith you are who you say you are. Mr. Bannon is struggling with his long-term addiction to alcohol, and he is now in his second day of purging his body of its physical addiction. The emotional process, as I'm sure you know, will be lifelong."

"Can he talk?"

"Oh yes, he can talk. But he talks about dragons and dead women, and I doubt you'd find it very useful."

It was her turn to sigh. *So near, yet so far.* "Look, I know you're not a doctor, Father, but I'm sure you've seen this kind of thing before. How soon do you think I might be able to get a straight story out of him, minus the dragon?"

"Today is Wednesday. I think Saturday at the earliest."

"Damn—Oh! Forgive me, Father, I mean ..."

She heard soft laughter on the other end. "If that is your worst sin today, my child, you may skip confession tomorrow."

"Thank you. For the information, I mean. And well, the forgiveness too. I'll talk to my sergeant and get back to you."

"Very well. I will await your call, Detective."

Ruiz nodded to her poster of Justice Sonya Sotomayor before leaving her cubicle to give her boss the semi-good news: she'd found the witness—although he was, at least momentarily, a madman.

Chapter Six

Jan. 3

"What's the status of your double homicide, Bailey?" Mankiller asked at their weekly squad huddle on Wednesday mornings

"Plea bargain, Sergeant. The assistant DA wasn't happy, but he was overruled. They've got a backlog just like everyone else. Our perp was looking at a possible death sentence, so when his lawyer offered up a guilty plea for life without parole, the DA took it." He checked his watch. "I'm due in court in an hour for the robbery gone bad, so I'll need to leave right after this."

"How about the floater, Ruiz?" Mankiller asked. "Anything to add besides dragons?"

"No dragons sighted, *Jefe*. I'm going to question the manager at the club some more this morning. He couldn't give up all the employee records because the accountant was out of town or something." She threw a suspicious eye at Bailey and added, "What's your impression of him, Bailey? He hiding anything?"

Bailey grinned. "I might not be the best to answer on the grounds—"

"That you're guilty of distraction?" Ruiz finished for him. Bailey's grin morphed into a smirk, and she added, "In other news, after I speak with the manager I'll drop in on the victim's roommate, see what she can tell me about the mysterious boyfriend. If I can find a picture of the girl with him, we'll be home free."

"And I think the proper response to that is *buena suerte*, Detective," Mankiller said without hope.

"*Gracias, Jefe*. I could use some good luck about now."

"We all could."

***

Lloyd Finnegan, owner and manager of the Gold Diggers Gentleman's Club, was a big man with big shoulders and a frown to go with them. He scratched at five o'clock shadow when he opened the back door for Ruiz that afternoon, then squinted in the glare from the piled snow. He looked unsure as Ruiz showed her badge but waved her inside. She was barely five foot two and one hundred and ten pounds; he didn't know cops came that size.

"Where's the other guy?" he asked. "The one making eyes at Lori?"

"In court," Ruiz said. *And regretting it.*

"I'll get the list."

The walls of the Gold Diggers Club wore nicotine like another coat of paint, a brown reminder of the days when smoking indoors was still allowed and was often used to obscure. A testament to how little Mr. Finnegan invested in his establishment. There was a thin film of dust on the ceiling fans and a stickiness to the floor that crackled as they walked. Around the stage, chairs were stacked up on tables. A mop bucket stood moldering close by, tinging the air with the smell of stale beer, and Ruiz wondered if the water was ever changed.

As they crossed the floor, her eyes scanned the sad little theater where illusions were sold by the drink. Her steps slowed as they passed booths with couches built back into the walls, half-hidden by curtains. Her stare lingered; the curtains suggested more private forms of entertainment.

"Totally legitimate, Detective," Finnegan told her, keeping his eyes fixed forward with long practice. "I tell the girls what kind of business we're running."

And I didn't ask. She pulled out a notebook and pen and made a note to herself about the secluded couches. You never knew when you had to come back with a warrant.

Finnegan led the way to a closet of an office, where he picked up a manila envelope. He shook it open and rifled through several pages inside.

Ruiz took a few more notes. It didn't matter if there wasn't much to go on. A pen in hand during questioning had two possible effects: it either got people talking or made them more careful. She'd learned to read either reaction. Everyone was a suspect until a case was closed.

"How many dancers work here?" she asked.

"Twelve or so, when I can get them to work," Finnegan said, still checking pages. "Turnover's pretty high. They might call in to quit. Sometimes they just don't show up. I put an ad out and get another one."

"What about Carly?"

"She'd been here nearly a year. Was one of my most popular girls—blondes usually are. Thought she was something, she did. Said she went to Julliard."

"You didn't check?"

"I don't give a damn about diplomas, Detective. Just the date of birth and a drug test."

Finnegan seemed satisfied with the pages and taped the envelope shut.

"Anyway," he said, passing it over, "like I told the other detective, I never saw her big-spending boyfriend clearly. But I can say he didn't fit the usual clientele."

"Oh?"

"Well, you'd think he could pay for better company." Finnegan held up his hands as Ruiz's pen paused. "I'm just saying it like I saw it: Brand clothes. Brand watch. Hundred-dollar haircut. Purple silk tie. He'd buy a drink for the seat, but soon as she was off the clock, they were out. Never looked like he touched it."

"Did Carly ever skip work with him before?"

"Nah. But that night, she said she needed a smoke in the back. Next I knew, she'd clocked out and they'd both disappeared. I'd have fired her ..."

"If she hadn't been murdered?"

Finnegan only shrugged.

Ruiz weighed the envelope in one hand. "And this is everyone working that night?"

"I keep good records. No one's going to accuse me of anything," Finnegan said pointedly.

"Are any of your workers friends?" she asked.

"Jan Trudy was Carly's roommate. They'd beg me to keep them on the same shift. Let them leave work together. New Year, Jan worked a double just to get the early train. She's in that envelope too." He sighed. "Anyway, I gotta meet the plowman in an hour, Detective. You need anything else, let me know."

"There've been a number of disappearances in this area," Ruiz said as she tucked the notebook away. "Tell your girls to be careful."

"They know. If they don't, it's on them. They can be replaced."

"Thank you for your cooperation, Mr. Finnegan."

"No problem, Detective. By the way, if you ever get tired of playing cop, I could probably work you into the schedule." He looked pointedly at her chest. "Some men like 'em small."

Ruiz had plenty of experience with this kind of BS from her days on the beat and looked pointedly at his crotch. "But not many women."

It took all her willpower to turn away without waiting for his reaction and to restrain a fist pump as she strolled out the door.

***

Back in her car, Ruiz tapped her notebook on the steering wheel and took a few breaths. In a world of several billion people, you inevitably ran into assholes, but it never got easy. If there was a zoo for them, Finnegan would get his own cage, an image that brightened her day. She counted to ten and let out a sigh, and then called Mankiller to share her lack of progress.

"What do you think, *Jefe*?"

"The roommate's next," he said. "See if she can remember a name or something useful. You're the—"

"I know ... the people person."

"Right, we'll go from there."

"Mm-hm."

"Unless you want to check up on our dragon-spotter?"

"Mmm."

"Well, don't make me be the funny one, Ruiz."

Ruiz glared at the phone and felt her frown lighten a little. "Sorry, Boss," she said. "That guy really got under my skin. You'd think there'd be some respect for the dead."

"Women like Carly hardly get any respect when they're alive."

"Yeah, I know. It's just ..."

"What?"

"Never mind. I don't have the words, *Jefe*, at least not polite ones."

"And that's stopping you?" Mankiller asked seriously. "I've heard you curse in—is it *three* different languages now?"

That got a little smile. She appreciated it.

"I'll never get used to it."

"Not something you'd want to, Detective."

"I guess not." That helped the smile. "See you soon, *Jefe*."

Ruiz hung up and then pulled on her seatbelt before punching Jan's address into the GPS and setting out.

At least one guy gets it, she thought. *Wonder if you realize how rare you are, Boss.*

Chapter Seven

Jan 3, cont.

Jan Trudy, Carly's former roommate, lived in a brick apartment building not far from work. At midday, the building resembled a hollowed-out skull. The windows were dark and the outside halls and stairways were pale and bare, stained with mildew and rust. It had seemed to glare at Ruiz from across the gravel parking lot.

"I should have known something was wrong," Trudy said.

"Don't blame yourself."

"I do, though."

In a two-bedroom apartment that smelled of instant ramen, Ruiz perched on the edge of a sofa that had seen better days. Once again, she kept her pen and notepad at the ready.

To her left, an armchair was piled high with clean laundry. From the look of things, Trudy had been folding it when Ruiz knocked on her door. Now Trudy sat beside the coffee table, folding an Adidas T-shirt. She was a thin, fit young woman with dark eyes and close-cropped hair. It was her day off from her second job, she explained, as if apologizing for her sweats. Her dark eyes were red-rimmed, haunted, brimming tears.

"You don't really think of it," she said. "It was only a couple of weeks. She didn't even drop his name, just say, 'Sorry, Jan, I gotta date.' She said I'd meet him someday if she got lucky."

She stopped to sniff and reached for the tissue box. Ruiz nudged it closer and wrote down what she could. There wasn't much, but Doc Stevens, the psychologist who worked with them sometimes, had told her about another benefit of taking notes: it reassured people, proved you were really listening.

"We didn't find a cellphone," Ruiz explained, "so anything you can tell us can help. Really."

"Okay."

"When did they start dating?"

Trudy drew a shuddering breath. "Maybe four, five weeks ago. First, she said she was meeting a friend, but, you know, she'd grin when she said it. I figured she'd tell me eventually. It's not like she'd had a lot of boyfriends. She was pretty picky, you know, in a good way. I mean ... Goddammit ..."

"Did she ever show you a picture? Maybe on her phone?"

Trudy shook her head. "She said he didn't like pictures. I mean, how stupid can I be?"

"It's okay," said Ruiz quickly. "Your manager, Mr. Finnegan, he said this man came by on New Year's Eve."

Trudy nodded shakily. "I saw him. I mean, the club's pretty dark, so Carly would tell me if he was there. But you don't pay attention when you're supposed to be dancing— better not to, really. I did see him briefly when they left, from across the room."

"What do you remember?"

"White, tall—taller than Carly. Dark hair, kinda short—I don't know, brown or black. He had a nice suit and a purple tie, silk, I think. I remember that 'cause no one wears a suit and tie to the Gold Digger."

"Anything else?"

"Yeah, he wore one of those long detective coats, the hat too. As they were going out the door he gave her the coat, and I thought, 'Okay, he's a gentleman, no worries,' you know? I mean ..." She shuddered.

"Would you recognize him if you saw him again?"

"Maybe. It was dark in the club. And some guy was trying to get up on the stage. The bouncer and me had our hands full." She shrugged. "I mean, I'll testify. Really, I'll do anything if it'll help."

Ruiz took a few more notes. "How often would they go out?"

"Sometimes she'd ask someone to pick up her shift. She was a doll, though, always made sure I had someone to walk me home, 'cause it discouraged Finnegan from offering us 'side jobs.'"

"What do you mean?"

Trudy sniffed again. She looked anywhere but at Ruiz, her eyes falling on the laundry, the kitchen. *Chores to do*, Ruiz thought. *I'm using up her time, but she's gonna do what she can.*

"I don't know if it helps ..." Trudy began.

"Better more details than fewer, right?"

Trudy nodded. "Okay, so Finnegan's a bastard. I mean, he's not exactly managing a casino in Las Vegas. He knows how much we get paid and has a good idea of our tips. He makes our schedule, so ... Sometimes he'll corner one of us before we leave a shift."

"What for?"

"To ask if we want to make some extra money. I always say no, and he drops it. Not everyone says no though, but no one talks about it. And I noticed they tend to get their name on the schedule more, get better shifts, the ones with more tips. Not always, but I'm kinda thinkin' ..."

"What?" asked Ruiz, maintaining her objective air but knowing already. *Bingo.*

"He's trying to pimp us out," Trudy snorted. "Wouldn't put it past him. Anyway, Carly got this idea. Said we should all walk home with someone. You know, witnesses. And they could say, sorry, someone's waiting for them, and not get crossed off the schedule. Pretty sure Finnegan didn't like that. He didn't like Carly, really. Maybe 'cause she went to

Julliard." She looked suddenly worried. "You're not going to tell him I said anything?"

"It's confidential."

"Yeah, sure. Um ... I mean, that's why this is so hard to believe. I never really thought Carly'd get in trouble with a guy."

Ruiz nodded and bit her tongue.

"I mean, she talked about this guy taking her to dance clubs mostly, and she liked to dance, so there were a lot of those ... He even bought her *roses*. I think I have something. Do you mind if I ...?"

Ruiz nodded, and Trudy stood up quickly, swiping a hand at her eyes. She ducked into the bedroom and came back with a dollar-store storage box patterned with tacky French motifs and the word "*l'amour*." She sat and eased off the lid.

"So, these might help. She put stuff in here after dates. The dead glow sticks are from the Euphoria on Ponca Street, she said—*really* nice place—and there are some receipts. She said he was always paying cash, though, figured he liked to flash his bills."

She passed the box carefully to Ruiz, who set aside her notepad to handle it with care. She didn't reach in but shifted the contents with her pen, turning it this way and that. She spotted something crackling near the bottom, a dried pink rose, half-closed and shedding petals.

"Is that one of the roses?"

Trudy swallowed and sobbed a little. "Yeah. For Christmas. No one had ever gotten her roses before. And they were the real shit, baby's breath and all that fancy stuff. But, you know, they coulda been dollar roses, she was just so happy. It's unbelievable."

There was potential there, Ruiz thought. If she could get Doc Stevens to take a look ...

She said, careful not to sound too hopeful, "Maybe we can search the stuff in that box for any fingerprints. It's a long shot, but it could help. Mind if I take this with me?"

"Go ahead, yeah, sure." Trudy nodded quickly.

"And if it's alright, I could take you down to the station to help with a police sketch."

"Sure, just don't tell Finnegan about, you know ..."

"Of course."

"I don't know what I'm going to do now. Her stuff's still here. I keep forgetting, you know? I can't believe someone would kill her. I mean, no one respects dancers, really, but you don't think someone would kill you. I don't even know her parents' number. It's all on her phone, but you said ..."

Ruiz spared her the details. Of course, they'd already made phone calls. "It's okay. Mr. Finnegan said you have a shift tonight? We'll get a car up here soon as possible, get you down to the station, then get you to work, how's that?"

The younger woman nodded again.

"If anything else comes to mind, anything at all, here's my card."

Trudy took the card and read it aloud. "Maria E. Ruiz, Homicide. What's the E stand for?"

"Esperanza."

"I've heard that in songs sometimes. Does it mean something?"

"*Esperanza* is kinda tricky in English. It can mean "wait," but it can also mean "hope." *And the more of one, the less of the other*, she thought. Then with a tight smile she added, "Call me anytime. If I'm not in, it'll go to voicemail and I'll call you as soon as I get the message."

"I will. Absolutely. Anything if it'll catch the bastard."

"Take care." Ruiz fought the urge to make any promises. She closed the notebook and headed back to her unmarked car. The parking lot was all but abandoned at this hour. Close

53

by, a bicycle had been chained to the surrounding link fence. The lock was still intact, but the front tire had been stolen and the back tire deflated. A siren sounded in the distance.

There had to be thousands of people buying roses on Christmas Eve, Ruiz thought. And the odds of any club remembering a certain couple were pretty much impossible. "Gotta hope Doctor Hammer has something better," she said to herself, tossing the notebook on the passenger seat. She'd pass her suspicions about Finnegan over to Vice, though. Might as well clean up the messes they could find.

Chapter Eight

Jan. 3–4

Father Tomas moved KO to a small private room so his struggle wouldn't disturb the other residents and to reduce stimulation while the man's brain was running wild, sensitive to the slightest noise or movement.

He offered to take KO to the hospital. They might not keep him, since he had a place to stay, but they could at least give him medications to ease his transition. KO refused.

"I know my weakness, Father," he said. "If they make it easy, I won't be afraid to go through it again. If I fail this time, I don't think I'll ever be able to try another time. I gotta make this fight to the final round on my own."

So, Gerry had been posted in a chair outside the room, and KO lay shaking in the bed in the darkness, alone, a bucket on the table beside him in ready reach and a pitcher of water beside it. He drank a lot of water. There was another bucket on the floor to deal with that.

Visions came to him in the darkness. His old manager, Howard, smoking a cigar, telling him he was a bum. He saw Amy, no longer the admiring child but an angry adult, shoving a bologna sandwich into his hand and telling him to get out and never come back.

Then there was the dead woman. Pale, so pale in the black mirror of the harbor at night, floating peacefully with the dark line across her throat. That line became a gill, and it flapped open slowly as she drifted away, farther and farther toward an inky horizon.

Then his ears filled with the roar of the dragon with a woman's face. Its eyes smoldered in the light of an exploding sky and the mouth opened to bare fangs of steel as it whispered his name. The dragon was hunting him in the cold night and his body shook with the need to run, run as fast and as far as he had ever run in his life. But the voice was everywhere, calling after him ...

Then he saw his face reflected in the dragon's eye. And knew it had found him.

He threw himself onto the floor, and when Father Tomas came to check on him before going to bed himself, he found the old boxer curled up in the fetal position, passed out beneath the bed.

At 2 a.m., Gerry knocked softly at Father Tomas's room. Gerry had walked through the same valley KO was now struggling through, recognizing himself in the former boxer who was fighting the toughest battle of his life.

"Yes, my son?" the priest asked. "Is it time?"

"Yes, Father," he said. "He's crying and shaking like a tree in a hurricane."

"Go to bed, Gerry, and thank you. Your watch is ended."

Father Tomas didn't knock this time, fearing it would only make things worse.

KO had climbed back into bed, but the sheet was pulled over his head and he lay shivering underneath, calling out from time to time to the accusing images and voices forming a gauntlet between him and sunrise.

He saw a dragon with a woman's face feeding on the dead woman in the water. The beast paused from its feast and looked at him, deep inside him.

"You're next," it growled and licked its lips.

Then Amy, her face warped with anger as she yelled at him to go away and never return.

"I'm sorry, Amy!" he cried out, now sobbing. "It's my fault, I'll never do it again, I swear! Don't throw me out, baby girl. Please."

"KO," Father Tomas said softly. "It's you and me here. And Satan. He's lived inside you a long time, and he doesn't want to leave. But remember, the Lord is with us."

He placed his hand upon the old man's shoulder. "Pray with me, my son, so the Devil knows he's no longer welcome. Take my hand."

A small, shaking hand slid out, and the priest took it. They prayed for a long time, the words unimportant for the rhythm of the prayers and the comfort of the small priest's hand in his held more meaning than words spoken on a cold dark night when the Lord of Darkness was fighting eviction.

Amy's face returned. She'd gone to work, and KO had been left to watch over his grandson, Taylor. When she got home, she'd found him passed out on the couch, drunk.

Taylor, where was Taylor? In his dreams he couldn't find the baby and ran through long dark halls searching as the cries of a frightened child led him in all directions. The fear and shame made his gorge rise, and he emptied himself into the bucket again and again before collapsing back onto the sweat-soaked mattress like a balloon drained of air.

Sugar Ray Leonard came at him with hands the size of bread loaves, hitting him everywhere at once. He couldn't hit back; he couldn't even block the blows, they came so fast, and he was rocking back and forth, bleeding, barely able to see, yet the hands kept coming. He made it to the end of the round and stood still, afraid to answer the bell to go again.

His corner man held out a bottle of whiskey and winked. "Have some of this, KO, and you'll whip his ass."

"No!" he cried.

Suddenly his corner man turned into Father Tomas, holding a glass of water to his lips. "Drink, KO. You need to drink more water."

He drank and slept far into the next day. And when he awoke, Amy, the corner man, and Sugar Ray were gone.

But the dragon remained.

***

KO staggered into the dining hall at seven, his face as marked by the night's battle as any bout in the ring. He ate a small portion of eggs and toast, washing it down with lots of coffee, looking at his hands as he held the mug. Almost still, like his mind. He hadn't gone this long without a drink since the day Amy had thrown him out. He felt like a small child learning to walk.

Father Tomas joined him as the old boxer was contemplating his second cup of coffee.

"How are you this morning, my son? Are you ready to join the rest of us?"

"I've wasted seven years, Father. I'm not throwing away another day if I can help it. I'm slow, but I'm moving. Might as well move forward. What's next?"

Father Tomas believed that the simple kindness of a warm meal and a place to sleep was the first step to restoring a man's dignity. He smiled, finding proof in the eager question.

"Nothing this morning except to move you back into the dormitory," he answered. "I believe being with the other residents is good for you and I don't think you need a private room anymore. You've made it through the worst of your physical addiction. The emotional need is another matter, and to address that I'd like to see you at our evening AA meeting, if you feel up to it."

"Do I need a sponsor?"

"Not necessarily. But I found you one. I've asked him to see you when he gets in around four. His name is Theodore. Everyone calls him Teddy. You'll see why when you meet him. He helps our local arabber tend to his horse and cart."

"I remember those!" KO smiled weakly—a bit envious of the mysterious Teddy. "The '*ay*-rabbers,' my father called them. They used to come around our neighborhoods here in Baltimore with their horse carts full of fruit and vegetables, always singing out what was in season. You know, Father, it's hard to find fresh vegetables in the neighborhoods where I grew up. The arabbers always had the best prices, straight from the farm, and came right by your front door."

"When I first came to America, my son, I was surprised at how hard it was to buy a fresh orange anywhere near the shelter. Back in my country, even the poorest of the poor have ready access to God's abundance."

KO sighed. "There ain't many arabbers left."

"Teddy's helping to keep the tradition alive."

"Any chance of me getting on with 'em?"

"We'll take things a step at a time. For now, help out here in the shelter. Attending a few AA meetings before you go back out into the world will arm you against temptation. I know life's been hard on you, my son. You've become a wanderer. Take some time to find your strength before you go looking for a home."

KO nodded. "I guess every fighter needs some healing after a tough match before going back in the ring."

Father Tomas turned his head curiously, reinforcing his birdlike appearance. "Does it help you to think of it that way?" he asked.

"Yes, Father. You're my trainer. I'll do whatever you say."

"Well, I have no experience with boxing personally." He paused, briefly touching his left shoulder. "But I do know God and I are always in your corner." He studied the new version of KO before him. "There's something else, my son. A detective called shortly after you arrived, asking if she could speak with you. I told her you weren't ready. I'm not sure you are, yet."

"What did she want with me?"

"She said she was from the homicide division and wanted to ask you about a murder you may have seen."

KO put his coffee cup down and looked around before lowering his voice. "You mean the dead woman I saw was ... coulda been *real*? I thought she and the dragon were God's way of warning me."

"God's ways are His own and no one can see His hand before we are meant to. If the dead woman is real, it doesn't mean God didn't mean for you to see her. Think on that, my son. Don't lose faith now after such a promising beginning."

"Don't worry, Father, I'm done quitting. Let me do something today 'cause I want to get this behind me as soon as I can. Could you tell the detective I can talk with them this afternoon?" KO stood, his plate in hand. "I think I need more eggs and coffee before I go one on one with a room full of cops, though."

"I think that's wise. I'll let her know."

After breakfast, KO was given a mop and a bucket to clean the shelter floor. He soon fell into the rhythm of dipping the mop into the water, wringing out the excess, then sliding the mop across the linoleum. It was almost like dancing, he considered. Well, slow dancing anyway. He wouldn't change the world by cleaning a floor, but maybe this dance over cracked, wet linoleum could start to change his life.

***

Theodore "Teddy" Harper was six foot six and two hundred and fifty pounds of muscle and bone. His boss joked that if the horse ever got sick, he'd hitch Teddy to the wagon instead, as he looked twice as capable.

Father Tomas introduced him to KO in the dorm. Teddy stuck out a huge hand and immediately pulled KO into the bear hug that gave him his nickname. "Mr. KO, sir, proud to meet you." He patted his back. "I used to watch you fight, back in the day."

KO pulled back and looked up at the neon smile above him. He gave his own, low-watt grin in return.

"Back in the day? Now look at me." He spread his arms to indicate the bunk and his tattered clothes.

Soon after they sat together with coffee in the dining hall. Teddy told KO his story while KO listened in fascination. The big man had once been a collector for a loan shark, until he'd been arrested. In prison, all his allies abandoned him.

"After serving my time, I couldn't find work. No one wants a crook," Teddy explained. He spread his arms. "Especially one my size." Still, he smiled. Everything about Teddy was big, especially his smiles. "I wound up on the street, collecting unemployment and a side of hangovers. I was a big man with a big chip on my shoulder. Then I found Jesus."

"Much the same as me," KO admitted. He was fingering the aluminum cross again. "I hit rock bottom, Teddy. I don't even know where to start."

"Where you start don't matter to Jesus, KO," Teddy said. "Just where you're going, that's all."

KO nodded. "Still ..." He watched the other men setting up a circle of chairs across the room. "I ain't never gone to an AA meeting. What d'I gotta do?"

"Take it slow. Get to know the others. Listen to their stories. Learn from what worked in their lives and what didn't. Share *your* story. Ain't nobody here thinks they're better than you. Like the Good Book says, 'all fall short,' but it's easier to get out of a hole if you got a hand up. Meeting's in twenty minutes." Teddy stood and offered KO his hand by way of example. He paused at a thought. "You might want to go pee first."

"Why?"

"Lots of stories, lots of time—takes lots and lots of coffee."

Chapter Nine

Jan 4, cont.

R uiz went by Vice to share her deductions about the Gold Digger's manager. They promised to let her know if they turned up something, and Ruiz left in a good mood. It'd be worth a month's pay to walk by Booking when they brought him in.

Little moments like that might undo a year's worth of harassment from jerks like him, she reckoned. A girl had to dream.

Her interview with Carly's roommate was less productive. A review of registered sex offenders was positive for three regulars at the club, but none of them resembled the well-heeled mystery man Trudy had seen leave with Carly. Ruiz trudged back to her office and found a note on her desk that brought back her smile. Her witness was making faster progress in detox than the priest had expected, and the man was ready to talk. The case needed a break. Maybe this was it.

She called the shelter back and after getting past the volunteer, she got Father Tomas back on the line.

"I got a note that KO can speak with us now?"

"Yes, Detective. He had a rough night, but though he's still very weak, his mind is clear. He's eager to get this all behind him and is ready to speak with you whenever you want. But our van has an old set of tires, and I don't trust it in this weather. I'd prefer you come here."

"Is it too late to come today?"

"Dinner is from six-thirty to seven, lights out at ten, but of course he'd be available any time you could get here."

"Thank you, Father. Expect me later this evening unless I call you back."

She left her cubicle, giving her poster of Sonia Sotomayor a high five but curbed her enthusiasm when she peered out the office window. Fat white flakes were drifting down already. She pulled her ski sweater tighter around her.

She knocked on Mankiller's door, and he was so deep into the report he was reading he nearly jumped.

"Our witness is dry enough to talk. Want me to see him today?"

"You have someplace else to be?"

"If you looked up from your screen, you'd note the arrival of the next Ice Age outside, and I don't have all-weather tires."

Mankiller looked outside, surprised.

He really does live in his own world sometimes, Ruiz thought, not unkindly.

"I've got all-wheel drive," he said, still looking out the window. "Let's go together. He may be a difficult witness." He added, turning his face back to her, "But you're still the people person."

"So you say, *Jefe*. I guess that's my superpower. Okay, give me a minute to grab my polar explorer outfit. I'll be right back."

***

Mankiller snorted when she poked her head back through the door. He wouldn't have said anything, but the parka had more padding than his sofa. The multi-colored cap of Andean wool and the fleece-lined boots over leg warmers just added to a certain ... look.

"You modeling for a Land's End catalog?"

Ruiz scowled at him over her muffler.

"Sorry, Ruiz. It's just you're usually the best-dressed on the force, though Bailey takes a close second."

"You laugh now, *Jefe*," Ruiz reached one stylish leather glove up to paw down the muffler, "but I'm not turning blue to make a fashion statement. The only reason I'm wearing thin gloves," she indicated her hand, "is because I can't get my trigger finger through that tiny hole with anything thicker."

"High fashion with a ballistic flair." Mankiller grabbed his scarf as she turned with a huff and waddled out the door. He fought the urge to reference penguins. *Not worth the risk*, he wisely told himself.

***

The drive to the shelter went smoothly. The streets were largely empty already and the plows were hard at work. Mankiller took it slow, and they arrived at the shelter just as the sun set. He glanced at his watch.

"Six p.m."

"The priest said they'd be serving dinner in a half-hour," Ruiz said.

Mankiller squinted through the snowfall as they hurried out of the car to the shelter door. As they arrived, it opened and a small man with frosting glasses peered out. He didn't look surprised when they produced badges, although he had to lift the glasses to see them.

Father Tomas introduced himself in the hallway. He took their coats as they stomped snow from their shoes.

"Get a lot of cops around here ... Father?" Mankiller asked.

"It comes with the work."

Father Tomas kept a rueful smile at the mild contempt he heard in the detective's voice.

"KO believed the dead woman was a vision from God," the priest explained. "Your presence tells me there's more to the story."

"Correct. New Year's Eve, he reported a dead body. Because he was drunk at the time, the cop who took him to the ER didn't think much of it, but it turns out KO was right. We'd like to see what more he can tell us." Mankiller exchanged a pointed look with Ruiz, then added, "He's currently not a suspect."

"Very well. I can take you to my office so you can speak with him in private. It shouldn't be more than five minutes."

"We could take him to the station."

"If you take him there, who would bring him back?" Father Tomas waved his arms vaguely toward the door. "And I would hate to make him leave the shelter in this storm."

"Fair enough, Father," Mankiller said. "Lead on. But we'd like to return to the station as soon as we can for the same reason."

"Of course. I'll hurry him along."

He paused before he left, adding, "KO has become quite popular here already. Most of the men from this area know of him, and they love listening to his stories of his days in the ring. They respect him, and that's good for him." He wiped clean his glasses while looking directly at the hard-faced detective. "Please don't take that away from him before it has a chance to take root."

Chapter Ten

Jan. 4, cont.

KO shuffled into the office, the battered old fighter clenching and unclenching his hands. Father Tomas seemed nervous when he'd told him that the police detectives had arrived to talk to him. If his corner man was nervous, KO reckoned he should be too.

The man at the priest's battered desk was looking out the window at the piling snow. KO caught the man's eye as he turned from the window, saw the judgment in them.

What for? KO wondered. Am I about to lose my second chance?

No. If this were the end, he'd already be in cuffs and a squad car.

The man gestured to the one vacant chair in the room. The other detective, a younger woman in a bulky coat, stood beside the empty chair. She looked worried, too. KO hoped it wasn't about him.

He sat and braced himself.

The man pulled out a notebook and pen. "Mr. Bannon, I'm Sergeant Mankiller. This is Detective Ruiz. We'd like to ask you a few questions about the body you reported three nights ago."

KO nodded politely. "Yes, sir."

"About what time did you see it?"

"I remember lights in the sky. Musta been just after midnight—fireworks."

"Do you remember exactly where you were?"

KO shook his head to clear it, like he might after taking a right cross.

"Not exactly, sir. By the water, that's all I can recall."

"What do you remember about your surroundings?"

"There was a ... a flashing sign. I can't get it straight in my head. The first letters were blurry. Best I could make out was C-O-P-E-N, or maybe O-C-P-E-N ... I dunno, it's kinda jumbled in my head."

The one called Ruiz put her hand on his right arm. KO stiffened but then remembered her from when she was a beat cop in the neighborhood.

"Hello, Officer Ruiz," he said, feeling a little less threatened. "Glad to see you moving up in the world."

She smiled briefly. "Thank you, KO. I'm happy to see you're still with us." She bent down so that her face was on the same level as his. "KO, the officer who took you to the hospital reported you saying something about a 'dragon vomiting blood.' Is that still what you remember?"

KO cringed. "Yes, ma'am." He looked down at his feet, at his new shoes that were someone else's old ones. Even with a fresh coat of paint, folks doubted him. "I, uh, I thought maybe it was like the burning bush Moses saw. A sign, a message to clean up my life ... 'fore it was too late. I wouldn't put too much stock in it. I'm an old punch drunk." He tapped his temple. "No telling what's in my head anymore."

Ruiz patted his arm with a patient smile. "Anything might help."

KO considered. "You think it's important, Detective?"

Sergeant Mankiller was less patient. "Tell me about the dragon, Mr. Bannon. Did it look like a Chinese dragon to you? Could you have been in Chinatown? There's a dragon mural there, a couple miles from the harbor, some dragon motifs on a few restaurants, too."

KO was startled by this suggestion. A real dragon?

"No, sir, not Chinatown. I remember the smell of the water. I couldn't tell you if the dragon was Chinese or not, but I know a dragon when I see it."

Ruiz caught Mankiller's eye. "Could we take him to Doc Stevens? Maybe he can help with the memory."

"Not tonight, we can't," he said.

Ruiz looked back at KO sympathetically.

"Mr. Bannon, I know you want us to catch whoever killed this young woman, or you wouldn't have told Officer Richardson what you saw," she said. "Now, it's late and the weather's getting worse. So how about we bring you to the station tomorrow and have you talk to Dr. Stevens? He's someone who might be able to help you remember. He's a psychologist who works with witnesses like you that have trouble with their memories."

KO relaxed a little. He wasn't sure about the hard-faced man, but he liked the way Ruiz talked to him. Like he was a citizen, not a bum. He nodded slowly.

"Sure thing," he said. "I'll do what I can, but ..." He wondered about the word 'doctor.' "As long as there's nothing chemical involved. I'm cleaning up. I don't want no truth serums or anything."

"Deal," said Ruiz.

Mankiller said nothing more, back to watching the snow. He nodded, thanked KO for his time, and told him to expect someone around one the following afternoon, then he and Ruiz left the office.

"Probably a waste of time," Mankiller muttered to Ruiz once they were out of earshot, "like he said, drunk—probably not much punch left."

"*Jefe*, I should call you Detective Cynic Holmes."

"Only if I get to call you Detective Penguin."

***

KO shuffled back to the dining hall, still staring at his not-new shoes. He didn't know whether to feel relieved or not, but he knew what a punch to the gut felt like. Was that it then? A dragon in Chinatown? Had he been making too much of nothing?

But no. KO remembered what Father Tomas had said about God working in mysterious ways. Dragon or not, he must be meant to be a witness. If this was part of God's plan for him, he would follow wherever it led.

***

After asking Father Tomas to have KO ready by one the next day, Mankiller and Ruiz stepped outside to find the storm had snuck up on them. The snow fell heavy as curtains, only getting thicker. Ruiz whimpered a little.

"It's not so bad," he lied.

They returned to the car, looking like a freezer in serious need of a defrost, and soon they were winding their way carefully down the streets toward the station, Mankiller driving.

After about five minutes, even at five miles an hour, the car was bucking and sliding down the avenue. Mankiller cursed. "All-wheel drive, it says," he muttered loudly.

"We're moving at a crawl, *Jefe*," Ruiz mumbled behind her muffler.

"Thanks, Ruiz, I noticed. But any faster and I'd lose control. At this rate we'll be at the station by ..." he checked the red line on his maps app. The ETA glared right back at him, "*nine?*"

Ruiz popped out of her cocoon to look around and pointed stiffly down the street. "*Jefe*, we're almost at South Linwood, that's Patterson Park off to the right, where I go running."

"We're probably on the sidewalk," Mankiller muttered, squinting as he leaned forward. It was like trying to drive with spiderwebs all over his windshield.

"My apartment is one street over. Just take a left on South Streeper."

"Ruiz ..."

"I really don't want to ride to the station and drive back by myself."

"So get a taxi."

"You see a taxi out here, *Jefe*?" She blinked out from under her hat pitifully. "We're gonna be buried out here!"

"If I leave a major street, I might never get home."

"Why don't we spend the night at my place?"

"No."

"*Jefe* ..."

"No way, Ruiz. People would talk."

"Only if we tell them." When he rolled his eyes, she insisted, "People will talk if they find me frozen to death, driving back all by myself, with my terrible tires—"

"That's your fault, you know."

"—when you could have *saved* me. I'm a tropical girl, in case you never noticed." She blinked innocently as she nestled back in her layers of insulation. "Besides, if we keep going, we'll just be stuck in your car all-night."

The car had already gone ice surfing twice during their short trip, and the snow kept falling thicker. Mankiller groaned in defeat.

"Okay, Ruiz. Two conditions: first, I take the couch, and second, no booze. Deal?"

Ruiz smiled victoriously. "Deal! Take the left, just before Sharky's Bar and Grill."

Chapter Eleven

Jan. 4, cont.

R uiz's apartment was the opposite of Mankiller's in almost every way possible. He had his designated work and sleep spaces, his telescope, bare sofa, and dollar-store plates. Ruiz had knickknacks. Celebrity bobbleheads? Ruiz had them everywhere.

Mankiller stared in disbelief at what one bobblehead's very small label insisted was the "Royal Wedding." He noticed a brass trophy gleaming on a bookcase with Ruiz's name underneath. He looked closely and saw it was a track and field trophy from a local high school.

"What's this?" he asked, pointing to the shiny female figure holding a laurel wreath aloft.

"A memory of my faded athletic glory, *Jefe*," she said before turning the trophy around. "I used to be a real threat on the relay team." She turned back to preparing her place for unexpected company. "Back in the day."

"Any other athletic accomplishments you've been hiding from me?"

She paused. "Not exactly. I did work as a lifeguard on the beaches. First thing they teach you is if someone grabs you, duck down, then you can spin them around and take control. A useful thing to know when you start dating, too."

"Noted. I'll decline a demonstration."

"And I can beat your butt in dominoes any day of the week." Ruiz scooped laundry off the couch, the elliptical, and every other imaginable surface before dumping it in a basket in the hallway, grateful her Victoria's Secret collection wasn't out for display.

"I've got leftovers if you want them."

"I don't like spicy food."

"Oohhh ... You *do* realize that Latinos in Baltimore eat what everyone else in Baltimore eats, *Jefe*? It's not like we're a different species."

"I just mean I don't like spicy food ..."

"Ha!" Ruiz stooped behind the fridge door and popped up again with a flat cardboard box. "Pizza! Supreme okay?"

"Oh, sure. But no mushrooms. If you can manage, I mean."

She grimaced. "After the autopsy ... No problem. I'll stick this in the microwave, then grab you a blanket and pillow."

"Fine." Mankiller picked his way to the right-angle couch by the television. Another thing about this place, he quickly noticed: there wasn't a nook or cranny by a chair without a basket of chocolate in it. He knew the stereotype that women liked chocolate—he'd even teased his ex-wife because she didn't. But he had never met someone that kept stashes.

I'll know what to bring if I'm her Secret Santa next year.

"You got a spare phone charger I can use close to the couch, in case I get a call?"

"I got one of those magnetic thingees next to the trophy. You can lay it there."

"Thanks. I can leave my gun there too, if it's alright. Looks like there's space if I move The Royal Wedding to one side."

"Fair enough, just don't disrespect the Royal Couple!"

Since the coffee table was covered in fashion magazines (Ruiz really was the best-dressed person in the department), Mankiller piled the bright throw pillows into an armchair.

Ruiz returned with the promised linens just as the microwave chimed. She dropped them behind the couch, then opened a cupboard and pulled down two plates with bright red stripes.

Soon, they were sitting at the kitchen island with pizza and iced green tea, talking about anything but the weather. The snow was falling like a slow-moving wall now, with no signs of stopping. Ruiz shivered just looking at it.

"Only one thing to do on a night like this ... You like cocoa?"

"Cocoa?"

"Don't get too excited," she added, bustling about the tiny kitchen, clattering utensils as she prepared to do battle.

It was *real* cocoa, too. She pulled a hockey puck of Mexican chocolate out of her pantry, pulverizing it into powder with a stone mortar and pestle before slowly stirring it into steaming milk over the stove's low flame.

Mankiller wavered between the couch and the kitchen, finally wandering back over to watch like she was brewing a magical potion, which she was.

"That's a lot of work for a cup of cocoa," he said. "Can't you just buy it in powder or syrup?"

"Sure you can, and the pricy stuff tastes about the same, but that's not the point."

"What is?"

"Part of why I enjoy cocoa is I like making it. I don't want to just drink it, I want to create it. I like to think of making cocoa as an art form." Ruiz tested the heat with her pinky. "It's the moments enjoyed together, not just the drink, *Jefe*." She sighed. "I tested out of Spanish in college, so I took Italian for two semesters. Kinda cheating, I guess, since they're so similar, but I learned a lot of Italian expressions. When I drink cocoa, I think of my favorite, *'il dolcente di fare niente,'* or 'the sweetness of doing nothing.' People are always rushing from one unimportant thing to another. Making cocoa forces me to take a moment just for me—and whoever's lucky enough to share it with me."

"Poetic." He watched her in curious silence. It *was* a nice moment. The smell of the chocolate blending into the hot milk while the world outside covered up with snow reminded him of a time when he was a little boy, watching his mother bake cookies. "You know, I haven't had cocoa since I was twelve," he said.

"Your loss. You said no booze."

"I did."

"You like cinnamon in it?"

"I don't know. I'll try it."

She threw a couple of cinnamon sticks in.

"You're spoiling me, Ruiz."

"I'm spoiling *me*, *Jefe*." She pulled two mugs from the cupboard inspired by an Andy Warhol painting, then added, "But you get to share."

She poured the cocoa from the saucepan and passed him a cup. While she dug out the remote from the couch cushions, Mankiller stacked the throw pillows on the carpet and took the armchair before settling in with his mug.

They watched an episode of *The Office* while the bitter and sweet of the cocoa slid down his throat. He'd never thought to make cocoa himself, avoiding chocolate entirely while he was married to make his wife happy. Maybe that should have been a first sign, he thought, an omen it wasn't going to work out. Not being able to be themselves in the same space.

He realized he was thinking of his ex again and tried to stop.

"That was the funny bit, *Jefe*," Ruiz broke in.

"I don't need a laugh track to tell me that," he evaded.

"How d'you feel about our little slumber party now?"

"It's better than driving in snow," he admitted. It felt mean, so he added, "The cocoa's nice, thank you. It reminds me of a snow day when I was a kid."

"I know how to treat a guest."

"Yes, you do, but it's time to call it a night."

"Tired already?"

"I'm an old man." He swallowed, still tasting chocolate. "You got a toothbrush?"

"I put one by the sink. Brand new." She pulled herself upright and shut off the television, then crooked a finger toward the bathroom. "Bath towels in the cabinet if you need them. *Buenas noches, Jefe.*" She smiled with a little wave and shut the door to her room.

After Mankiller did his due diligence with the toothbrush, regretfully scrubbing away the last bit of cocoa, he shut off the lights and bumbled back to the couch in the near dark, then lay down and pulled up the quilt. She'd put a fresh case on the pillow, and it smelled of something flowery.

For a couple of hours, he listened to the muffled quiet of the city outside the apartment walls as he tried to surrender to sleep. It got quiet in Baltimore when it snowed, this southern city with occasional northern weather, the only sounds the occasional scrape of a snowplow trundling by or the distant blaring of emergency sirens. Otherwise, the world outside was a quiet haze of snow and blurry yellow lamplight. He curled up beneath the blanket, savoring the warmth on a cold dark night while he reviewed the day's events.

He thought of KO, staring at his feet and going on about signs and dragons. A simple man. That might help. Too simple to lie convincingly.

Mankiller didn't really go in for faith. Statistics were a fact of life on the force: about twenty-five hundred homeless people were on the streets of Baltimore any night; the younger ones turned to drugs, but the older ones preferred traditional poisons, ready at retail. Sometimes the habit followed the homelessness; sometimes it came the other way around. In both cases, it might be preceded by a life worth running away from, but there was no general rule. It was like that question about the chicken and the egg. No big problem had easy answers, even with all the numbers.

But when Mankiller thought of drunks, his images weren't of people huddled under bridges but of men shouting behind chain-link fences or wandering long winding roads to nowhere in the hills of eastern Oklahoma. Some people went off to see the world like he did; others took a shortcut—down the mouth of a bottle.

Becoming a cop seemed the natural thing to do after leaving the Army. He'd been looking for answers since the morning he found his older brother, John, shot dead in his car by the playground where they used to play. The coroner called it a suicide, persuaded by the gunshot wound to the right side of the head of a left-handed man, made by a gun beside him no one knew he owned. His brother had been a drunk, and it seemed the local authorities preferred an easy answer over one taking more work than they thought John Mankiller's life was worth.

After time as a cop himself, Mankiller thought of another reason the locals would be eager to sweep his brother's murder under the rug. They'd have to call in the Oklahoma Bureau of Investigation to handle a capital murder case, and they probably worried what outsiders might learn about a small police department run by a chief whose only qualifications were as a military policeman in the National Guard that employed his untrained cousins. A dead "Indian" was a cipher in their world.

Because his mother was Catholic, it nearly killed her when the young priest refused to do the funeral, saying suicide was an unforgivable sin. His brother's funeral was attended only by him, his mother, and two of his brother's old friends from his days on the high school football team. He knew his brother hadn't fired the bullet into his head, but John had put himself on the path that led to his death as surely as if he'd pulled the trigger. Knowing the crowd his brother ran with, they should all be dead or in prison by now. Sometimes, justice took care of itself.

But he vowed that day to take the longer, harder path, first to the Army, then college, and finally to the police academy. He was still looking for answers but knew this was the right path for him. A warrior's path.

Mankiller fingered the St. Christopher medal around his neck, a gift from his mother on his first Communion. He still wore it in memory of the giver, not the faith it represented.

His brother had had one, but what good did it do him? *I've made my own way, no thanks to you, Christopher.*

He rolled over, his hand dropping to his side, and sleep finally pulled him gently away from the dark of the winter's night to a darkness of his own.

Chapter Twelve

Jan. 5, Saturday

D r. Arthur "Doc" Stevens was a clinical psychologist specializing in post-traumatic stress disorder. He'd accepted part-time work here because he sensed the void to be filled. Coming in on the weekend was par for the course. He'd spent a few years in the Air Force and was used to working where he was both needed and avoided. Policemen were diggers and hunters. It was easy for them to get stuck in that frame of mind, to think everyone was hiding something out of shame, but Stevens knew better: some people were just scared.

He was seated at his desk when KO entered but stood to greet him. The desk placed a physical barrier between doctor and client, giving them a wall of sorts to hide behind until they were ready to drop their shields. There were so many little things that helped the suffering feel at ease, right down to the comfort of the chairs and the soft color of the blinds. Stevens's office didn't look anything like the rest of the Spartan police station.

"Mr. Bannon, is it?" Stevens slowly polished the glasses on a cloth before putting them on. He smiled reassuringly.

"Oh, I've never been a 'mister,' sir. Just KO's what I know."

"KO, then."

Stevens sat back down behind the desk and lightly folded his hands on his notes. "Tell me a little more about yourself, KO. You've been homeless for some time, you said?"

"Seven years, more or less."

"How d'you wind up there?"

"Kinda a long story, Doc."

"Oh, I've heard a lot of stories here, KO, and I don't mind them long. What was it? Family trouble?" KO didn't answer at first, so Stevens added, "The sergeant said you wanted to avoid drugs, in case I thought they might help you relax for the interview. Something to do with that?"

KO flinched a little but said, "Drugs were never a problem for me, Doc. Just booze. It's just, I don't want to add anything worse, y'know? Drink's enough, ain't it, I mean, to mess your life up?"

"It has been for many. What was your life before?"

"I was a fighter, but one day my manager ran off with my share of the gate. Didn't know what to do. It's hard to make it without someone to promote you. I only knew the ring."

"It must have been hard not to give up."

"I didn't give up, Doc, not right away." KO thought of one time in life he had given up, but he wasn't ready to share it.

"So what did you do?" Stevens asked.

"Tried to make it as a trainer."

"That's resourceful of you."

KO shrugged and wrung his rough hands. "I was a middleweight, though. Big money's in the big men, and they didn't want a guy my size telling 'em how to fight."

"You felt the odds were against you?" Stevens removed his bifocals and folded them. "The underdog?"

KO nodded. "Yeah, I worked with the young fighters at one gym after another, but if it wasn't people leaving, it was the place closing down. Boxing ain't what it used to be, Doc. Now it's all mixed martial arts. Cage fights. Less sport, more show." He sighed. "While I was still fighting, I got married, had a daughter, but I lost all that. Fighting's the only thing I know and, well, soon I couldn't make the rent. My wife went home to her mother with my daughter, Amy, and soon after, I went to the streets. Hoped it'd be just 'til my luck turned, but it kept turning worse and I started drinking.

"My daughter went out on her own and took me in for a bit. She's real smart, that girl, nothing like me. She's a pharmacy tech and coulda been a pharmacist if I'd helped with her schooling, but the drink ... One day, she came home from work after leaving me to watch the baby and found me passed out on the couch. The baby was fine, thank God, 'cept for a full diaper, but Amy changed the lock and told me to never come back. Seven years later and look at me. But I got my sign. I figure it's time to make my own luck."

"I respect that. One good way to get back on your feet is to help others, like in this case with the woman you saw ..." Stevens shuffled his notes, but kept his eyes on KO, waiting for his nod, then continued, "I read from the interview notes you could smell water."

"That's right. Like dead fish in a dumpster."

"Is there a particular place you sleep along the harbor?"

KO shook his head. "I usually don't go there in winter. Too cold, not too many steam grates—and the boat owners get angry when you're near their toys."

"So why were you there that night?"

KO shrugged. "I went to watch the fireworks. I drank to stay warm and fell asleep too soon. Then the fireworks woke me, and I saw ... what I saw."

Stevens set aside his pad and pen and pulled a small analog clock from a drawer of his desk. It had radium highlights on its numbers and hands. He set it by a map of the harbor, and KO studied both curiously. He turned the map of a harbor around on the desk.

"Does anything look familiar?"

KO made a vague line with one finger. "Probably ... the north shore, east of the Inner Harbor, that's all I can say for sure. Coulda been anywhere along there. Sorry."

"You didn't smell food cooking?"

"No, sir." He shrugged. "I mean, maybe I didn't smell it over the smell of me. Sorry, wish I could do better."

Stevens nodded slowly. "If it's alright with you, KO, I'd like to try some simple hypnosis. It might help your memory come back."

"Isn't that like a spell or something?"

"Not at all. It's just a way of helping you focus; you're still in control, sorta like being buried in a good book. You okay with giving it a shot?"

KO clenched and unclenched his fists, then nodded. "Okay, Doc. Got nothing to lose. Just don't make me crow like a rooster or nothing."

Stevens chuckled and promised before he stood and closed the Venetian blinds. The hands of the little clock glowed in the dark. He tapped the clock. "Just relax and watch the second hand moving around the circle. Count down slowly from twenty-five. As slow as you like. When you're relaxed, we can begin. We'll stop any time you want."

KO settled deep into the office chair. At first, he fidgeted, but soon there was only the second hand and the man's soft voice.

"I want you to go back to that night, KO. Go back to that winter night when you fell asleep. You're on the dock, KO. Something's woken you. What do you see?"

KO's voice came slow but calm from deep in his chest. "A ... rainbow. A rainbow on fire. I see ... the lights shining on the water. All the colors. Fire in water."

"What do you hear?"

"The *boom* ... like a voice from Heaven."

"A voice?"

"Telling me I'm lost."

"What happens next?"

"Something hits the water. Something big. I get up. I walk to it. It's ..." He swallowed hard.

"What do you see, KO?"

"It's a young woman ... a-a girl, really. Only twenty or something, but her hair's white in the water ... pale. So's her face. There's something across her neck, a black line, but I don't know. It's like ..." He shuddered. "It's like a gill flapping open and closed as her body rocks in the water ..."

"Look away, KO. Look around. Look at the dock. What else do you see?"

"A ... flashing sign. Purple letters. Neon. Off and on."

"KO, I want you to look closely at the sign for me. What does it say?"

"I can't read it. Makes no sense, the letters."

"It's alright. What letters do you see?"

"The first two are a blur. O ... C ... P ... E ... N, or maybe it starts C ... O. I'm not sure about the first two letters. Maybe there's others. Maybe I can't see it all."

"Can you turn around again, KO? Can you tell me what you see above the water?"

"I ..." KO grew rigid in his chair and clawed his temples, shaking all over. "I can't, Doc. I don't wanna go back. There's a dragon! Don't make me stay there ...."

"It's alright." It was, the psychologist admonished himself. He shouldn't rush this. "It's alright, KO. You don't have to look. That's very good. Now, I'm going to turn the clock away from you, and I want you to follow my voice, back into the room where we're sitting right now. In my office, in your chair, all the way back to me."

KO blinked as the clock turned away. He squinted uneasily as the doctor opened the blinds.

"Sorry, Doc," he said. "I can't remember more than that."

"You did fine for a first session, KO, and there are other methods we can try if we need to go further. This is just the simplest one." Stevens made a few more notes. "Would you be willing to go with a detective back to the harbor and see if anything rings a bell?"

"I can try, I guess."

The psychologist considered this. KO seemed guileless and clearly doing his best to help. "The thing is, KO, this memory of yours, of the dragon?"

"The vision."

Stevens didn't miss the conviction. "Visions can stem from reality, KO. They usually fade like a bad dream unless they feel important. You had a vivid enough memory to see this dragon again while you were hypnotized."

"What's that mean, Doc?"

"It means you saw something but didn't know what it was. It might be evidence, something pointing to where you were, something pointing to whoever killed that young woman."

"I'm sorry, Doc. I wish I could remember."

"With your permission, I'd like to talk to Sergeant Mankiller about this. After that, maybe you and he or another detective can drive around the harbor and see if something jogs your memory. If that doesn't work, there's still one other thing we can try."

"Yeah?"

The psychologist closed his notebook. "Let's cross that bridge when we come to it."

***

Stevens sent KO to the diner next door for lunch with a ten-dollar voucher from the police department, then sat down with Ruiz to report.

"How'd it go, Doc?"

"The first session's usually the hardest, but we've established trust. He's easily hypnotized, thank goodness, or we wouldn't have accomplished as much as we did."

"Can we use what he says under hypnosis in court?"

"It's kind of a gray area, but if his memories under hypnosis lead to tangible proof, then that proof could be introduced into evidence. For example, if he identified someone based on a memory he regained through hypnosis, a defense lawyer could, and probably should, object, as such memories can be manipulated by the hypnotist. The person under hypnosis wants to please the voice of the person who's guiding them. But if they recall a red truck with a certain license plate as being at the scene of the crime, and a red truck belonging to a suspect with that license plate is discovered later as a result of the memory, then it can be introduced into evidence. The defense lawyer could still object, but it would probably withstand the challenge."

"Fair enough," Ruiz sighed. "What else?"

"First off, I think he's being honest with you. I don't see anything that makes me think he's holding back or lying, but there's something there in his memory that's really scared him. It will probably take a couple more sessions before he can face it, if ever."

"He's an ex-prize fighter. What could scare a man like that?"

"A vision from God." Stevens sighed. "That's what he thought it was, anyway. I think there's more to it, but he needs to be willing to look."

"I wish we could give him time, Doc, I really do, but the lab's got nothing so far and the trail could turn cold. Can't you speed it up?"

"A trip to the harbor might be good for him, you know, get back on the horse that threw him. That's fairly simple. The other method isn't really."

"And that is?"

"If he were alright with drugs, we could try hypnosis again in conjunction with some diazepam to help him relax, but barring that, there's only one other option. It might be doomed as well."

"What is it?"

Stevens sighed. "Have you ever heard of situational-dependent learning?"

"Like the Pavlov thing?"

"Not exactly. It's about learning two things at once."

"Like what?"

"For example, how many song lyrics can you recite?"

"I dunno, hundreds probably."

"Okay."

"Okay what?"

"Let's hear a recitation. Um, *La Vida Loca* by Ricky Martin."

"You *and* the sergeant, Doc? It's like you think I live in the Spanish Dimension."

"I happen to like that song. But don't sing it. I want you to recite it, like poetry."

Ruiz sighed. "Fine. Uh, 'She's into superstition, black cats, and the moonli—' I mean, 'voodoo dolls,' right. Um, 'I gotta ... dodo doo doo ...' Uh, sorry, I can't remember the rest."

"You see?" said Stevens with a satisfied nod.

"See what?"

"You learned the words with the music. Now you can't remember one without the other."

Ruiz laughed. "You're singing that one at karaoke next office party, Doc."

"I accept my punishment, Detective, if it will prove my point," Stevens chuckled. "But in KO's case, the association is even stronger than the lyrics of a song without the music. It's called state-dependent memory, a variation of situational-dependent learning. Several studies have described people who learned or experienced something when they were drunk or high on drugs but were unable to recall them later when sober. But if they became intoxicated again, the memories returned. They were drunk when their brains encoded the memory, and it's almost like a key. They must return to the same state they were in when they formed the memory to unlock it."

"Wait. You're saying that for KO to remember where he was that night ..."

"We may have to recreate the environment *and* his physiologic state when he saw his dragon. You would need his permission, obviously, but yes, you'd have to take him to the harbor at night and get him drunk."

Ruiz sighed and pushed away her coffee. "You're right, Doc. I think we're screwed."

Chapter Thirteen

Jan. 5, cont.

The market had been crazy all day, so Marty returned to his boat after work and turned back the tarp to climb in and unwind. The heater in the cockpit wasn't made for the long cold spell they were having, so wrapping the boat in the tarp reduced the leak of cold air inside, leaving only the front window uncovered so he could enjoy the view of the harbor.

He found it easier to relax in his own little kingdom, kick back with a Scotch, fantasize that he could let go the mooring lines, power up the engine, and sail off to who knows where ... He could be lazing off the Florida Keys in four days. Someday, when he had his nest egg squirreled away, he'd sell everything he didn't want to take with him and do just that.

He was sitting in the saloon, watching the water taxis rush around, when he saw an old black man with a crooked nose walk up to a couple waiting on the dock. The tall middle-aged man's face was mahogany brown and looked to be in good shape, while the younger, obviously Latina, had a lean face, her body enshrouded in a large puffy jacket. Marty didn't like the look of any of them. No friendly greetings. No waves. Certainly not some meeting up of old-time friends. And now they were walking the dock, back and forth, the taller, gruffer man sometimes stopping to point at a storefront, the water, even the boats.

The Florida Keys evaporated, and Marty felt the winter chill catch up to him. Cops. Had to be cops. Cops looked like poker players even when they were just drinking coffee.

Sure, there could be a million reasons why they were walking along the harbor, but there was only one that mattered to him. Marty cracked open a window and sat down below it, listening.

***

Mankiller spent the rest of the afternoon driving KO around the harbor, stopping at docks, and seeing if the waterside brought anything to mind. The briny air ate away at the snow, but the cold was all the sharper for it.

Around five o'clock, Ruiz came by to check on them, hefting the notes from the day's interviews pointedly. "Any luck?"

KO was walking the length of the dock a few yards away, looking at every spar and post.

Mankiller shook his head. "How about you?"

"I'll have the sketch for you soon enough. The roommate described about half the men in Baltimore, but maybe if she saw him again, she could ID him, though she doubted she could testify in court."

"Figures. Anything on this 'copen' thing?"

"*Nada*. I got a few receipts from Carly's dates with her mysterious and wealthy boyfriend, but they're a long shot."

"So where does that leave us?"

Ruiz explained the last card Stevens might play. Mankiller grimaced.

"Should we tell KO before or after the AA meeting?"

KO circled back, his hands dug deep into the pockets of his winter jacket, his shoulders stooped.

"Sorry, Detectives," he said at last. "There's just nothing in my head but that dragon and the sign."

"We've already been to every Chinese restaurant within a mile of the north harbor."

"I told you." KO shook his head. "Nothing smelled like that."

Mankiller bit off a remark about the stink of whiskey. It wouldn't help. None of this was helping.

"Okay, one last thing," he said. "Stevens would like to meet with you again on Monday. That alright? You could talk, or try the hypnosis again, this time on a drug, see if you can see this dragon more clearly if you relax."

KO was already shaking his head.

"Okay, barring that," Mankiller went on, "meet with him and try to jar something loose. It might help you remember. One o'clock all right?"

"Sure thing, Detective. I'll do what I can."

"You are planning on staying at St. Roch's Shelter for a while, aren't you, KO?" Ruiz asked. "We need to know where to find you."

"It's where I need to be, Detective. I got some hard work ahead of me, and that's the place to do it."

"So long as you can stay sober," Mankiller said. "You start drinking again and Father Tomas will make you leave. We need you to stay dry and in one place, at least until this is over."

"I intend to stay dry for the rest of my life."

He believes it—for now, Mankiller thought. The best liars lied to themselves, he knew.

KO looked the detective in the eye. "Look, Detective, I know you don't like me."

"I never said that."

"You don't have to. I mean, I don't like me, and I won't like me 'til I clean up and get my act together," KO said. "I gotta do it now. Not a drop more."

"Look, KO. I appreciate your cooperation," Mankiller said as he rubbed the back of his neck. "It's just that I feel the bodies of these young women piling up, and it's getting to me.

You gotta understand I'll do whatever I can to catch this guy." He sighed. "OK, enough preaching, let's give you a lift back to the shelter before your AA meeting."

"Thank you, Sergeant."

"Yeah, don't mention it."

The trip back to the station from St. Roch's was silent until Mankiller laughed.

"What's so funny?" Ruiz asked.

"Just what we need. A drunk who won't drink."

"You can't blame a man for trying to get his life straight, Boss."

"But we both know he's gonna fail. Might as well do it now and help someone."

He turned silent as he navigated the slippery streets of a wintry Baltimore until they approached the station, but finally said, "Does Doc really think hitting the bottle would bring the memory back?"

"There's a chance, *Jefe*, but whatever we do, we gotta respect KO's choice here. He's really trying." She nudged his ribs. "And he ain't dumb. He knows exactly what you think of him, no matter how you try to hide it."

"Yeah, I guess you're right about that. If he didn't learn that in the ring, he must have on the street. You gotta have skills to survive as long as he has."

"He could be the key, Boss, but we gotta be gentle with him, or we'll break him."

Mankiller knew Ruiz was making sense, and he usually appreciated her optimism but today he felt trapped by it, unable to explain why he was so pessimistic. That would be getting too close, wouldn't it? Too close to talking about his ex and his brother and everything else your coworkers didn't need to know about you.

"We can't wait for his vision or whatever it was to come back to him on its own, so we need another way to catch the bastard," he said at last. "And soon, before Romeo gets any new ideas."

***

"That was a close one," Marty muttered.

When the lady cop had mentioned the name *Carly*, his breath left him for a moment.

He glanced up just once to watch the three walk away toward a dark-blue sedan. The old man wore regular clothes, but there was something to that shuffling walk that Marty thought he recognized. The drag of homeless trash. *What a laughable idea. Something like that trying to take me down. Me. Still …*

He stayed put for a few minutes, clicking the rim of his empty glass against his teeth. "Maybe a bit too close."

He was just thinking about the cop saying something about a dragon when his phone suddenly blasted Bon Jovi's *It's My Life* from across the room. Marty jumped, then scrambled across the floor on all fours.

"Shit … shit-shit-shit …"

He made a mad grab for it and jabbed the *ignore* button, then lay on the tiles, listening.

Nothing.

Cursing his panic, Marty checked the call record. "Dad, you bastard …" Bon Jovi burst into song again, and he punched *accept* and pressed the phone to his ear. "Hey, Pops."

"Marty, where are you?"

"I'm taking Friday afternoon off. For the stress."

"You sound out of breath."

"Yeah, I was, y'know, running. Getting the dopamine flowing."

"Marty, I wanted you at the board meeting. You know I had to make an excuse for you."

"Sorry, Pops. I didn't know you needed me there."

"You're more than just a nine-to-five employee, Marty. If you're going to run this company someday, you're going to have to start taking things more seriously so people will take you more seriously. We were going to talk about the new charity initiatives ..."

"Right, right, yeah, Pops, I know. And y'know what? I've been thinking on that. 'Cause I do care. You know I do."

"Glad to hear it."

"In fact ..." Marty unfolded himself and crept back to the bar. He pulled open a few drawers. "I was just thinking about that, the whole 'second chance' thing ..."

"Were you now?"

Marty dug out a notepad and pen. "'Cause I know a guy, just some guy, was telling me about this shelter that's got people looking for a new start. Nice place. AA program and everything. Nice priest works there. I think his name's Tom ..." Marty scribbled out "Kayo Bannon" with a question mark, then added a few more notes.

"I'm impressed, Marty. Sounds like you've been doing your homework for once."

"Give me some credit, Pops. Anyway, I could go there, find you a few candidates in a week or so."

"Where's this?"

Marty smirked and read off the pad, flipping the pen across his fingers. "St. Roch's Shelter," he said. "I gotta hunch, Pops. It'll be good for us both."

After they hung up, Marty organized his notes. He'd been no great student in college, usually paying some nerd to write his papers, but he'd loved movies, especially gangster movies. As he considered his next move, he channeled his inner Michael Corleone, mumbling, "Keep your friends close, but your enemies closer."

Chapter Fourteen

Jan. 5–7, Friday to Monday

That evening, KO found a note on his bunk in Father Tomas's thin script asking him to come by his office. When the fighter walked in, the man was hunched over the keyboard for his old desktop computer. The machine was under a dustcover most days and looked like it ran on vacuum tubes.

The small priest looked up from the screen. A faint sheen of perspiration shone on his forehead like the frost on the leaky window beside him.

"Something the matter, Father?"

"I've been asked to give the sermon tomorrow at the noon mass at St. Joseph's down the street. English is my third language, and I'm probably as nervous as you were when you went into the ring. I'd be grateful for your prayers."

KO was warmed by the confidence. He didn't think the little man was afraid of anything or anyone but smiled his support all the same. "You, uh, asked to see me?"

"Yes, KO, for two reasons." The priest rolled his rickety chair around the corner of the desk so the two men could sit directly across from one another. In his homeland, there were few things more disrespectful than not facing a man when you talked to him, and he still thought so. "First, how did the interview with the detectives go? You were gone a long time. I worried they might have wanted to detain you."

"Sorry, Father, I should have called. I'm not used to having someone worry about me." KO felt his face flush a little. "They had a lot of questions. I did the best I could, then I rode around the harbor with the sergeant, tried to see if anything helped me remember more. You spoke to him?"

"He doesn't seem to care much for priests—or this one, anyway." He shrugged. "An attitude I am not unfamiliar with. He's also very ... grim. But determined. I was surprised."

"Why, Father? Policemen smile a lot where you come from?"

The priest shook his head, his lips a tight line. "No, they're not very happy men anywhere. No, it was not his stone face that was unusual, it was his desire to catch a killer."

"But, Father, that's his job."

Father Tomas smiled sadly. "This killer chooses the type of women my colleagues usually see at the women's shelters. Poor women are at the bottom of society, as they are in my country. This sergeant cares that they are murdered, even if he is bitter. In my country the police would not bother. I dare say in this country there aren't many who would either."

KO considered this. "I hadn't thought of that. Would you say he's doing God's work?"

Tomas sat back, surprised by the question. "Yes, I believe in a way, he is. I'm glad to see you're alright, KO. I suppose I should get back to my composition ..."

KO stood to leave but turned on a thought: "You said there were two reasons you wanted to see me?"

Tomas slapped his forehead. "Yes, of course. The man Teddy works for has slipped on the ice and hurt his back. I'd like you to go in his place on Monday when Teddy goes to out. The pay is only twenty dollars for the day, but it will give you some gentle exercise. You're probably still a little weak from your ordeal, but the work is not strenuous and if you get tired you can ride in the wagon. Is that acceptable?"

KO couldn't stop his grin. "Be an arabber for a day? Sure thing, Father. Hope I don't have to sing, though. That'll drive away the customers!"

"Then go talk with Teddy. He usually leaves by five. I'll tell the cook to give you an extra helping at dinner tomorrow night. You'll need it, if only to help with the cold. Oh, and go by the clothing storeroom where donations are held. Pick yourself out some boots and warmer clothing. You'll need them, too."

"Thank you, Father. Er, if you need an audience to practice with your sermon, um ... I mean, I'm only good at listening. Can't say my eyes were ever much for reading, but I could help."

"Your offer is greatly appreciated, KO."

KO was hungry, but he set off down the hallways toward the storeroom first, his toes itching as he thought how cold the docks had been that afternoon. He eventually found a warmer coat for his adventure on Monday, along with a pair of boots that would do him well, and left the other shoes behind. Someone else might need them more.

***

KO observed a Sabbath the next day, napping, playing dominoes with the other residents, and sharing his stories about his days in the ring, for which he always had a ready audience. He was hardly in fighting trim, but the rest, plentiful food, and sleeping in a bed were already having a noticeable effect on his energy level. His brain, no longer battered by surges in chemicals, was quieting down and his hands were steady once more. Tomorrow, they'd be useful. As was usually the case with such occasions though, sooner or later, someone asked about his famous fight with Sugar Ray. He would always shake his head and say, "Some other time."

Monday morning, KO woke to Teddy shaking his shoulder while it was still dark—and surely freezing cold outside.

"Rise and shine, my man. Time to feed the multitudes."

KO groaned before he rolled out of bed and dressed. *Just like a training run—in the Antarctic*, he decided. He looked down at his new-old army boots. They were insulated. Outside, the faint gleam of the streetlights off the snow told him he'd chosen well. He'd need all the insulation he could get.

"You warm enough?" Teddy asked, smiling as big as ever.

KO threw a dark-blue scarf around his neck and put on his gloves. "Guess I'll find out quick enough. Let's go."

They arrived at the stables a little after five-thirty. The smell of horses, straw, and horse manure was a new experience to KO, but not unpleasant after years on the streets.

"Like Santa's stables," Teddy laughed. "Am I right?"

KO spotted a knot of elderly white men hitching the ponies while others loaded fruit and vegetables onto the carts in crates. They were dressed in overalls and sporting chin beards, and KO smiled at how the men looked like well-fed Santa's helpers.

"Who are these guys?" KO whispered. "They're too big to be elves."

Teddy slapped KO on the back. "Mennonites, my man, from the countryside."

"They're not arabbers?"

"No, but they're the ones who make this possible," Teddy explained. "They grow our food on their farms or buy it for us wholesale, and I couldn't take care of the horses without them. They're production and management—we're sales. We split the profit. Works for me."

He waved KO over for introductions and KO got to see the daily exchange. The brief conversation in the stable was marked by puffs of fog from each speaker, mixed with the steam coming off the animals. Money from the previous days' profits changed hands between the arabbers and the farmers, then the Mennonites went back to their farms and the arabbers went onto the streets.

Teddy and KO's cart had a brown pony with graying flanks. She was named Spirit, though she seemed to have little of it that cold morning before sunrise. The farmers had already put a thin blue blanket over her before she'd been hitched up, but it took a firm pull on her bridle before she'd leave the barn.

Once they left the smells and relative warmth of the stable, the light breeze off the harbor felt like icy needles. It searched for any cracks in KO's winter armor and began pricking the tips of his ears. KO pulled his head turtle-like into the heavy navy pea coat's collar.

"Where to first?" he asked.

The cold didn't faze Teddy, who grinned like it was a fine spring day. "A coffee shop, of course," he announced. "We'll wait 'til sunup. Ain't nobody getting out of their warm bed in fuzzy slippers this early for a few tomatoes."

"Then why come so early?"

Teddy jerked his thumb back toward the stables. "The farmers. They gotta get back to plow the fields and milk the chickens—you know, farmer stuff—so they call the shots. Let's have a cup of something warm before we freeze our butts off. Come on."

They led the horse the two blocks to a small coffee shop with the name "Aromas" on the sign above the door.

Teddy pulled a thicker blanket from under the driver's seat and threw it over Spirit after they parked, then he pulled a carrot off the back of the open wagon and held it in reach of her mouth. The pony either nickered or grumbled, it was hard to tell which, but the carrot vanished in two bites.

"Okay, old girl, you got your sweets," Teddy said softly, stroking her gray-brown muzzle for a moment. Turning to KO, he nodded toward the door of the café. "Now it's our turn."

Beside the door, a small neon sign proclaimed it open in blinking green letters. KO stared at it a moment. Something nudged his thoughts ...

"Well, don't stand there staring."

It was gone, lost to Teddy's voice and the thought of hot, steaming coffee.

***

After a coffee and a donut, the sun finally crawled over the horizon and the temperature began to rise to something just below freezing.

"Okay, my man," Teddy said, his smile brighter than the winter sun, "time to do our thing."

Outside, Spirit had shown her disapproval for being left out in the cold with a pile of recycled hay steaming behind her. Teddy reached under the driver's seat and pulled out a small shovel.

"Time to earn your coffee, KO. Can't be leaving a mess." Teddy ceremoniously handed KO the shovel, then fetched a bucket hanging from a hook at the back of the cart. "Just hang this back on the hook after and we'll dump it later."

A month ago, KO couldn't have imagined himself scooping up fresh horse dung in the freezing cold, but now he laughed. His life had taken many unexpected turns, and this wasn't the worst by far.

KO's job was to lead the horse as Teddy sang out in his rich baritone, "Cantaloupes, potatoes, sweet corn, and yams! Come get your greens from the arabber man!" KO would stop the wagon when a customer emerged from a storefront or doorway.

Teddy did the selling, putting the money in a waiter's money belt. All transactions were cash only, and Teddy noted every sale in a green, cloth-covered notebook. "The

Mennonites are God-fearing people," Teddy explained when KO noticed this, "but they're tough businessmen. I gotta account for everything we sell today."

"What happens if they think you're cheating them?"

Teddy shrugged and waved cheerfully to the last customer at their stop. "I won't. But it'd be hard to prove, so they look for honest men. If they thought I wasn't straight with them, they'd get someone else to man the cart. A business like this relies on trust, and I respect them for giving men like me a chance." He beamed again as KO took hold of Spirit's bridle and they set off again. "This is a good gig. I've got two more weeks at the shelter, then I'm moving into a place Father Tomas set up for me. It's got its own kitchen, so I need the job."

"Is it hard, living on your own wages?"

"It'll keep a roof over my head. The farmers let me buy five dollars of produce every day at cost. That'll go a long way along with the food stamps and my share of the profits to keeping my belly full." Teddy spread his arms to indicate the neighborhood. "This ain't easy street, but it's heading me in the right direction. I'm happy to see you going the same way." He paused to stroke Spirit's nose. "C'mon, my brother. Let's sell some fruit."

Just then, they passed a bar. The wind changed, and the smell of stale beer from the dumpster washed over them. KO and Teddy froze. Teddy's smile was gone, his face hard, filled with a hunger KO understood at once, and he felt a chill other than the cold as the debt collector Teddy had been suddenly appeared before him. They exchanged looks before KO nudged Spirit forward once more, the only sound that of the old pony lumbering down the street.

"Hey, Teddy," KO said after they'd gone another block, his voice husky from the cold and the lust the fumes had awakened. "How long do you have to stay dry before you stop wanting a drink?"

Teddy shook his head as though to clear it. "I don't know, my man. I'll tell you when I do."

The last stop of their long day was at a retirement community, a one-story building set at the end of a cul-de-sac. It sat back far from the road, surrounded by trees and a snow-covered lawn.

KO and Teddy were greeted like rock stars, the few dozen residents converging all at once with smiles and waves of excitement. Some came out to buy a bundle of celery or an apple, others just to chat a minute and stroke Spirit's flank. A few shared a carrot or a freshly purchased apple with her.

"Where's Moses today?" one old black man asked. He wore a Korean War veteran ball cap on his head. "He on vacation in the Bahamas? If so, tell him to say hello to Sydney Poitier." He pronounced the last name "Poh-tee-aa," and the small crowd laughed together.

Teddy turned on his neon smile. "Moses slipped yesterday, and he's resting his bony butt at home. It'll be a few days 'fore he's ready to haggle over yams with you again." He hooked his thumb back at KO. "But we got us a celebrity here today. None other than the famous Kyle 'Knockout' Bannon. Him and Spirit been getting along so well, I think he'll be a jockey next week."

"KO Bannon?" the Army vet said. "I thought you was dead."

KO looked down the street for a minute before looking the man in the eye. "To tell the truth, for a while, I was."

More than one of the residents nodded. They understood how a man could draw breath but be dead to the world.

"Welcome back," the old soldier said.

"I remember seeing you on television," laughed another man, elbowing his way between two friends for a spot on the step. "You went up against Sugar Ray. I remember that. Eight rounds against Sugar Ray Leonard. Man, that was some fight!"

KO tried not to frown. "Oh, it was a good fight for Sugar Ray; was an ass-whipping for me!"

"Don't matter. You did your best," said a woman, smiling across an apple at him. "Ain't nothing like seeing a local boy in the ring against someone like that. You're a hero to me, KO."

Her sentiment was echoed by smiling and nodding faces surrounding them. KO was overwhelmed by the welcome, the sense of belonging. After a day under that detective's stare, he'd started to wonder if anyone would really think of him as more than an old drunk. He swallowed.

Teddy noticed a tear at the corner of KO's eye and gave him a strong pat on the back.

KO managed, "It's good to be back. Think I'll be staying this time."

On the way back to the stables, Spirit plodded wearily while Teddy hummed to himself in rhythm with her steps. At one point, he leaned sideways to nudge KO out of his quiet.

"Well, what do you think of your first day as an arabber, KO?"

"More than I could've hoped for, Teddy." KO smiled a moment, then stared at the growing shadows.

"You know," Teddy said, "I noticed you looking kinda serious back there, when they mentioned Sugar Ray."

"It's just that's a time when ..." KO shook his head. "It's not who I am anymore, is it?"

"Who you was is a part of who you are."

"Well, I was kinda thinking. That's the one time I gave up. Really gave up."

"What d'you mean, brother?"

"I heard the bell. I knew I could go back in the ring, but I knew he'd just bust me up some more. It was the eighth round ... I couldn't believe I'd made it that far. I had some fight left in me, too. I should've gone for it. Maybe we would've gotten more fights, made it big. Maybe Howard wouldn't have bailed on me if he thought I was worth staying for."

"Ah, no matter how you tell it, KO, this Howard was a crook. There's no making you the bad guy in the story. You're an honest man. Take it easy on yourself."

"I dunno, Teddy. Maybe I was afraid of making it big. Maybe I ... maybe I wanted to fail."

"Let it be, brother. Today is all we've got." Teddy gave the reins a pull and steered Spirit around the last bend. "And y'know, you thinking about it? That means you learned from it. And next time you hear the bell, you'll get up. Count on it."

Chapter Fifteen

Jan. 13, Monday evening

A familiar drama was unfolding outside a bus terminal as the snowfall thickened to a blinding veil, one familiar to Jillian Meyers. She glared at a blinking Chyron on the nearby schedule board. One by one, the departure times were blinking to canceled. She pressed her phone closer to her ear, trying to hear over the drone of other grumbling commuters.

"No, it's fine, Mom. Dinner's in the freezer. Just ... yeah, just fill the tub in case the pipes freeze again. The buses aren't running. I'll get to work another way. Really, I can deal with it. Love you too ... I ... Look, Mom, I gotta go. I'll be fine."

She punched off her phone and growled up at the gray clouds. It was certainly *not* fine, but you said things to parents.

From across the street, she spotted the promising glow of headlights from a steady stream of bright yellow taxis. They were sliding up to the curb and flying away again as travelers from the bus terminal crowded the sidewalk, all as desperate as she was. She stuffed a hand into her pocket, mentally counted her dollar bills and change. She had a protein bar. That would get her past dinner ...

Eyeing the foreboding sky again, she made a sprint for it, her gym bag clanking at her side, her other hand waving, desperate to be seen in the growing dark.

She hit the curb and skidded, saw the last taxi slowing as it approached, and hurried toward it. She was cut off by a tall overcoat that whipped open the door and dove inside.

"Hey, asshole!" she shouted, beating a palm on the glass. The taxi jerked to a stop as the thief spoke to the driver. She was already turning away when the window rolled down.

"Hey, sorry! Did I cut you off?"

She hesitated and turned back. A handsome, bewildered face leaned out the window and she suddenly felt embarrassed. "Sure, fine, whatever."

"There's room, get in. This is no cold to get trapped in."

She hesitated, then sighed in relief. If she lost her cab, she'd lose her shift. The man pushed open the door and she dove in, wedging the sports bag between them pointedly.

He told the driver, "Sinclair Marina."

"Drop me off at the corner of Southeast and Elliott," Jill said.

"Sure thing," said the driver, then shut up because he'd once gotten a bad Yelp review for being "too chatty."

Jill shot the interloper a sideways look. "You live by the dock?"

"I was working late, and sometimes I go to my boat afterward to unwind," he said easily. "I really didn't see you," he added apologetically, then eyed the bag. "You work out?"

"Is that a pickup line?"

"Not at all. I'm just desperate enough for conversation to state the obvious."

Okay, she admitted to herself, *that was kind of a funny line.* He wasn't bad to look at either. Still, there was a reason she'd gotten the gym membership.

"Yeah, I work out," she said to test him. "You probably can't tell by this jacket, but I could whoop your ass."

"Thank you for not doing so when I stole your cab!"

He looked a little pale, so she laughed despite herself. She admired a man who could take a sting. "Nah, don't worry about it, um ...?"

"Marty."

"Marty." She offered a hand. "Jill."

"Maybe I can make it up to you sometime when I'm not chained to a desk, Jill, or, y'know, out at sea," he laughed. He looked back ahead, then sideways again, opened his mouth, seemed to think better of it, then did it again at the next block. "You know, there's a—ah, never mind."

"What?"

"There's a pancake house down the street where I like to get my breakfast-for-dinner," he explained. "I mean, it's kinda the opposite way from Elliott, but I'd pay for the cab."

"You're a glutton for punishment is what you're saying."

A little smirk twitched at the corners of his mouth. "Uh ... nah. Just for pancakes, for now."

"Sorry. I got work tonight. Thanks for the offer."

"Sure."

The cab crawled on through the snow. Marty cleared his throat as they pulled up near his stop. "Um, would you like a rain-date, um, snow-date? A date?"

"You serious?"

He shrugged. "Why wouldn't I be?"

She could have answered that most men didn't like women who called them an asshole. She decided not to.

"Sure, hang on a sec."

Marty paid the driver as she dug out a memo pad. "No weeknights," she said as she wrote. "I work two jobs." She passed the page. "But if on the weekend you're in the mood for ..."

"Pancakes?"

"Pancakes. Or something. Give me a call."

He flashed a charming smile, then ducked out into the snowfall. Jill sat back in the cab as it pulled away, her stomach fluttering a little. It had been a while since she'd had a date. Maybe things could get better than fine.

Chapter Sixteen

Jan. 14, Tuesday

Father Tomas sent word for KO to come to his office after breakfast. Winter cost the shelter in heating bills, so he kept it cold and dressed in layers. The priest looked more like a fluffed-up owl than ever in his baggy black overcoat. KO took a seat in the only other chair, unconsciously patting the pocket where he kept his sobriety chip.

The priest said, "You're doing well, KO. Frankly, better than most. Teddy's boss is ready to go back to work and I think you're ready for a regular job outside of the shelter, though I'll miss seeing the floors here shine as much they do."

KO shrugged at the compliment. "I used to clean up the gym for extra pay when I worked as a trainer, Father," he said. "Guess I owe the gym owners for the experience. Any openings?"

"Possibly. Apparently, you still have fans. I got a call last night from a Mr. Hightower about a hiring initiative aimed at local shelters. He'd heard you were here and said he had an opening for a janitor, so your experience would be put to good use. The pay is better than anything I could hope to find for you on my own. You could start as soon as this week if I call him before noon."

KO liked the sound of that but teased, "What's the rush, Father? You anxious to get rid of me?"

The little priest wagged his finger. "The shelter policy is ninety days, and we need to show progress to keep you here."

"Just kidding. A paying job ..." He shook his head. "Ain't had one of those in a long while."

"With these wages, you could afford your own apartment. I'd like you to go to his office for an interview. If you get the job, wonderful! You can save up for a security deposit here for another month or so. But you don't have to accept it if it's offered if you think it's not the right fit for you. You can try your luck elsewhere. What shall I tell him?"

"Give me the address, Father, and I'll catch the bus this afternoon."

"No need. He said he could have a car here at one o'clock. You've time enough to get ready. I'll let them know."

KO smiled. His smiles were becoming more frequent and deeper, showing off the gold-alloy crown on his right canine. He'd bought it with his first winnings as a fighter—a reminder of better days.

"Thank you. Looks like my luck is about to change."

"You're working hard, KO. You deserve it."

***

KO changed into a white shirt and clean, dark trousers before running a brush through his graying hair. At the shelter closet, he exchanged his army boots for a pair of black shoes. They may have once belonged to a cook, as grease embedded in the leather made them impossible to shine, but they had grip that would help him on slippery floors. KO hadn't had new shoes since he'd wound up on the streets. If he got this job, he resolved, he would put something on his feet that hadn't been shaped by another's.

Having done all he could to look presentable, KO put a pen in his pocket, said a quick prayer, then headed outside. At one on the dot, a big black SUV with tinted windows pulled up at the shelter entrance. KO had never seen a car so clean in the middle of winter.

It couldn't have been anyone but his ride, but he approached warily. For a moment, his reflection stared back at him darkly from the driver-side window, and he almost didn't recognize the reflection as his own. The well-groomed respectable man who stared back at him looked like a citizen. Was that who he was now? Maybe not yet, but perhaps who he was becoming.

His study of this new self was interrupted by an automated hum, and the glass slid halfway down. A young man with a part in the middle of his hair stared at KO out of an interior that could have belonged to a spaceship. He wore a white shirt and black tie. The look reminded KO of a Mormon missionary he'd met once, which made meeting him in an expensive car feel even stranger.

The driver said, "I'm looking for Kyle 'Knock Out' Bannon."

"Are you Mr. Hightower, sir?"

The young man snorted a laugh. "Mr. Hightower doesn't drive his own car, not at work anyway. I'm Tommy—the gofer." He didn't open the window further. Instead, he looked KO up and down. "You're him?"

"KO, that's me."

"I'll take your word for it. Guess you're retired from the ring?"

"You could say that."

Tommy jerked his head toward the back. "Get in, if you're coming."

He hit a switch somewhere and the back door opened soundlessly. Holding his breath, KO ducked inside and buckled up.

They headed west toward downtown, and KO kept his hands clasped in his lap the entire way.

"What's it like, working there?" he asked, trying to get the silent chauffeur to open up.

"Pay's good. Hours regular. I do some acting but nothing that would pay the bills. Until Hollywood calls ..." he laughed, and KO felt a little better. "Mr. Hightower runs the show, but you hardly ever see him in our area; he's trying to get his son to learn the business."

KO wasn't sure what to say to this, but Tommy seemed ready to carry the conversation on without any help.

"I say, good luck with that! Gladys rules the office, though. You'll meet her soon enough. She won't like you, but don't take it personal. She doesn't like anyone except Mr. Hightower, *Senior*. She's been with the firm since he founded it. I think he'd fire everyone else before he'd let her go."

"Even his son?" asked KO in surprise.

Tommy laughed and shrugged.

A cluster of tall office buildings loomed ahead. "Almost there. Good luck with your interview. Mr. Hightower Junior can be, well, hard to predict. Let's hope today is one of his good days."

KO clasped his hands tighter. All this for a janitor position?

Eventually, Tommy turned the car into a parking lot the size of a small stadium.

"Thank you," KO said when the door silently opened. "For the ride and advice."

"Wait a sec," said Tommy as KO stepped out and stared up at the skyscraper. "I'll walk you in. We can't have you getting lost."

KO waited. He looked up at a sign marking the spot they'd just parked in. It read, "RESERVED. HIGHTOWER SECURITIES."

Tommy led KO across the parking lot, then through a polished foyer with multiple reception desks and high glass windows. The signs were all silver and brass, etched neatly with capital letters. Around a corner stood a line of elevators with pinstriped doors that opened with a pleasant chime.

Tommy waved KO in and punched a button halfway up the panel.

No going back now, KO thought.

He watched the numbers count to fifteen as Tommy pulled out a smartphone and texted distractedly until the chime sounded again. Tommy stuffed the phone away and led KO down a hallway with carpet so thick it muffled their footsteps.

They stopped at a dark-brown oak door with a brass plate. It too read, "Hightower Securities," and Tommy shouldered it open.

KO thought they would walk into an office but found himself in a lounge. Ten leather chairs were arranged around the room with brass pins for accents and lion-footed legs that sank into the thick wine-red carpet. There were no magazine racks and no vending machines, just a coffee cabinet in one corner beside an ivory-toned water cooler. The coffee machine was polished to a black shine and there were real mugs standing on a kind of warmer plate. The people who worked here had time to *brew* coffee.

KO was afraid to move, but Tommy strode straight to a desk beside the door across the room. He glanced back and beckoned impatiently for KO to follow.

Typing at a computer was an older stick-thin woman with dyed red hair, a pale face, and bloodless thin lips. Even from across the room, the odor of stale cigarette smoke wafted like a well-used ashtray. The name "Gladys Prince" glinted on the desk's nameplate above the title "Executive Assistant."

Gladys wore half-moon glasses on a glittering gold chain. She gave Tommy the barest of nods, but at the sight of KO, she stood and leaned forward, looking at him over her glasses like a librarian who'd just found a mis-shelved book. KO fought the urge to look down and check to see if his fly was open.

"You must be Mr. Bannon," she said in a gravelly, tobacco-scarred voice.

"Yes, ma'am, that's me."

"Well, you must be very important. Mr. Hightower said to bring you right in. Thank you, Tommy, I'll take it from here."

"I'm gonna get lunch then. Good luck." Tommy wandered out without looking back.

Gladys slipped from behind the desk as KO walked toward the inner oaken door. Its lettering read "M. Hightower, Jr." KO reached up, but Gladys knocked first with a pointed glance that strongly suggested she was concerned with the state of his hands. He tried to stop wringing them by holding them stiff at his sides.

At a summons from within, she pushed the door inward.

"Thank you," KO said again.

"His next appointment's in a half-hour," she said in reply, then turned back to her work.

KO swallowed and shuffled inside, letting the door fall closed without touching it.

The office reminded KO of a public defender's, only this place was several stories higher with a lot more brass. Everything was oak and wine-red carpet except for its wall-to-wall window that framed the desk and chair of its only occupant.

The young man looked to be in his mid-twenties, sitting with his fingers laced atop a green blotter. There were pens on his desk that looked too fancy to use. Beside these were a letter opener shaped like a crusader's sword, a file tray, and a bit of metal that might have been art or a puzzle. KO had never seen enough of either to be sure.

He tried not to stare at these too long because the man was busy staring at him. He was tall, even sitting down. After years in the ring, KO immediately judged a man's size by what his boxing weight category would be. As a middleweight, KO could not have fought over one hundred and sixty pounds. Years on the street had robbed him of at least fifteen pounds of muscle. This man was probably between two-ten and two-twenty, a heavyweight. He wore a suit jacket over a turtleneck, so no tie. The look bulked up his shoulders to match his waist. His short hair stood straight up, and he seemed amused by KO's arrival. As KO approached, he stood and offered a hand. Definitely a heavyweight. The man was nearly a head taller than he was.

"Mr. Bannon? Please, have a seat."

KO took the nearest one while Mr. Hightower sat back down and pulled out a notepad and pen as KO sized him up. Despite his fine clothes, he looked like he could take a hit. Maybe two. He just didn't need to. He had gofers for that sort of thing.

Uncapping the pen, the man flicked his eyes up once, more subtle than Tommy, but with clear intent.

Sizing me up too, I guess.

"So, why are you here?" the man asked.

KO's stomach tightened as the question caught him off-guard. "Beg your pardon, Mr. Hightower, but Father Tomas told me you were a fan of mine."

"What? Oh, right. That would be my father—Mr. Hightower *Senior*." He sighed, turning back the notebook cover. "*The* KO Bannon, living legend—it's all before my time, sorry."

"Thank you for your invitation, just the same."

Marty wrote something on the notepad, then smiled. It was a salesman's smile—a bit too shiny and tight.

"Well, I'm going to be running this company someday, so now and then I get to do the interviews. I've been looking over your recommendation from Father Tomas. I'd like to ask you a few questions."

"Sure thing."

It wasn't like talking with Dr. Stevens. KO sat on the edge of his seat, wringing his trouser leg in one hand, trying to keep up with the questions and maintain eye contact. As the questions and answers were exchanged, KO found himself dodging and weaving like he was back in the ring, trying not to let his nerves make him ramble. He kept his answers simple, sharp, on target.

The questions got a little personal toward the end. What had he been doing for seven years? How was AA going? Why change now?

KO had been willing to share his story with anyone up 'til now, but that salesman smile pushed back like a counterpunch with every question.

"I figure it's about time," he said, deciding to leave out the details unless they were asked for. "I'm not going to live forever. I've been given a second chance, and not many get that. It'd be wrong not to take it and make something respectable of myself. Do better by myself and others."

Mr. Hightower (Junior) studied KO for a long time after this answer. KO couldn't tell if he was taking his words seriously or about to laugh and began to think this was all a cruel joke.

At last, the businessman sat back in his chair with a sigh. He tugged at the collar of his turtleneck and the veneer of the showroom cracked into a cold, careless grin.

"Well, Mr. Bannon, you've said the magic words. My father has this idea he's calling the 'second chance' initiative. We fill low-skill labor positions at our company with men and women who need a second chance to get their lives back in order. My father's very Catholic, you see. He sits on various boards within the Baltimore diocese. He asked around for names, and yours came up. I figure anyone can hold this position if they've got grit, but my father wants you. You know why I'm telling you this?"

KO shook his head, then remembered to speak and said, "No, sir, though I'd thank your father for his faith in me."

"I mean," said the other man, leaning forward, "I've got just one more question for you: When could you start?"

"Anytime, sir. Tomorrow, if you'd like."

"Well, I couldn't offer you a ride every day. You'd have to make your own way to work. And there'd be duties besides cleaning. Errands to run, maybe some copies to make. You'd have to set up the coffee every evening, get it ready for the next morning—or folks will not be happy around here, I'll tell you."

KO frowned, a little confused. "Would I be working for you then, sir?"

"For Gladys, mostly. She can show you what we expect, but you'd mostly be on your own. You'd hardly see me." He put back on the grin. "Don't worry, she's a dear once you get to know her. So, your hours'd be nine to six, an hour for lunch. As for dress, wear clean clothes every day. Black pants, white shirt. No ties though. Tommy will be green with envy. Any questions for me?"

KO looked around the fancy office, then down at his less-than-fancy shoes. It sounded too good to be true, a job made just for him. And for good pay, too. "You mean I'm hired?"

"If you want the position, I don't see any problems. Just don't punch anyone—unless my father asks, I suppose. Might make his day."

"Oh, that's the old me, sir. I'm not—"

"Just a joke, Mr. Bannon. You'll get used to it."

KO had to take a moment to understand what had just happened. Just an interview, just talking, but he felt like he'd gone twelve rounds without a break.

"You won't be disappointed, Mr. Hightower."

"I'm sure I won't," he said, then added, "Just call me Marty."

They both stood and shook hands.

He broke open a wide, charming grin, but KO still couldn't help but see a salesman behind it. Strange. Must be what a company man always smiled like, though KO couldn't figure out what he was selling.

Chapter Seventeen

Jan. 18, Saturday

Jill had agreed to pancakes that afternoon, which led to drinks at the nearby bar, then a visit to his boat for a cruise of the harbor by moonlight. He didn't take long at it, not as much as usual. A pity really. But it had taken over a week to get her routine down for the initial "chance" meeting, and he had needs.

Later, Marty ran his "lucky" silk tie through his fingers, savoring the feel of it, almost liquid, and he imagined it was still warm from her neck. He shivered as he relived that magical moment watching the spark in her eyes fade away, feeding that dark place inside him that no one else ever saw— and lived.

This time, when it was over, he decided against weighting the body before dumping it. The cops were onto him, anyway, and it pleased him to let them know that he knew. Cops liked to remind people of their power, but they'd never be his equal.

Time to show them who they were dealing with. He liked to play video games and he'd played this game of cat and mouse with the cops long enough. He was ready to level up.

***

Jan. 21, Tuesday

Winter deepened. Ice and snow built up in layers with mud, and car exhaust dyed hills of it gravy-brown on every street corner. The cold sank its claws into everything and kept its grip, even as the days inched toward February.

Leads were going as cold as the streets.

"Dragons," Mankiller muttered. "I need something I can use."

Ruiz was making a roundabout way to his desk and had been for the past fifteen minutes. She had her usual stops, including the coffee machine and the printer, checking in on other cases with other detectives before taking the last leg to his office. She had a file tucked under one arm and tapped a finger on it pointedly when she entered.

"Anything?" Mankiller asked.

"My informants haven't seen anyone suspicious that matches our profile, and the recent Jane Does don't fit the MO. Still, there's some good news."

"What?"

She passed him a photocopy from her file.

"Vice gave me a heads-up. They've got a warrant to search Finnegan's office at The Gold Digger Club and personal effects for proof of solicitation, and here's the file of his criminal record, under the name James Finn."

Mankiller whistled. "The law of unintended consequences. I like it."

"Well, after what that creep said when we were alone in the club, I'm not shedding any tears." She coughed. "I may just happen to wander by Booking when they bring him in."

"Go for it."

"Karma's a bitch, but I didn't mind lending her a hand this time. Too bad Bailey can't be in on the bust. He'd love to swoop in and rescue his ... damsel?"

"Sir Galabad." Mankiller shrugged. "You really believe that guy? Dating one of those girls he interviewed!"

"People all have different ideas about romance, Boss. It'd be a story to tell the kids."

"Yeah, when the kids were of legal age. I wonder if they'd be born with tattoos." He reached for her file. "You mind if I look anyway? Your informants may have seen something important and not known it."

"Here's hoping." Ruiz handed over the folder. She hesitated, then said, "Maybe it's time, *Jefe*."

"Time?"

"To put out an ad. In the paper. Offer some reward."

"Every Tom, Dick, and Harry would have a story."

"We need *some* kind of story."

"Yeah, one without dragons in it," Mankiller sighed.

The front desk phone rang a moment later, and Davis began waving from across the room. "Sergeant! Line six."

***

Mankiller and Ruiz shivered their way into the morgue after lunch just as Dr. Hamera was bustling forward to meet them. She looked pleased with herself.

"You're going to be happy with this one, Sergeant."

"Bold choice of words," Mankiller grimaced.

"Anything new?" asked Ruiz.

Hamera beckoned them down the lane to the newest arrival. At the table, she set aside her notes, pulled on her gloves, and neatly folded back the sheet.

Ruiz relaxed a little: no jarring scar gaped up at them. But the face looked almost as pale as the sheet, and nothing like the pictures in their growing file.

Mankiller gazed stonily at the still form of Jill Meyers, former kickboxer, waitress, and aspiring actress. Science said that humans came from the water, long ago, and he believed it. "Floaters," bodies that were recovered from the water, began to look more and more like fish the longer they remained submerged: gray, bloated. As much water as flesh, as the body returned to where it had come from millions of years ago.

"She was underwater a lot longer than the last one," Hamera said, "but her appearance matches the missing girls you're following. My supposition that the last floater was a rushed job is supported by these ..."

Hamera uncovered the woman's arm and carefully handled the wrist. "A narrow rope or cord, tied tight. Here," she set down the arm and moved to the foot of the bed, turned back the sheet there, "and on the ankles. With the amount of bruising, I'd say she was tied up at least an hour before she died. But there's no sign of a struggle. Otherwise, there'd be ecchymoses around the knots."

"So she was bound after she was drugged?" Ruiz suggested.

"Right. That would explain the traces of Valium we found with Ms. Wyatt. The contusion on the back of this woman's skull doesn't belong, but it's not the cause of death. It's fresh, but it wouldn't have knocked her out."

"Maybe she got it at the gym, kickboxing," Mankiller explained as Ruiz checked the file. "That was the last anyone saw of her."

"Cause of death?" Ruiz asked. "Her throat isn't cut like the last one."

"Probably strangulation," Hamera answered. "Or, rather, garroting. If the material is soft and wide, a person can be slowly strangled without leaving external marks. I'll know for sure once we open her up."

"So, Carly Wyatt must be an outlier, like you said."

Hamera nodded. "And still your best bet for catching him. This john is a clean-freak, whoever he is. This body came in here tidy except for what it picked up in the salt water. He feels safe, wherever he is, or he wouldn't take so much time."

"Then why not weigh it down? Why risk us finding the bodies now?" Ruiz asked.

"He probably reads the paper and knows the jig's up," Mankiller said. "Or maybe ... he might be taunting us."

"What do you mean?"

Mankiller grimaced. "You know the psychology, Ruiz. It isn't about sex; it's about power. Strangulation is as much a power trip as it is a means to kill someone. Might even be the only way our perp gets release."

Ruiz suddenly wanted to hit something or someone. Very hard.

Mankiller turned back to the pathologist. "So, to transport the body to the harbor, he'd need a car or a place nearby."

"KO said he heard a splash," Ruiz pointed out. "He must be close to the harbor to dump the bodies there."

"KO also said he saw a *dragon*."

"Mmm. Anyway, it's progress," said Hamera. "I'll have this in the full report on your desk by this evening."

"It's weird, though," said Mankiller. "First the streetwalkers, then a dancer, now a boxer. They've got almost nothing in common except how they look. How does he meet them? What's the connection?"

Ruiz opened her mouth to say something, then shut it hard. Mankiller didn't miss her hesitation but said nothing. She'd tell him when she was ready.

Meanwhile, the killer was playing with them, leaving behind a trail of breadcrumbs. For now, they had to follow as best they could.

***

"The speed limit's twenty-five, Ruiz."

"On a sunny day."

"I mean it's not five." Mankiller looked up from turning pages in a file. He glanced at the road, then Ruiz clutching the steering wheel, peering through a light fall of snow. "You're doing fine, Detective Penguin. If you feel the tires start to slide—"

"I know, *Jefe*, roll with it, not away. It's just ... this weather is crazy."

"Which is why you're learning to drive in it—in my car, by the way."

"Why does it have to keep snowing? There's plenty on the ground already."

Mankiller shook his head and turned another page. He sighed. "Forget the dragon a minute. What's by the dock that's dry and private?"

"We can rule out hotel rooms."

"Okay, I'll bite. Why not a hotel room?"

"Because he's got kinks."

"I think his problems go way beyond kinks, Ruiz."

"I mean, he'd have to make sure it was the same setup every time. Even if he checked in as a John Smith, he'd have to make sure he had the same room, same bed."

"Is that how kinks work?"

"And, assuming he's done all the murders in the same place, there'd be a record. He wouldn't want a record, even with a fake name. Besides, he's *rich*, *Jefe*. He'd have a cave."

"A what?"

"You know, a cave? A lair? A secret hideout? Like you and your little observatory where you look at the stars."

"I knew I shouldn't have told you about that."

"I mean, I have a cave too, but I horde fluffy pillows and bobbleheads there."

"And chocolate."

"You *looked*?"

"I didn't have to look, Ruiz. It was everywhere. Watch the light here."

"I see it. Okay, I'll admit, these all-weathers are great. I'll get some—after you drive me home." The tires slid a bit and

Ruiz's endearing smile didn't quite make it through the grimace this time. She re-centered the car in the lane.

Mankiller settled back in his seat and continued reading the slender file they had on the latest victim. Jill Meyers was survived by a widowed mother. Senior citizen. He swallowed hard, knowing soon they'd have to ask her into the station. He tried not to think about it.

"So," he said, "not a hotel or motel then. Maybe an apartment. Somewhere no one would notice."

"Near all those clubs and fancy restaurants? Come on, *Jefe*, you're making this too hard."

"Look, she left with the guy. They all *left* with him and then they were killed—why arc you pulling over?"

"Hear me out." Ruiz pulled the parking brake. "In the twenty years you've been on the force, when have you ever blamed the victim?"

Mankiller sighed and dropped the folder in his lap. "I've been around the block, Ruiz. I've seen killings, robbery, domestic abuse, kidnappings. I'm not blaming the victims; I'm looking for patterns of behavior that help me understand how he finds them and earns their trust. I want to understand how Romeo gets women to go with him to their death, and I'm not getting any better at it."

Ruiz shrugged. "Not much to understand. No one asks to be murdered. Murderers do it anyway. You know this. I know this ..."

"Not everyone takes risks that leave them alone with a killer."

"*Life's* a risk, *Jefe*."

"Fair enough." Mankiller sat back in his seat, but he was thinking about Anne again, how she'd waved a finger in his face too, right before saying, "*I left you enough clues, didn't I?*" He tried not to think about it because he still didn't know what they'd been. He drew a deep breath. "I don't really know how to put this without sounding like an asshole ..."

"Try me."

"I don't understand women."

She deflated as much as her puffy coat allowed. "Well, I know you've been a detective more years than me, but I've been a woman more years than you'll ever be."

"Do enlighten me." After a beat, he added, "Please."

"You once said you became a cop 'cause of all the stuff your family went through when you were a kid."

"And ...?"

"And I became a cop because of women like Carly and Jill. I don't blame them for what some predator does to them. I mean, look at me, right? Young, healthy, attractive—"

"I'm sure I'm not allowed to comment, but sure, two out of three."

"Thanks, *Jefe*. Look, I got lucky. I've got a family that made me work hard for what I wanted. Got skin tough as nails. If I had just my looks—Lord knows, right?"

"Er ..."

She dug her elbows into his ribs. "C'mon, *Jefe*! You think some little girl woke up on her first day of school and dreamed of dodging handsy drunks as a pole dancer, paying bills with money she had to iron first?"

The image hit him late. He felt a blush creep up his neck.

"Life hit, and it hit hard. All these victims, they were just trying to keep their heads above the water and then something *nice* came along. Carly went to Julliard. You have any idea how much work that takes? It's a dancer's dream."

"But then why not play it safe?"

"I know these streets, okay? I know the guys who *try* to pick up chicks from the guys that *do*: they're not idiots. They know what mothers tell their daughters to look out for. They know how to *look* safe and respectable. They're hunters, *wolves*. It's not the woman's fault; it's the wolf's."

Mankiller sat in silence, turning her words over in his mind. She was right. He knew she was, both about the wolf and his blindside. He wanted to ask her about Anne but was too afraid of what she might say.

"Whoever this john is," Ruiz continued, "he'd look respectable and he's got a nice setup to lure them in. We'd be wasting time running around motels and shoddy apartments. He's selling fire-in-the-sky romance: roses at Christmas, chocolates on Valentine's Day. And fireworks and a kiss at midnight."

A thought clicked ... He scribbled down a note before it was lost.

"And meanwhile," Ruiz continued, "women like Little Carly and now Jill the Boxer, they're just living paycheck to paycheck, and their world's this narrow tunnel. They live for hope that it'll get better, but they're alone, mostly."

"Ruiz, say that one more time?"

"Not the whole thing? I really don't want to park here any longer while the snow piles up."

"No, I mean, about the fireworks."

"Why?"

"Because I'm an idiot."

He should have known better. Ruiz smirked and patted his shoulder. "This is a big step for you, *Jefe*. Glad I could help."

He brushed the hand aside. "Not about that. Just drive, okay? We need to get to the station. KO has a session with Stevens today and I want Stevens to debrief you after."

"You gonna tell me what's going on in your head?"

"We were talking rooms, but Carly's body was dumped in a hurry—no bag, no weights, nothing. The killer had to have been *near* the water. The dragon KO saw was above the water."

"So ...?"

"So what do rich kids keep by the water? What's their cave?"

"Not a hotel."

"Not an apartment either. Detective, we're looking for a boat."

Chapter Eighteen

Jan. 21, Tuesday cont.

"I hear you've got a new job, KO."

"That's right, Doc. Working downtown. I'm getting so good at making coffee, I might work up to Starbucks someday." KO smiled.

Stevens liked that smile. It had been slow in coming.

"How's it going with AA?"

"My sponsor, Teddy, is a big help. Like he says, the best person to get you out of a hole is someone who fell into it themselves. I wish we'd had more time working together as arabbers, but this job came along and it's the best one I've had since I left the ring. Things finally seem to be going my way."

Stevens knew how much work KO had put in to have come so far so quickly and hated to break the mood, but he had to ask his usual question eventually.

"Wanna go dragon hunting today?"

The smile faltered.

Stevens was certain KO had seen something that frightened him besides the dead girl, and he knew it was important. Maybe a movie poster or ad for a new TV series? *Game of Thrones* was big now, and there were a lot of ads for the next season. But Stevens suggested nothing. Suggestions could build false memories.

KO wasn't nervous anymore because Stevens never pushed him too hard or too far, but he was never able to look directly at the dragon in his vision and describe it. Now he shook his head. "Sorry, Doc. Every time I get to that place in my head, all I wanna do is run away as fast as I can."

"Okay. Let's work on the sign you saw then. Care to take a spelling test for me?"

He gave KO a list of common words, all misspelled. "KO, I want you to correct the spelling of these words the best you can. There're twenty words, so I'll give you five minutes. Care to try?"

The fighter shrugged. "Sure thing. I was never very good in school, but I'll do my best."

KO finished in two minutes. Of the twenty words he'd been given, he changed the spelling of twelve, nine of which were still wrong.

Stevens kept a poker face as he graded the test. "So, you say you were never very good in school. Were you ever held back, maybe moved to another class?"

"Yeah, Doc. I had to repeat seventh grade. I dropped out right after ninth."

"Did your teacher ever mention you might have dyslexia?"

"My teacher said I might be stupid."

"Well, that was a different time, wasn't it?"

"Don't worry about it, Doc. Good thing I was better with my hands, or I'd never have made a living."

The psychologist nodded at this. "Dyslexia doesn't have anything to do with intelligence, KO. It just means your brain sees some letters backward or mixed around. There's help for that these days."

"Nah, Doc. I am as God made me. I can read enough to get by and do my numbers pretty good. Thanks anyway. Anything else?"

Stevens paused. It was probably now or never, he reckoned. *Time to play my last card.* "There's one last thing we can try to help you remember, but it's a hard one."

"What's that?"

Stevens cleared his throat before he took the plunge. "There's a chance that if we recreate the moment, your mind might be able to recall what you saw at the harbor that first night."

"You mean imagining, Doc? I tried that already, you know. I really did."

"This would be different, KO. You see, strong memories, including trauma, are often triggered by familiar conditions. If we take you back to the harbor at night and you have some drinks, it's possible you'll remember exactly what you saw and where you saw it."

KO's eyes widened as he slipped a hand into his trouser pocket.

"Doc, I told you, I made a promise to God, to Father Tomas, to Teddy and my friends at AA that I was never gonna drink again. When I was out with Teddy selling fruit, we walked by a bar and when I smelled the booze ... I mean, it took all my strength not to crawl inside the dumpster and lick the bottles. I'm dry today, right now, but I don't know if I ever drank again if I could stop it. I can't ..." He swallowed. "Next time, the dragon might be coming for me."

"I understand," said Stevens patiently. "You fought your way to sobriety. You're not sure if you can do it twice. It's only a suggestion."

KO nodded, tears in his eyes, his smile gone. "There's a demon waiting for me in a bottle, and when I drink it, the demon crawls inside and tears me down. I don't know if I'm strong enough to go another round with him."

Stevens nodded, both disappointed and proud of the man at the same time.

"Alright," he said. "Let me know if you change your mind." He stood and walked around the desk, his hand out. "Unless something new turns up, this is our last session. I admire how much you've improved these past couple of weeks, KO. I'm proud to know you and wish you well."

The old fighter stood, took the man's hand, and saw the respect in the psychologist's eyes. Respect. He was getting used to it again.

No, KO resolved, getting drunk again wouldn't help.

***

Ruiz brought Stevens' final report into the sergeant's office.

"Bad news, *Jefe*."

"There's another kind?"

"Not lately. Doc did a spelling test on KO. He's got dyslexia. His memory of the weird sign is probably nothing more than that. I'd bet he got his 'C's and 'O's mixed up. He was probably just looking at an 'OPEN' sign."

"Great. All we have to do is find an OPEN sign and we're halfway there!"

Ruiz grimaced sympathetically. "That's not all. Doc asked KO if he'd be willing to have some drinks at night along the harbor."

"That 'situational' theory?"

"That. He refused. Said he was never gonna take another drink. Stevens didn't feel like arguing it, figured he'd lose the man's trust, and frankly, didn't think it was ethical to try to convince him and put his sobriety at risk."

"So, we've struck out in the witness department."

Ruiz closed the file. "Sorry, *Jefe*, but it looks that way for now."

"That it?"

She shrugged.

"Any crumbs you can give me?"

"Doc said we should still check in on KO every couple of weeks for a while. Sometimes these memories come back on their own, get triggered by something. He has no idea how likely that is."

"Barely better than nothing. Maybe I can convince the priest to talk him into it. It's a long shot, but I hate looking at dead women on a slab with nothing to show for it." Mankiller rubbed the back of his head, his old nemesis making an appearance. "Anything on your search for dragon boats?"

"Funny you should ask. Dragon boat racing is a big thing in the summertime here, but they're kept in boathouses for the winter. No way KO would have seen one of those walking along the harbor. I had the boys down in IT do a scrub of marina records for any regular boat with a dragon name. Found a *Smaug*, a *Dragon Wagon*, and a *Green Lizard*. Two are down in Florida for the winter and the other's been in dry dock in storage while the owner looks for a buyer."

Mankiller's headache slithered to the front. "Well, keep at it. Might be time for less Detective Google and more Sam Spade."

"What do you mean?"

"I mean, use some shoe leather and go down to the marinas. I've never owned a boat, but the folks who do tell me the things are always breaking down."

"So, check with the mechanics?"

"Maybe one of them can remember a local boat that has something dragon related."

Ruiz half-bowed her head. "So, *that's* why you get the big bucks."

Mankiller rubbed his temples. He'd need a dark, quiet place to lie down soon. "Yeah, and good thing. It almost pays the alimony."

***

Mankiller met Father Tomas in his office later that day despite a now throbbing head. The small priest was sorting books in his library while his dinosaur of a computer sat with a blank word processor page on the screen. Mankiller got the impression of a college student up late working on a paper ... or procrastinating on it. Still, when Mankiller repeated his request Tomas gave him a cold, hard no.

"I've assured his employer that Mr. Bannon is committed to staying sober."

"So, we'll do it on the weekend. We'd be with him the whole time. This murderer is killing women, then vanishing without a trace. Maybe some spirits will smoke him out."

"That," said Father Tomas, "is a joke in poor taste."

It hadn't felt like a joke. Mankiller glanced back down the hall from the priest's office. He could hear Ruiz talking in hushed tones to the big man called Teddy. She was apparently getting along better than Mankiller was.

"Father, there's a murderer out there," Mankiller said bluntly. "This isn't just some shot in the dark. This is science."

"Memories come back in many ways, Sergeant. Mr. Bannon has made a vow to God. As his spiritual guide, it is my duty to help him keep it."

Mankiller nodded, his face neutral. *Vows.* "Could you at least tell me where he's working?"

"You wouldn't question him in front of his employer, would you?" Father Tomas asked sharply.

"I'm a cop. I go where the trail leads."

"You think I'm fighting a losing battle, don't you, Detective? You believe Mr. Bannon and all the men here are lost causes."

"I don't think anything of anyone I haven't met," Mankiller said. "But, yeah, it just so happens I've met a lot of lost causes."

"In your line of work, I doubt you have any need to see the ones who succeed," Tomas pointed out. "I have. It's worth the effort. Every man has a right to a new life if he's willing to work for it; a right to second chances and to dignity."

Mankiller paused, remembering why he never touched a bottle. His brother, John, had ambitions once, making the final fall worse.

"Yeah, well," Mankiller said at last. "I'm not a drinking man myself. I don't want to encourage it, but I do want to find a murderer. I think if it's to save a life, it's a vow worth bending."

"And will a life be saved?" Father Tomas shook his head. "If you've never been taken with an addiction, I don't expect you to understand, but you're not the only person in the life-saving business. The Lord calls all kinds."

"Forgive me, but I'm having trouble understanding why KO would be 'called' to sobriety right when this is the only way to save lives."

"Then perhaps it is not the only way." Father Tomas paused a moment, then said, "There are no easy answers with faith, Sergeant. In my case, I grew up in the Democratic Republic of the Congo. It was and still is far from what a democratic nation should be. I was barely ten years old when my much older cousin had me 'conscripted' as a child soldier—a kinder word than kidnapping. And thanks to him, I got these."

Father Tomas surprised the detective by tugging off his priestly collar, then carefully removing his shirt. Mankiller gasped at the scars crisscrossing the small man's chest and back, clearly marks of torture—one in his left shoulder an old bullet hole, puckered and ringed with a hard black scar. Whoever had treated it hadn't done a very good job.

"If you're seeking a murderer, Detective, then one stands before you. I killed my first man on my twelfth birthday."

Father Tomas passed his hand over his eyes, as though to wipe the memory away. "He was tied to a post, crying with fear. Shooting him was my 'graduation' ceremony. The last life I took was a child I killed before her pleading mother. I was fifteen."

"Damn," Mankiller said softly, not knowing what else to say.

Father Tomas nodded. "Yes, Detective. Damnation of the deepest order. My parents named me Justice Dibwa, and if I'd received the justice I deserve I'd have been killed long ago. Instead, I wound up in a program for child soldiers developed by UNICEF, and a Portuguese priest named Tomas Gonzalez showed me the way to salvation. Justice Dibwa could never atone for his sins, but as Father Tomas I have yielded up that burden. Christ led me out of Hell, and I have dedicated my life to helping others find their own path back to God, whatever their Hell may look like. I will not help you throw a man back in when he's doing all he can to climb out."

Mankiller could not meet the priest's eyes. Suddenly, the small man seemed larger than anyone he'd ever met.

"I'm sorry, Father," he said at last. "I respect what you've gone through." Then he raised his head and watched as Father Tomas replaced his shirt and collar and became a simple priest once more. "But I'm also trying to save people in my way. I meet with the families of the dead. I see the pain in their eyes and it follows me into my dreams. They ask me why but I have no answers other than I do all I can to stop the killers from killing again. It only makes it harder if I know there's something more I could have done. I couldn't forgive myself if I lacked the will to do it."

"And I honor you for taking on that burden, Detective," Tomas said, "but the Apostle Paul wrote, 'We now see through a glass darkly; but then face to face.' We might not understand now, but when the Lord offers a path and we follow it, we can trust a reason will present itself once we are ready to see it."

"With respect, in my line of work there isn't time to wait that long."

"But this short-term solution, this scientific method, might yield you nothing while doing irreparable damage. I will not encourage it."

Mankiller recalled a line from Shakespeare, how did it go? *"Though she be but little, she is fierce."* Tomas was a man, but the mild little priest had a steel within him as fierce as a Marine storming a hill, and he knew when he was fighting a losing battle. He chose a compromise.

"Look, Father, could you ask him if he'll talk to me about it again, at least, when he's had time to think it over? In the end, he should decide either way. He's not going to survive out in the world without you unless he starts making his own choices."

The priest took a seat at the computer and considered the blank screen. "I will ask him, Sergeant, but I won't help you convince him."

"That's fair."

Mankiller bid him a good day and collected Ruiz. As they headed out, he seriously considered plunging his head into a snowbank to take away the pounding and the image of the enormous scars on a fierce little man.

Chapter Nineteen

Jan. 22, Wednesday

K O was hard at work at the table of the office's small break room. He had cleaned the surface carefully of crumbs and ketchup before laying a sheet of the firm's stationery down to begin his letter, and now he worked intently on his lunch hour to the exclusion of all else, even forgetting about his packed sandwich.

> Dear Amy,
>
> I'm writing from my new job in downtown Baltimore. I know it's hard to believe. So did I. I waited a few ~~wekes~~ weeks, and I'm using this paper to show it's true. I know you don't have a lot of reason to trust an old drunk, but I've got good news about that too. I got an AA sponsor! I've been going to AA meetings for three weeks now at ~~Winebamu~~ St. Roch's Men's Shelter, and I'm clean now. Clean enough to hold a job.
>
> I know I haven't been there for you, Amy, but I want you to know I think of you every day. I think of the kind of man I should be for you. I'm doing my best, Amy. I'm saving up to get out of the shelter and make a new life. And I know it'll be a while before you might ever want to see me again, but I want you to know I'm ~~gonna~~ going to keep trying. I believe God has given me a second chance ...
>
> Dad

Gladys had been waiting for something ... anything to re-establish her authority outside the executive offices. In the past, the custodian had always worked under her supervision, but Marty had made KO his own special project, like a pet. Something suspicious was going on, she was sure of it.

She had been the first employee Mr. Hightower Senior hired when he started the company and had seen it through the financial crash. In theory, Gladys was his EA, but his demands were few and young Marty couldn't keep his own for very long. So, the father asked Gladys to "take care" of Junior while Hightower Senior coasted into his final few years in the firm. He knew Gladys wasn't overworked but did not begrudge it of her, given what they'd been through together.

Gladys admired her "real" boss, and he treated her with kindness and respect. His son—not so much. The only saving grace was she could give him as good as she got as he didn't have the power to fire her.

But now Marty had shown up with this homeless bum, this "KO," and because this old man had once been good at knocking down other men, he was treated with more kindness and respect than she'd ever gotten from that privileged snot.

She saw KO struggling with a pen (apparently his own) and a sheet of fine bond paper. She looked closer and saw with some satisfaction it had the firm's letterhead. He hadn't noticed her yet. Perfect.

"And what do you think you're doing?"

He sat upright and dropped the pen, clicking as it bounced on the floor. KO's eyed fixed on the furious Gladys, glaring over her half-moon rims at him.

She snatched the paper up.

"I-I was just, uh, writing a letter, ma'am," he stammered. Stooping, he fumbled for the pen. "I waited 'til lunch hour and—"

"This is the *company* letterhead. Where did you get this? Were you going through my desk?"

"No, ma'am, never. I asked Tommy for it."

"Tommy? And he let you have it? I ought to have you both fired!"

"Please, Ms. Gladys—"

Gladys held the paper out of reach. "Hightower Securities is not a trashy *motel* with cheap stationery to spare writing to some girlfriend."

"It's not—"

"This is for company business only. You should know better."

"I just ... I ..."

A calm voice broke in from the doorway. "Something the matter, Gladys?"

"Mr. Hightower," Gladys said primly. "I was just explaining to Mister Bannon that company stationery is intended for company business." She glared at KO, "and only company business."

Marty was wearing a turtleneck again today and had his jacket slung over one shoulder, like someone out of an ad for upward professionals. He even grinned like one until he noticed KO's face.

"What's going on?"

KO listened as Gladys gave her version of events with a dramatic flourish or two.

She must really hate me. Maybe she resented someone as rough as him for finding a place in her world of thick carpet and shiny brass fittings. Not for the first time, he felt out of his depth. It was *just* a letter. No one had said there were regulations about paper. He'd even brought his own pen ... KO's chest felt tighter and tighter, like the moment in the ring just before the bell for round one.

Marty was saying, "Gladys, I think you're overreacting. KO, you okay?"

Taking his daily newspaper out from under his arm, Marty gave KO a light tap on the shoulder. KO stared fearfully at the captive letter in Gladys's hand, unable to explain its importance. Marty groaned.

"Now look what you've done, Gladys. Let me see that." Marty took the letter and scanned it quickly. Then he chuckled and shook his head. "Ah, c'mon, Gladys. It's a letter to family. This is right up Dad's alley."

"Mr. Hightower—"

"Mr. *Hightower*, yes. Now be a dear, Gladys, and go have yourself your tea and sandwiches—and a cigarette. I know when you're all nerves. I'll take care of this."

Gladys turned on her heel and strode off in a rasping huff, her head bloodied but unbowed. This was far from over in her mind—a ceasefire, not a truce. Marty looked back at KO, and his smile faded as he handed the note back to KO as if it were made of glass. KO took it and held it to his chest.

"KO, you a'right? That your sandwich?"

"Um, my pen fell and ..."

"I got pens a-plenty in my office. Grab the sandwich."

Moments later, they were behind the door, barred against Gladys's imminent return. Marty fetched KO a tumbler of ice water from a drinks nook, then leaned on the desk and looked him once over. He opened a drawer and pulled out a fresh piece of stationery, an envelope, and a better pen than any five-and-dime would sell.

"Here, use these."

"Sir, I ..."

"My company, my office, my paper."

KO took the tools with great care.

"This Amy—your daughter. Any other children?""

"No. Only Amy. Her mom passed on a while ago. She lives here in Baltimore, got a house and everything all on her own. I'm proud of her. She used to be of me … a long time ago."

"And she hasn't seen you in a while, I take it?"

"No, sir. We, uh, well, she tried letting me home once, after her man left. She figured 'family first' and all. I couldn't hold a job, though. I get some social security every month, but I spent my money on drink, so … she kicked me out. I deserved it."

"And that was how long ago?"

"Seven years. I call on holidays, but, um, she usually won't take my calls, so …" KO tried to shrug but it looked more like a spasm. "I thought, what with Tommy saying it was alright, that I would write using the stationery to prove I was doing better. I mean, why should she trust me?"

Marty switched on his salesman smile. "Tell you what, KO. You finish your letter. I'll add a little note of my own and I'll put the company address on it for you, use Gladys's stamp and everything. That way it's doubly official."

After the tornado had torn through his nerves, KO felt the sun had come out. "Thank you, sir, I mean Marty. That would be … That's more than I deserve."

Marty flinched a little, then boosted the wattage of his smile. "Yeah, well. Look, I know I said you'd get your own rides from here on in, but why not catch one home with me tonight? You look like you took a bit of a shock."

***

The look Gladys gave KO when she left for the day would freeze a pot of coffee in August. He knew she could make his job a lot harder, and he didn't want to be watching his back. But the damage was done.

Still, anger was a heavy burden, KO considered as he finished mopping the break room. Maybe that was why Gladys was the way she was. KO thought about his anger at his old manager, Howard. He had been carrying that weight for a long time, blaming all his troubles on how the man had wronged him.

Maybe it was time to let that go. He thought back to the sermon Father Tomas had wrestled out of that old steam-powered computer on his desk: "When I was a child, I talked like a child, I thought like a child, I reasoned like a child, but when I became a man, I put away childish things." The priest had gone on to say that when you blame someone else for your troubles, you don't take responsibility for making things right. Maybe it was time to put his own burden down so that he could move forward on his own two feet.

Like a man.

"Hey, KO."

KO looked up as he stowed the mop bucket in the utility closet. Marty was waiting with his briefcase, still wearing that million-dollar smile.

"Ready to head out?"

***

Marty kept his eyes on the road and hands on the wheel. He wore fancy leather driving gloves and didn't seem bothered by the falling snow. He took the long way back to the shelter, citing his wisdom of Baltimore traffic.

"So, what's it like at the shelter? They treat you pretty good?"

"No complaints ... Marty." KO nearly stuttered over Marty's first name. It must be a new-fashioned thing. He felt like he might be kicked for breaking rank. He looked out the window at the city still under an icy siege. "Food's good, and as long as you got earplugs for the snoring, sleeping in a real bed sure beats cardboard in an alley."

"From what I hear, you made a hard right turn in your life. Why now?"

Marty's smile was the cold, shiny salesman version, but he seemed interested all the same. *Maybe he's been smiling like that so long, it's normal for him,* KO thought.

"Everything a'right?"

"New Year's Eve I saw something, but, well … I still don't know for sure whether it was real or a vision from God, or maybe something real God meant for me to see." He kept looking out the window.

"Now you've got me interested, KO. A vision?"

"Part of it was real, though," KO explained. "I …" He hesitated. "I saw something while I was drunk. Had to tell the police about it."

"You saw something? What, if you don't mind my asking?"

KO hesitated. The sergeant hadn't said anything about not telling, and there had been a story in the paper. "I thought I saw a dead girl," he said. "The next day she was found washed up on the shore in the harbor."

Marty let out a low whistle. "Pardon my French, KO, but *damn.*"

"The police have been trying to help me remember where, even brought in a doctor who hypnotized me, but nothing worked. You, uh, you won't tell anyone in the office? Your father …"

"Don't worry about it." Marty's hands tightened on the wheel, his fancy gloves creaking slightly under the strain. "That must be a lot of stress. What do you remember so far?"

"It was around New Year. There was fireworks, a splash in the water, and the dead girl—that's all I can recall."

"Nothing else?"

"A sign I couldn't read straight. I have trouble reading anyway. It was dark, and I was drunk. I didn't even know where I was ... After that, I knew I had to clean myself up. I could have done more if I hadn't been so drunk."

"It's not much to go on. So, what now? More hypnosis?"

"No, I'm done."

"Really?" Marty's grip on the wheel relaxed, just a bit.

"Well, the doc told me he had one idea left, but I can't."

"Oh? Come on, KO, buddy, don't leave me at that. What is it?"

"He thought if I went back to the harbor at night and got drunk, like I was before, maybe I could remember where I was."

"Damn! You gonna do it?"

KO shook his head. "No, Marty. I took the pledge. I ain't never taking another drop. I don't know if I could give it up again if I broke my promise to myself and God. One thing they teach you in AA is that it's all or nothing. And I'm all in."

"Honesty. I like that in a man. I hope your daughter sees the new man you've become."

***

Marty switched on his smile for the rest of the drive while he considered his next move. Like he'd thought, a bum. But even without the booze, he had a weakness. You could never have too much insurance.

They turned onto the back street near St. Roch's Men's Shelter.

"Say, KO, did you mail that letter from the mail drop in the building?"

"No, Marty. I was so shook up I forgot. I can drop it off tomorrow. Why?"

"Well, from what you've told me, she might not believe you've got a job. She might think you stole the envelope and the paper. Why don't I hand it to her myself? Then she'll know you're telling the truth."

KO shifted in his seat. "It's a hard thing to say, Marty, but you're probably right. She got no reason to think I'm not still the drunk she threw out. Would you really do that for me?"

They pulled up to the shelter and Marty extended his hand. "If I wouldn't do it, I wouldn't have offered. You got the address written out, right? I'll drop it off on the way home."

KO pulled the letter from his jacket pocket and worried it in his fingers. Marty tried to keep his eyes off it while holding his breath. Finally, KO passed it over and Marty patted his arm.

"Just, uh, don't make me look bad, KO. Remember your pledge. You don't want to let me, her, or yourself down."

"It means a lot to me, you saying that, Marty."

"I don't say what I don't mean. Good night. I'll see you tomorrow."

"See you tomorrow, Marty, and thanks for everything. I won't let you down."

Marty nodded pleasantly, his foot itching for the gas pedal. "I'm sure you won't. Stay sober, and you've got a future with us. Don't forget that."

KO turned and shuffled to the shelter door while Marty drove away, considering his next move. He'd have to play his next cards carefully. He dropped the envelope on the seat beside him and pulled out a small notepad.

He jotted down the address on the envelope while idling at a red light, murmuring. "A nice little insurance policy."

Now it was up to KO to choose if Marty would need to cash it in.

Chapter Twenty

Jan. 22, cont.

When KO returned to the shelter he found a grinning Teddy waiting for him by his bed with a ready bear hug.

"What's this about?" KO asked.

"I'm moving out tonight, remember? Come to give you a present before I go. I wanted to hand this to you myself."

He held up a blue poker chip. Like the green one, it was thick and sturdy. KO dropped his hand into the pocket of his trousers, his fingertips finding the familiar ridge there as he had so often over the past month.

"I already got a green one from Father Tomas," he said.

Teddy didn't stop beaming. "The green one's your welcome chip. Since I'm moving out, I thought I'd give you your one-month sober anniversary chip a little early just in case I'm not there the exact day you make it. It's both a reward for what you've done and a reminder of how far you still have to go. As your sponsor, I get to give it to you and I didn't want to miss the day, just in case." He rubbed the back of his head and cleared his throat. "I didn't tell you this before, KO, but you're the third man I've sponsored but the first one to make it this far. I'm proud of you. Here, take it."

KO took the chip from the big man's hand and looked at it. He pulled out the green chip and put them together. The ridges and grooves fit snuggly together. Just plastic, maybe, but they felt firm and full of promise. Another milestone.

"Thanks, Teddy. I'm grateful for you standing by me." KO hesitated, but if this chip was another sign, he couldn't have asked for a better one. "Hey, before you go, you got a minute?"

"Sure, man. What is it?"

They sat on the bunk and KO explained what Doctor Stevens had suggested.

"They want you to drink again? Why?"

KO was grateful for the practice he'd gotten telling Marty. "The night I turned around, it was 'cause I found a dead girl's body. It was New Year's night. She'd been murdered. I was drunk, so I can't remember much. A doc I talked to at the station thinks the only way I can take the cops back to where I found her is to return to the harbor and get drunk like I was that night. What d'ya think?"

Teddy thought a minute, not rushing the question. "They sure you'll remember if you take a drink?"

"No."

"Do you want to take a drink?"

"Truth is, right now ..." KO rubbed the two chips together, "yeah. Real bad. I know it's the last thing I need, but it's still got a hold on me."

Teddy nodded gravely. "You worked hard to get here. Don't throw it away. If it was me, and it ain't, I'd politely tell the cops to get drunk and go jump in the harbor themselves."

KO slipped the chips into his pocket and felt his shoulders unwind. "Yeah, I think you're right. Thanks, Teddy."

The big man stood and dropped a hand on KO's shoulder. "Just 'cause I'm moving, don't mean I'm not still your sponsor. I'll be two blocks away, and I'll keep coming here for meetings. You ain't rid of me yet. Any time you need someone to talk to, even just to listen, I'll do my best to be there. The Devil's more patient than most people. If he tries to sneak up on you, last thing he wants is you asking for help. You ain't alone."

They embraced, and Teddy left to gather his things into a duffle bag. KO watched him go, one hand squeezing the hard, round chips in his pocket.

That'll be me in about six weeks, he told himself. I just have to hold on.

***

Ruiz knew the best way to find someone who worked on boats was to go where the boats were. That afternoon, she knocked on a sturdy door under the sign: *F Shwiller, Custom Boat Cabinets and Repair.*

She heard the clank of a metal tool falling on concrete, profane muttering, then the stomp of heavy boots. The door opened, and a middle-aged man with thinning red hair and an even redder nose stuck his head out, his bifocals nesting on top of his head.

"Excuse me, Mr. Shwiller?"

"Is me." She recognized a Boston accent. "Got it on the first guess."

"I'm Detective Ruiz, Robbery/Homicide. I'd like to ask you a few questions."

Shwiller looked Ruiz up and down, then squinted at her badge without bothering to recover his glasses. He looked unhappy with what he saw.

"Yeah, Officer, ya here to look for suspicious anythings? All the boat pieces I got here I either got from the boat owner or I can show invoices for."

Ruiz couldn't think of anything suspicious a shop like this would have, but the question made her think there might be. Were there "chop shops" for boats like there were for cars? She smiled at the vision. Maybe there needed to be a video game named "Grand Theft Kayak?"

"No, Mr. Shwiller, I'm not accusing you of having stolen property."

He didn't budge from the frame nor open the door any wider. "Then can we make this short? I work solo, so when we're talking, nothing's getting done. Maybe it's because I like working alone, or maybe no one's willing to work fo' me. Maybe a bit o' both."

Ruiz would bet on the latter.

Shwiller crossed his arms. "Ya still ain't told me why ya're here."

She shivered in the evening breeze coming off the harbor. "I'm looking for a boat, or at least I think I am. I thought maybe you could help me find it. Can I come in?"

He snorted but stood back to let her into the tepid warmth of his shop.

The workplace was in a semi-permanent state of disarray. Ruiz had seen desks with similarly organized chaos. Some people just worked better with their trade spread out to all corners of the room. The workbench was currently occupied by a sheaf of wires resembling an octopus cyborg.

Shwiller closed the door and offered a stool, the only visible seat in the workshop. Ruiz brushed most of the woodchips and sawdust off to join those on the floor.

"If ya're looking to buy," said Shwiller, "I don't think ya can buy the kinda boats I work on with just a cop's pay." He pulled out a workbench for a seat. "I could fix ya up with a rowboat, maybe, if ya can pay cash."

Ruiz laughed. "It's not for me, it's for an investigation."

Shwiller's eyebrows knitted. "What kinda investigation? I need a lawyer?"

"No, Mr. Shwiller." She pulled out her notebook, checking for his response. None. "But you've seen a lot of boats in the harbor and I hoped you might know one matching the description a witness gave us."

His eyebrows parted and he leaned forward as he considered her words. "Lady, these rich guys think they're unique little snowflakes. They're like a supermodel who won't wear their favorite dress to a party if someone else is wearing the same style. They try to make each boat as different as they think they are."

"That's promising."

Shwiller shook his head. "It's irony for ya: in the end, they all look and act pretty much the same."

"So nothing stands out during repairs?"

"As long as they pay up on time, I don't much notice anything on their boat that ain't broke."

Ruiz wondered if Sam Spade got this kind of grief, but what the hell, she was already here. "Well, I think you'd notice if they had a dragon."

Shwiller whistled. Ya'd think so, wouldn't ya? Nah, I've seen cobras, rattlesnakes, anacondas, and sea serpents painted on the side or stern of a hundred boats in the harbor."

Ruiz was overwhelmed by the reptilian possibilities but plodded on. "Maybe you could give me a list of sea serpents, and we can start from there."

Shwiller scratched his head. "It's not like I keep a file or anything, but ... tell ya what, I'll write down a list of names I can recall and send an email in a day or so." He stood up and started moving papers and folders beside the workbench, revealing a small PC buried underneath. "I can't promise it'll be all the boats in the harbor or even all the ones I've seen. Just the ones I can remember. Will that get ya out of here and me back to work?"

"I could come back tomorrow and pick it up, if you like."

"No need. I know how to use a computer. I promise to send ya the list before the end of the week. Deal?"

The man was under no obligation to do anything and he hadn't flinched at the notepad. His deal was better than nothing; at least she'd have proof for Mankiller that she'd spent some shoe leather.

Ruiz carefully printed her work email address on the back of her card and handed it to the man. "Thank you, Mr. Shwiller."

He shrugged. "Don't mention it," he said, adding as he turned to go back to work, "to anyone."

Ruiz stopped halfway to putting her notebook away. "Oh?"

"I just get the feeling some of my clients don't exactly make an honest living. If I get the rep of being friendly with the cops, well, they'll go elsewhere."

"Fair enough, and if I ever need a rowboat ..."

"You'll know where to find me."

Chapter Twenty-One

Jan. 22, cont.

The neighborhood was bare but neat, the hallmark of poor people doing the best they could with what they had. There were lawns, but none decorated with snowmen. All the sheds were locked. Some windows had bars on them.

Marty strode up the front walk, his shoes crunching on haphazardly scattered rock salt. He took the steps of the porch on tiptoe: each one still half-covered in snow. Noting the peeling paint on the stair rail, he jabbed at the dollar-store doorbell stuck to the frame. A window was open despite the cold, and he smelled the starch-water aroma of boiling pasta.

He didn't have all day, so he jabbed the bell again.

A curtain moved back, then fell before Marty could spot a face. A moment later, the sound of a chain, a sliding bolt, and a deadbolt marched up the doorframe, but it didn't open.

"Ms. Sellers?"

"Are you the police?"

"I'm not a cop, no."

"I don't owe anyone money. You stay around, and I'm calling 911."

"I'm not a loan collector either. Maybe you've heard of—"

"The good word? Have that here already. I don't need your 'more accurate' Bible translation or your tarot readings or some alien superpowers, or whatever you're selling."

He'd been to some shady places, but Marty had never heard a voice so polite and poisonous at the same time.

Thinking fast, he pulled a business card from his suit pocket. "Actually, Miss, I work with your father."

The door cracked open. There was still a single chain in place. Marty flinched at the dark, serious eyes of the woman staring up at him, but when she didn't speak, he carefully offered the card. The eyes flicked down at it, then back up at him. She didn't take it.

"Is he dead?" she asked.

"What? No, he works for me. This is just a courtesy call."

Reluctantly, the woman took the card and glanced over it. "Sorry—suits usually only come here if someone's already dead. Or they want money," she said, still guardedly. "My father doesn't live here, and he's not welcome. Hope he isn't bullshitting you. I don't talk to him anymore, so I don't really have anything to say to you. Now, unless you're not holding a giant check for a hundred grand, I have to get ready for work."

"Wait just a min—" Marty jammed his toe in the door and instantly regretted it as the woman slammed the door hard and he barely pulled it clear. He raised a fist, fought the urge to beat on the wood. Instead, he jabbed the doorbell again. "Ms. Sellers? I'm your father's *employer*."

"I'm calling the police if you don't go away now."

"He's not in any trouble. I'm just here to deliver a letter from him, then I'll be on my way."

The door cracked open again. Amy Sellers glanced back once down the narrow hallway behind her. "I'm not going to read it, but fine."

She didn't stick out her hand, just held it up behind the chain. *Careful, this one.* Marty passed the letter over.

"I know his story," Marty said. "I'm here because I think you should too. He's turning his life around. You don't have to do anything with that, but he knew you wouldn't believe him without proof."

"Yeah, well, thanks."

Marty took a step back and the door shut again. He could just make out the shadow of Amy watching him through the window. Fine then. He turned and hurried back to his idling car.

"What a bitch," he muttered, glancing back at the house.

A moment later, he cruised down the street and out of the godforsaken neighborhood, blasting Bon Jovi on the radio.

***

Amy rechained the door, then slid the bolts back into place. She considered the letter, leaning back against the door and hefting it to feel the weight. It was thin. Probably only contained a page, but it was heavy, the address a fancy embossed copperleaf deal. She'd never gotten a piece of mail this nice.

She shook her head and strode back down the hallway, dropping the letter in the wastebasket near her charging phone. She shut off the stove and drained the pasta, then turned to her fellow chef, standing on a footstool at the dining table, slicing the main dish with a child-safe knife.

"How're those hot dogs coming, Taylor? We gotta get you fed and next door to Mrs. Henley before I go to work."

"Almost ready," he said with the seriousness of a surgeon. "Who was that, Mommy?"

"That was Mr. Hightower, your granddaddy's boss."

"He didn't want to stay for dinner?"

"No, baby. He doesn't like mac 'n' cheese with his hot dogs."

"More for us then."

"Amen and amen."

***

Amy worked the graveyard shift at an all-night pharmacy a couple of miles away. She hated not being at home at night with Taylor, but the extra pay that came with a late schedule paid the mortgage. She returned from Mrs. Henley's and turned off the smile she wore so Taylor didn't worry.

She reached for her phone and glanced down at the fancy letter in the trash again.

I'll just keep thinking about it.

Sighing, she picked it out of the basket, leaned back against the wall, and opened it. It was short but earnest. Amy couldn't help smiling at the misspellings and crossed-out words.

Dad was never good with words.

She sniffed and reached for a handful of tissues, then pulled her Bible off the bookshelf and folded the letter carefully inside.

"Maybe we'll get a miracle this time, Dad," she said and tapped the Bible with her forefinger three times, like she had his nose years ago after their "sparring" matches.

She'd read it again later, she promised herself. If it all worked out.

Chapter Twenty-Two

Jan. 23, Thursday

Mankiller stared at the calendar. Another month ending. Yet no closer to catching the man feeding on the hopes of desperate women. He had no idea if getting KO drunk would help or not but knew that any day he'd get another summons to the morgue, and his frustration would grow. If only KO could feel the burden he felt to stop the killer and bring him to justice, he might reconsider his vow for one night at least. Just one night.

Father Tomas was right; Mankiller didn't know much about addictions. But he knew it wasn't all about a moment. It hadn't been with his brother. If there was something as simple as an on-off switch, the alleys and overpasses wouldn't hold so many lost souls every night, and Father Tomas could take up golf.

Father Tomas. Mankiller had to admit he'd underestimated the man, taken in by his soft words and thick glasses. Sure, the priest no longer carried a rifle, but Mankiller recognized him for the warrior he was. They'd get no help from the priest convincing their only witness to raise a bottle to his lips.

If only KO saw what we see, heard their words.

He tapped his pen a few times on his blotter to help himself think. One person stuck out. As far as he knew, her daughter had been the first, or at least the first whose parent insisted their daughter hadn't run off. When other girls matching the girl's description had also disappeared, Mankiller had taken her side. That's when the file started, along with the first suspicions pointing toward a murderer with a particular taste in victims. Three years later and the file was thicker, yet they were no closer to catching the man adding pictures to the file.

If she was willing to share her story again …

He hesitated. Was this right? He knew what Father Tomas would say, but Mankiller had his own scars, just deeper. He pulled out the file, opened it to the first page, and wrote down the contact phone number. He took a deep breath before calling it.

"Hello, Mrs. Faraday? This is Detective Mankiller from Robbery/Homicide. Would you mind coming in tomorrow at one? I don't want to get your hopes up, but we have a possible witness. I'm hoping your testimony could help him remember something helpful. You can? Thank you. Come to the desk sergeant; I'll have him call me when you arrive. Thank you."

He hung up the phone and returned the file. Trying not to think of the darkness of the interrogation room ahead of him tomorrow, he swiveled in his chair and looked out the window, hoping for stars, but all he saw were winter clouds. In times like these, he yearned to see the constellations, to look through his telescope and marvel at the purity of a creation far removed from a world where people's lives were so cheaply thrown away, either by their owners or all too often by others.

Chapter Twenty-Three

Jan. 24, Friday, 9:00 a.m.

G ladys was itching for a cigarette when the phone rang. "Hightower Securities, Ms. Prince speaking." She kept her irritation out of her voice, a skill built from years of practice. "How may I help you?"

"Good morning, Ms. Prince. This is Detective Ruiz from the Baltimore Police Department. I'm calling about a witness for an ongoing case who works for your company, a Mr. Kyle Bannon. I'm sorry for the inconvenience, but we need him to come in for some questioning. We'd like to send an officer to pick him up at your office around noon. Can you confirm his availability?"

Gladys's need for nicotine was replaced with a more potent drug—revenge—but kept her voice perfectly professional. "Just one moment, Detective," she said. "Let me confer with our director, Mr. Hightower Junior. It won't take a moment."

She hit the hold key and considered. Wouldn't the shelter have mentioned KO was part of an investigation?

Maybe it had; maybe Marty hadn't.

Gladys had had a bad feeling about Marty, even when he'd been just a boy, but his father always had an excuse. Then one night at an office party, Gladys found a young intern in tears in the ladies' room, two buttons missing from her blouse. That was all it took for Gladys to know her gut was right, but by the next day the promising young woman had left the internship with only a hastily typed-up letter of resignation.

Gladys had tried to tell Mr. Hightower the real reason, but Marty was in the office that morning before she arrived, ready with his boyish smile and saying it was all a misunderstanding complicated by too much alcohol on both their parts and he'd got it swept under the rug.

Gladys must have examined the signature on the resignation letter a dozen times against its original, but she couldn't prove anything. And that hadn't been the last time she'd smelled a rat.

Well, let Marty think she was some old witch in his father's good graces; she'd do everything to make Junior's life as painful as possible. Short of embezzlement, his father would never fire her, and Marty knew it.

All this ran through Gladys's mind in the space of two breaths before she decided what to do. Time to tighten the screws and see how Marty reacted.

She preened a bit, dripped a couple of eye drops into each eye to keep her vision clear, then checked her mascara for good measure. She took the two steps to the door and gave it two sharp raps.

When he barked, "Come in," she opened the door with the care of a surgeon entering an operating room. Spilling blood effectively was, after all, a matter of precision.

Marty was scowling at the monitor on his desk. Gladys knew petroleum futures were not going the way he'd predicted. It was a day to ponder whether it was time to sell and cut losses.

"What is it, Gladys?" he asked, not looking away from the red numbers on his screen. "This isn't a good time."

"Of course, Mr. Hightower, I apologize. But thought you should know I have a Baltimore Police Detective on the line."

The reaction was more than she could have hoped for. It was very quiet, but Gladys had paid her way through college at the card table. The old poker player in her could see the direct hit. Marty's head jerked toward her as he looked up and his pupils dilated.

Interesting, she thought. *Useful, maybe.* She filed it away. This was turning out even better than she had hoped.

Marty cleared his throat and clasped his hands. "And what do *they* want?"

"They want to know if Mr. Bannon would be available for questioning today, around one p.m. An officer would come by at noon to pick him up and, I assume, return him after." She paused, waiting to see how he played the hand she'd just dealt him. After an awkward silence, she asked in her sweetest voice. "Is that acceptable?"

"Yes, yes, of course, but tell them to wait downstairs. We don't want our clients seeing them here at the office."

Gladys nodded but wasn't finished. "I agree completely, sir. Oh, but that does remind me, Mr. Bannon's thirty-day evaluation will be coming due in two weeks. By the terms of his contract, we can separate him within the first thirty days without cause. Are you sure you weren't hasty in hiring him? Has he mentioned anything about the police before?"

"We did a background check."

"But this is new, isn't it? If he has continuing involvement in some sordid affair ... Think of our reputation. Police coming in and out, tramping through our reception area. Perhaps you should tell your father there's a chance of some scandal and look for more ... stable employees?"

Marty shook his head, and all his careless charm returned. "I know you don't approve of him, Gladys, but Dad says that helping people who don't need help is just an exercise in making you feel good about yourself."

"But you said ..."

"I said we did a background check, Gladys. KO shared this police issue with me. He's helping in a murder investigation, and I don't think we should penalize him for being a good citizen. He's an asset, really. Worth keeping close."

"You didn't mention this before."

"Are they on hold?" Marty added, still smiling. He fiddled with the mouse on his desk.

Gladys nodded, ever the dutiful executive assistant. Fine. She'd concede this battle but not the war. "I'll just let them know we'll have him ready, shall I?"

After confirming the time with the detective—and insisting Mr. Bannon not be kept from his duties longer than necessary—Gladys tracked KO down in the copier room. He was carefully adding the fine black toner powder to its receptacle, holding the packet away from his white shirt. It was the only shirt he'd ever worn to work.

Gladys reset her poker face and announced, "The police are coming for you, Mr. Bannon."

KO went very still. He did not, as she had hoped, spill the powder all over his shirt.

"Yes, Ms. Gladys," he said, resuming the task. "I imagine they have more questions?"

His calm acceptance was disappointing, but she couldn't expect to draw an inside straight every time. "Yes, that's what the police detective said, anyway. They'll be here at noon, and I expect you to be downstairs waiting for them. We'll not have them up here. We've a reputation to preserve. Do you understand?"

He shrugged. "Is there anything else?"

She turned on her heel and left, ignoring the question. Fetching her purse from her desk, she strode off to her favorite balcony. Soon she was puffing away at her morning cigarette like The Little Engine That Could.

Fighting with KO wasn't any fun because he never fought back, never raised his voice, never appeared to lose his temper. Perhaps she should just let him be. At first, she'd thought he and Marty might have some sort of under-the-table arrangement, but maybe it wasn't his fault Marty treated him with kid gloves. KO certainly didn't seem to expect it.

And she had to admit, the coffee had never been better.

Marty, on the other hand ...

One day he's going to slip up, and I'll be there. No one can look that perfect all the time. She reflected on his reaction when she said the police were on the line as she watched the smoke drift away into the gray winter sky. A look like that could give you hope. *Everyone has something to hide.*

***

Marty stared at the door after Gladys left. He knew his father thought more of her than he did his only son. While Marty's favorite fantasy involved lazing about in his boat off the Keys, a close second was watching her being escorted out the door by security, her brass ashtray and potted plant in a cardboard box. On really bad days there was something worse, but, no, she was too close to the family. *Pity. A bag of bones like that would sink without any weights at all.*

A cardboard box full of personal possessions was a distant second, but it would have to do.

Chapter Twenty-Four

Jan. 24, Friday, 12:00 p.m.

"This is not going to go well, Sergeant."

"I expect it to go horribly, Ruiz." Mankiller slowly turned pages of the thick file on his desk— now a file of all the missing girls and the two known murders. If he'd noticed the formal title, he pretended not to. "But I'm not changing my mind."

"There are other ways to warm up a cold case," said Ruiz. "Please don't do this."

"We need more details, Detective. That's the cold hard truth; otherwise, this john'll keep killing and this file will grow thicker."

"And if it doesn't work? What's the cost?"

"The decision is mine, Ruiz. You can hate it all you want. Hell, I hate it. If you can think of any other way, I'd like to hear it."

The trouble with having a staring contest with your boss was he had to look at you. Mankiller was cold today and fixed on the task at hand.

"I've thought about this a lot." Mankiller stood up and shut the file in his hand. "It's time KO understands what's at stake. Really at stake."

"And what about what's at stake for him?"

"I care, Ruiz, but I care about the dead girls and their families more."

"Well," she said, "I don't have to pretend to like it."

Mankiller slammed the file onto his desk. "OK, Ruiz, time for some tough love. You're a cop. You're a damn good cop, or you wouldn't have made detective. You did a fine job walking through the playgrounds and keeping the pedophiles away from the kiddies. Mothers were happy to see you. You made them feel safe. Storeowners probably offered you free coffee for the same reason. You were a badge-wearing sheepdog, there to keep away the wolves. But wake up. We're not the guardians. We're the enforcers, and to do that we have to go from being a big cuddly sheepdog to a wolfhound so we can think like the wolves. We get called in when the bad guys slip through, and no one, trust me, no one is happy to see us. We deal with the lowest scum in the city, and if it was your sister that turned up floating in the harbor you wouldn't shed a tear over trying to get a drunk to 'take one for the team' and bend his vow for one night."

"You're right about that, Sergeant. I'd be willing to use a hot poker on anyone who could lead me to the bastard that did it—which is why I'd never be allowed on the case."

"There are other sections in the department, Ruiz. You like catching pimps? Human trafficking is a major problem, and you could do a lot of good in Anti-Crime. Maybe that's a better fit for you. I know you asked for Robbery/Homicide. Now that you see what's involved, maybe you should reconsider. I'd make it easy for you and it wouldn't be a mark against you on your record."

All five feet two of Maria Esperanza Ruiz went into the answer.

"I'm a cop, Sergeant. I fought to get here to catch the bad guys, and I'm right where I belong. You say we're the enforcers. I see it different. When someone breaks the law, I mean seriously breaks the law, it throws the community out of balance. Trust breaks down. Just like my dad's car shop, we restore that balance when people see justice being done.

"The majority of the other cops are white men, okay? When they hit the streets, they're like some great white hunter on an African safari, studying the local wildlife and the primitive natives. I live in the neighborhood. I eat here, I shop here, and I get my hair and nails done here. Some old *abuela* tells me about her grandson working as a messenger for a drug dealer so I can bust him before he gets into bigger trouble. Why? Because she knows me and trusts me to do the right thing without cracking his head open. When my shift is over, I don't go back to my nice little house in the 'burbs ... No, I stay right here because these are my people, and this is my home. I knew KO on the streets, and he always reminded me of a king in exile. He had been noble once, and some traces of it are still there if you know where to look. I'd like to see him win his fight for self-respect. I don't think getting him to hit the bottle 'one more time' is going to help that."

Mankiller snorted. "Poetic, but it doesn't help us clear the case. Are you in or out? I need to know that now so I know how to stage this."

"I'll do what you say—as long as it's legal ... but I still don't approve."

The staring contest went on until Mankiller finally nodded and rubbed his neck.

"Never asked you to," he said. "If we're done here, wait for KO to show, then take him to the interrogation room and position him like I told you."

After Ruiz left, Mankiller went to the bathroom and took two large headache tablets, washing them down with tap water. He turned to leave but turned back to the sink and took a third one. After that, he returned to his office and sat waiting for the call from the desk sergeant. Mankiller sighed and fished for the chain around his neck with the Saint Christopher medal, taking it off and holding it in his hand.

He hadn't prayed in years, and he hadn't been to confession since his brother's funeral. Now he looked at the image of the patron saint for travelers. *I guess that covers all of us, doesn't it? We're all on a journey to somewhere.*

He balled the medal and chain up in his hand, dropped it inside his desk drawer, and slid it closed. Then he waited for the phone to ring and the curtain to go up.

***

KO showed up at the office at twelve-thirty. His worried smile made Ruiz hate herself even more.

"Hello, Detective. Is there something new?"

She wanted to say he was looking well, standing straight, holding himself with respect. But Ruiz just jerked her head down the hall from her cubicle. "Sergeant Mankiller will be questioning someone about a cold case. We think it involves the same man who murdered the girl you saw. The sergeant wants you to listen in, to see if it jogs your memory. It's a long shot, I won't lie, but it's all we've got."

KO nodded. "Sure thing, Detective. Whatever you say."

"I'll go with you."

"You don't have to."

"I don't mind." She pushed out of her chair and fell into step.

She led him to a viewing room one door past the interrogation room. Here a long table and four chairs faced a one-way mirror running the length of the wall. In the interrogation room on the other side was a shorter table with a chair on either side. A tape recorder was locked to one side of it.

"We'll need to be quiet and keep the lights off," Ruiz said in a tight voice. "Otherwise, we'll draw attention. They should be here in about ten minutes. Would you like a cup of coffee while we wait?"

"Sure, thanks," KO said, surprised.

"Milk or sugar?"

"I've never had cop coffee before. Black, I guess."

"It's a bit strong. I'll have it right up."

KO sat down in the chair Ruiz pointed to. When she came back with the coffee, she sat to his right. Mankiller's instructions had been very specific: He wanted the old fighter to see the visitor's face.

KO sipped his coffee and his eyebrows rose. "You weren't joking," he said.

"Yeah." Ruiz tried to smile. Failed. "Sorry, but this is rather serious."

"I understand, Detective."

"I don't doubt that."

Ruiz gritted her teeth, hating herself for what was about to happen. She pulled out one of her cards and wrote down her personal number.

"KO, I know you've been trying your best to help us. Maybe watching this interview will help you remember, maybe not. Doc said something might come to you out of the blue."

She handed over the card. "I've put my cell on the back here. If you remember anything new, I don't care when, please call me right away, okay?"

KO took the card respectfully, knowing how much trust she was giving him by sharing her private number.

"Sure thing, Detective. I promise."

Mankiller entered the interrogation room and turned his back to the mirror. He was followed by a stooped white woman in late-middle age. Her mascara had bled into the dark circles under her eyes.

He gestured to the other chair, and she sat, then he glanced briefly at the glass. Ruiz gritted her teeth, reminding herself he couldn't see her. She thought he could at least look sorry.

The voices came through a speaker mounted on the wall above the one-way mirror, slightly muffled, much as the glass tinted the whole scene dark.

"Thank you for coming in today, Mrs. Faraday." He opened a file. "I know this is hard for you."

The woman nodded weakly. "I'll do anything to help, Sergeant. Anything."

Ruiz held her breath as KO went very, very still beside her.

The woman glanced at the one-way mirror. "Is anyone back there?"

"Yes, ma'am, my colleague and the witness I told you about, the one to a recent murder. Is that alright?"

"Yes, of course."

Mankiller started the tape. Business as usual, unaware of Ruiz's eyes boring holes in the back of his head.

"Today is January seventeenth. The time is one p.m. This is Sergeant William Mankiller. I am interviewing Ms. Martha Faraday on case number HM-131 on the disappearance and presumed murder of Lily Faraday ..."

***

"Mrs. Faraday, I'll need you to take us through the events of the day your daughter disappeared, and of those the few days after."

The woman looked at the mirror in the back of the room for so long that KO felt she was searching for him. He felt goosebumps rise along his arms and chest. Once the interview started, he knew nothing, heard nothing, except the woman's tired, rough voice, pinned to his chair by the emptiness in the woman's eyes. He'd seen that look before ... every time he shaved.

"I understand, Sergeant," she said. "Anything I can do to help you catch the monster that took my baby is worth it."

KO wouldn't remember exactly what he heard next, but the story was crystal clear.

Lily Faraday, seventeen. A girl with braces and friends, with hobbies and homework. She'd been a cheerleader and popular at school; she liked to read, shop, and hang out with friends. Her mother described the way she'd looked the night of her prom, the pictures she'd taken. There'd been a fight with her boyfriend in a fancy restaurant, and she had stormed out while he stayed behind to pay the bill. When he went outside, she was gone, and he figured she'd taken a taxi home. Later someone said a girl matching her description had gotten into a nice SUV with someone, but all they could recall in the lights of the parking lot was that the car looked expensive and had tinted windows.

There were the frantic phone calls the next day. Weeks stretched into months. Now it had been three years.

There was pain in the woman's voice—twisting her face with grief, with anger. But there was drive too, a hunger for answers, for resolution. Her voice struck him like a roundhouse to the jaw.

"It's him," he whispered. "Has to be, doesn't it?"

Ruiz whispered back, "We think so. This missing girl looks just like the others we're looking for, and the two found in the harbor. The guy's obsessed with girls with a certain look ... like Carly, the woman you saw."

A wave of nausea swept over KO as he sat in the dark room, watching the woman open her wounds for his benefit. No. The wounds had never closed, as fresh today as the long night three years before as she'd waited by the phone—for a call that never came.

Ruiz went on, more quietly, "Usually, we wouldn't want witnesses or victims to meet or hear testimony from one another, but Sergeant Mankiller thought it would be helpful in this case. The disappearances have been happening closer together, and now with the last two bodies less than a month apart ..."

"I understand, Detective. So that other woman, the ... kickboxer?"

"Yeah. And there could be another by now. This guy's getting more and more active. The more women he kills, the more he wants to kill another."

KO's stomach clenched.

Did he have the blood of those others on his hands? If his coffee cup had been full of whiskey at that moment, he'd have drunk it in one go. To help remember? Or forget?

***

Ruiz watched the weight of the grieving mother's words slowly grow on KO, watched his head hang lower and lower. Her stomach was in knots, not just for him but for herself, for being part of this.

Maybe Mankiller was right. Maybe Homicide wasn't the right choice for her. He'd certainly been right about the difference between a beat cop and a detective. Before, her job had been to protect the public, a sheepdog watching over the flock. But now, just as he'd said, she was a hunter. She'd have to think like a wolf, but how to keep from becoming too much like them?

Either way, we chose this path, didn't we, Jefe? she thought. *But what right do we have to put that burden on anyone else?*

Mankiller ended the tape. "Interview concluded at one-thirty p.m., January twenty-fourth, 2014. Mrs. Faraday, thank you for agreeing to speak with me today."

She stood with a sad dignity. She'd told her story of loss many times before and no longer believed in miracles. She knew the detective couldn't make any promises. None she'd believe anyway.

"Every time," she said weakly, wiping her eyes, "it's like living through it the first time." She looked at the mirror again. Her voice was rough, dry, hewn from flint. "Just catch that monster."

She walked out of the room in silence, the echo of her pain lingering long after.

Mankiller put the tape in its case and labeled it. Then he stacked it with his paperwork, walked out, and shut off the light. The two-way window went dark.

KO and Ruiz sat in the darkened viewing room, neither speaking. Both started when Mankiller came in and hit the lights.

He sat down next to KO and set the papers on the table, then clasped his hands over them. If Ruiz hadn't known him better, she'd have thought he was about to pray.

"KO, I'm sorry for what you just heard."

Ruiz looked away, jaw clenched.

Mankiller went on, "I want you to understand that the man who killed the woman you found is still killing. You understand that?"

"I do."

"He enjoys it," Mankiller went on, grim. Relentless. "He's clever, careful, and ruthless. He won't stop until he's caught and brought to justice. I respect your courage in trying to improve your life, but this isn't just about you. How many more young women have to die before you see that?"

Ruiz and Mankiller waited. Finally, KO stood, ran his hands down his trousers, and straightened his collar. He asked quietly, "And if it doesn't work out, then what?"

Ruiz looked at Mankiller, who didn't answer.

"I know you don't like to hear this, Sergeant, but the last time I tried to do the right thing, protecting that poor woman from some rich white boys, I wound up in jail. I hurt my family all over again. My own daughter, who hadn't said ten words to me in years, got the call to bail me out." KO leaned forward until his nose was only inches from Mankiller's. "Now I got a chance to get my life straight, to earn back what I've lost, and you're asking me to 'do the right thing' again when it might not even work. I'm sorry, Sergeant. I really am. I'm sorry for those dead girls and their families, but I'm sorry for my family, too. I'm sorry for the years I threw away. I finally get the courage to put my life back together, and you're asking me to risk it all on an idea, on a big *maybe*. I've done everything else you asked, but I'm not going to do this. It's too much." He turned away and stared into the darkened glass, shaking his head. "Too much ... If we're finished, Detective, I need ... I need to get back to work."

Ruiz looked at Mankiller.

"Yeah," Mankiller said, "we're done." He walked to the door and paused there. "Now you've seen what we face with every missing girl who winds up dead. I can't force you to choose, but I asked you to come in today because I want you to hear their family's voices at night. I want you to see their tears. I want you to carry their pain the way I do. Maybe one more drink won't help, but maybe it will. The worst thing that happens is you fail."

"And that's what you don't seem to understand, Sergeant. It's not just me I'd be failing."

Mankiller nodded to Ruiz. "Have a cruiser take him back to his job." He gave the ex-boxer one final look before walking out, muttering, "Ours is far from over."

Later, as Ruiz passed by the men's room, she heard someone throwing up.

I hope so, she thought, then felt a twinge of guilt. *Another one for confession.*

Chapter Twenty-Five

Jan. 24, cont., 2:30 p.m.

Marty hid in his office the rest of the day.

Don't panic. Don't panic. You panic, you screw up. He left word with Gladys that KO should return to his usual duties when he returned. No use letting him out of their sight.

He shut down his PC and leaned back in his chair, scrolling the internet on his phone. He opened Wikipedia and made a few random searches, his knee jostling under his chair until he stumbled upon the phrase "situational-dependent learning" and punched that into the search field. He found an excerpt from 1835 telling of an Irish porter who forgot what he'd done when he sobered up but remembered perfectly when he was drunk again.

Marty read a bit further, making sure it wasn't just Victorian nonsense, and found several more reports within the last twenty years. It was a real thing. He read on as the sky darkened and sent all his office calls to message. He was staring down at the parking lot when the police car pulled in and watched KO climb out and shuffle back into the building.

"Shit," he hissed.

***

Later that night, KO got another ride home.

"This police sergeant has it in for me, Marty," said KO, as tired as if he'd just gone fifteen rounds.

"I thought you told him no."

"I did. I meant it, but ... he's not gonna let up until I agree to get drunk to help them."

"That's harassment!" Marty snapped. "You should get a lawyer. This isn't your fight."

"Watching that woman in tears, Marty ... What if I could help her?"

Marty was silent as the streetlamps swept by. "I don't want to be mean," he sneered, "but will you listen to yourself, KO? Really, listen?"

"What do you mean?"

"You're being gaslit. That means manipulated."

"He wants to catch the killer."

"And that's on you? He's the cop," Marty scoffed. "No, that's not even what this is about."

A few more streetlamps and shadows passed.

"What is it about?" KO asked.

Marty sighed. "Take it from me, KO. Better yet, take it from Gladys."

"Gladys?"

"You know how she's up to three packs a day? It's not because she said she wanted to spend that much money on cigarettes. It's because she kept saying 'just one more.' That's you, right there ... Just one more. Just one more drink. It'll be good. It'll help people. It'll do everything, but mostly it'll be *a drink*. That's all this is. I hope you don't mind my being frank."

KO slumped. "It did make me want to drink real bad."

"See?"

"Felt like I needed it."

"There. Exactly what I'm trying to tell you."

KO sighed like a tent collapsing. "You're right, Marty. It's just the Devil trying to get in the back door."

"Just the Devil," Marty said with a nod. "You got a new life ahead of you. Don't let some cop who can't do his job push his problems off on you."

"I don't think he's that bad," said KO. "Father Tomas says he just seems desperate to catch the bad guy."

"Shouldn't mean becoming one, yeah? Stick to your guns. Think of your family. You're *their* good guy."

There was more silence. The car slid a bit on the salted road. Other cars flashed by as mere headlights rushing in and out of the dark.

"Yeah, you're right, Marty. Thanks for hearing me out."

"You need a man in your corner, right?"

"Right," said KO, but he was quiet the rest of the trip, the image of the mother searching for him behind the mirror lingering as they rode through the dark and freezing night.

Chapter Twenty-Six

Jan. 24, cont., 5:00 p.m.

Father Tomas was making his evening rounds in the shelter before heading to St. Joseph's to hear confession when he saw KO in the day room, studying the sports page of a newspaper. "Good evening, KO. You're back early."

KO's head jerked up, startled from his meditation on basketball scores.

"Oh, hi, Father. I didn't see you come in."

"I trust everything is alright?"

"Everything at work is fine, I guess."

His twitching hands said otherwise as he laid the paper down.

"But not fine everywhere?" Tomas asked, sitting down beside him.

"Not everywhere, no. The cops called me in today. More questions."

"At work?"

KO nodded shakily.

Father Tomas considered going straight to his office and picking up the phone. There were words that could be said. Apparently, the detectives weren't brave enough to dare the shelter again. But the moment passed. In the end, his anger would achieve nothing.

Instead, he sat beside KO, picked up the paper KO had just put aside, and considered the scores as well. In his culture, time was not something to be rushed through but savored, especially time spent with friends. He knew when to talk and when to listen. Now was a time to listen, and he waited for KO to speak.

"They made me watch a woman being questioned," KO said at last. "They think her daughter was murdered by the same person who killed the woman I saw."

"That was cruel," said Father Tomas. "It must have been very difficult for you."

KO looked at his hands, and Tomas guessed he was thinking of the ring. It was where his mind always went when he struggled.

"One of the toughest in a long time. And the thing is, Father, it made me want a drink. Not to help that woman or the police, but to help *me*. To escape."

"What did you tell them, my son?"

"I told them no. The last time I stuck my neck out to help someone I landed in jail. I've helped them all I can."

"I see."

KO crossed his arms across his chest, hugging himself tightly. "Do you think I did the right thing, Father?"

"I have never known a situation where alcohol made things better, especially when the Devil was trying to make them worse."

"But didn't you say the detective was doing God's work? If I help him, aren't I?"

"KO, I've seen what you've accomplished and I'm proud of how far you've come. I cannot advise you to put all that at risk on some theory. They are asking too much of you."

The priest sat in silence with this troubled member of his flock as they both digested the problem KO had brought him. Then he stirred.

"Do you know who St. Roch was and why he is so dear to me?"

"No, Father. Who was he?"

"He is the patron saint of invalids and the falsely accused, and I think you are falsely accusing yourself of responsibility for the murder of these poor women. You freely told the police what you saw, and I admire you for it. It is not your responsibility to place yourself at risk to solve these crimes; it is that of the police. You have done all that you can. Leave the rest to them and to God."

KO nodded. "You sound just like my boss, though he's kinda rude about it. I guess you're right. It's funny, but if I didn't *want* the drink so bad, I think it'd be easier to say yes. I've knocked this Devil back, but I ain't knocked him out. I'm not free yet."

"I'm here in your corner, KO. So is God. Isn't that enough?"

KO gave a sad smile. "When I'm enough, Father, it will be."

***

Marty went straight to the boat that night. The bright blue tarp he'd bought at the home goods store was draped around the figurehead. He was proud of that figurehead. He'd had it custom-made. That was the problem.

Obvious. Too obvious.

He had already tried to change his berth since the cops were snooping, but docking spaces weren't easy to come by. Some were passed on in the family, like Ravens season tickets. Even if he could move the boat downriver ... No. A thirty-minute commute would turn into two hours. He couldn't give up his refuge so easily. He wouldn't.

That left only one option.

Marty spent the rest of the evening online. He sipped the good Scotch and searched websites, looking for just the right marine mechanic. It looked like most of them had gone south for the winter with the snowbirds, and the snowbirds' boats.

Chapter Twenty-Seven

Jan. 25, Saturday

Ruiz planned to visit the harbormaster's office first thing Saturday morning. Armed with the addresses on a computer printout, she'd go around the north harbor taking pictures for KO to study. Something less traumatic, hopefully, than attending victim interviews.

The office was on skeleton crew on weekends, and she nodded to Bailey as she went to her desk. She glanced once at Mankiller's darkened office out of habit, then remembered she was still mad at him.

At least Shwiller, while eccentric, had delivered. Perhaps he had delivered a bit *too* well, but that was her fault, wasn't it? Of all the mechanics in the Baltimore harbor, she'd chosen an anti-social expert in draconic imagery. The list he sent was two and a half pages long and the elaborate font made her squint.

"Forty-seven boats," she muttered. There were dragons, lizards, even dinosaurs. Snakes too. A *lot* of snakes. There was even a "chupacabra"—not a dragon, but the foreign-sounding name apparently made the list for its exotic sound.

It was a lot, but if one of them was the food of KO's nightmares, it would be worth the effort. As the late great Wayne Gretzky had once said, "You miss one hundred percent of the shots you don't take."

Speaking of which ...

Ruiz searched the news for dates of hockey games. She was going to get something for this overtime. There had to be a game tomorrow.

Please, please, please ...

Ruiz hated the cold, but she loved ice hockey. Every boy her mother tried to set her up with had hated hockey, she reflected. No one understood her love of watching very fit men crash into each other. (She also had a not-so-secret affinity for the Highland games. Large muscular men throwing things in skirts? Did there need to be an explanation?) Still, it was no fun going alone.

"Will I never find true love?" She glanced up at the poster of Sotomayor. "I know, I need to focus." Sotomayor continued looking strong and positive. "Yeah, you're right, but he's giving me overtime for this."

Overtime would take some of the sting out. Lunch along the waterfront on this cold gray day would help too. A shame she'd be eating alone.

When Ruiz got to the docks, the gray was depressing, and she wondered how people in Sweden kept from slitting their wrists before the end of February. She pulled out her phone twice before dialing.

"Good morning, *Jefe*."

"Good morning, Ruiz. Anything to report?"

"I am up to my ears in lizards," she said sweetly. "But I'm using some of that shoe leather you like so much."

"Do tell."

"I've got my list. Why do guys like lizards so much?"

"Girls like them too."

"Why do rich spoiled guys like lizards so much?"

"You do know what dragons do in stories?"

Okay, maybe she'd forgive him. A little. "You're giving me overtime for this, right?"

"You're not enjoying the fresh air this Saturday?"

"Oh yeah, great fun. Care to join me? Actually ... there's a nice family-run place I know. It has a dock in back. They buy fresh crabs right off the boat."

There was a pause. Ruiz imagined he was eyeing a stack of dirty laundry or something else his schedule forced him to put off until weekends.

"Sure. Why not? Where should we meet?"

"Harbormaster's office. I'm there now."

"I'll be there in half an hour. I'll bring coffee, unless you'd rather have cocoa?"

"Nah, coffee's better. No one makes cocoa as good as I do, and I won't settle for second best. Probably why I'm still single."

Mankiller had no answer to that. "Right. Coffee it is. On the way."

"Doesn't mean I've forgiven you, though."

"We'll talk about that."

Well, she thought after she broke the connection, *at least he remembers the cocoa.*

***

After three hours of all business and snapshots, they'd visited twenty of the boats. Ruiz took several shots at different angles of each one, especially of any parts dragon related. Satisfied and hungry, she led the way to a water taxi station. Soon they were pulling up to a large restaurant shaped like a boat, lights glittering in every window.

"When you said 'family run,' I imagined some small shack with oyster shells in the parking lot," he said.

"Well, Captain James has been around for about forty years, so maybe they started that way," she laughed. "Come on, I could go for some hot chowder before we tackle the last names on our list."

The waiter took orders for their drinks—more coffee—then asked the infamous question, "Will this be together or separate checks?"

When Mankiller paused, Ruiz cut in, "Together." She looked across the table at her wary boss. "My invite, my check." She winked. "Just don't order the lobster, or we'll wind up doing dishes together."

"I was afraid you wouldn't talk to me again after yesterday."

"I didn't like it. No, wrong: I hated it. And you, for making me sit there in the dark and watch him suffer."

"I'm the bad guy, I know ..."

"But I understand why you did it; you wanted him to see what was at stake from our perspective so he'd agree to take that drink. I felt ... dirty afterward. I went to confession this morning, you know. Haven't been there in, well, too long. You used that woman's pain against an innocent man and made me part of it."

"I don't think of someone holding back from helping people as innocent."

"Yeah, but you can't convict him of the crime of self-preservation, *Jefe*."

Mankiller sipped his coffee in silence. He'd been a cop long enough to know when to listen.

"Hey, I like you," Ruiz insisted. "I respect you. You're a good detective and a good boss most of the time. But since you brought it up, don't ever ask me to be there again if there's a next time. I can't take it."

"I didn't enjoy putting him through that."

"Uh-huh. You don't enjoy catching bad guys either—but you do like being right."

He nodded. "You got me there, but in my defense, I've saved lives before by doing unpleasant things. Nothing that could cause a case to be tossed out of court, you understand, but yeah, I'll push a boundary or two to get a predator off the street. That's gotta count for something."

He looked out the window to watch the large ships creep in and out of the harbor. The ocean was a long walk from Oklahoma and the concept of water stretching beyond the horizon still seemed like science fiction to him.

"So, you're saying it's your decision, *Sergeant*, how far to go, how hard to push an innocent man?"

Mankiller returned his focus to the young detective across the table. She so wanted to do the right thing, to protect and serve. He envied her.

"I was telling KO the truth, Ruiz. Looking into the eyes of the family after, trying to make sense to them what happened, trying to give them hope we'll catch who did it—without lying? It's the worst part of my job. And one of the reasons I bust my ass, and yours, to catch these bastards is so I don't have to do it that often."

"You ever think about giving it up? Maybe you're the one who should be busting pimps. That should keep you away from the morgue."

He shrugged. "It's what I do. It's who I am."

"Yeah, but I don't know why." She leaned forward. "You're driven, *Jefe*."

He watched the boats some more as she sipped coffee.

"I just know what happens when these things are let go, Ruiz," he said at last.

"What's that supposed to mean?"

Mankiller kept his eyes fixed on the boats. "You really want to know?"

"I asked, didn't I?"

He told her about John Mankiller, about what happened when biases and fear turned a case cold, only pausing when the server brought the coffee pot for a refill.

"Thank you for telling me," Ruiz said once he finished.

Mankiller took a long swig of his coffee, his throat suddenly dry. "My brother was a drunk—he said so himself.

But his death was swept under the rug too quickly. I should have pushed the local cops more. Maybe seeing who pulled the trigger get what they deserved would have helped my mother and me. I'll never know—and I never want to not know again."

"I still don't approve of what you did, but it helps to know why."

"Yeah, well, I know I was harsh with KO, but I'm hoping I planted a seed. I won't do it to him again, I promise. Now we wait to see if it bears fruit."

"Hopefully, before the next murder." Ruiz raised her mug. "I'll drink to that."

He raised the mug and gave hers a careful tap. "Forgive me now?" he asked.

"A little, *Jefe*. Let's just say you're on probation until further notice."

Mankiller risked a smile. "Fair enough. As long as I don't have to wear a monitor."

She gave a slight grin in return. "No need. I'm a Puerto Rican *chica*, *Jefe*. I've got spies everywhere. My two aunts in Baltimore have seven children between them, all girls. I call them my CIA, 'Cousins in America.' There's nothing that goes on in our neighborhood I don't know about."

The rest of the afternoon they spoke little, but the tension between them was gone. She'd had her say and he'd heard her. He wouldn't repeat using another person's pain as a weapon against a good man trying to become a better one.

Once they'd finished their sweep of marine reptiles, Mankiller wished her a good evening after she got him to agree all her time at the harbor was "on the clock."

Ruiz splurged on one last cup of coffee by the waves before heading home, thinking of the look he'd given her when they'd clicked their coffee mugs in a toast. Had he blushed, just a little?

She shook her head. "Really gotta stop daydreaming, Maria," she muttered. "Overtime pays better than dates anyway."

Still, maybe she should have asked what he thought of ice hockey.

***

Marty found a website for a local marine mechanic. There were impressive photos of custom woodwork he'd done for clients, and he was still accepting work. Marty called the number and got the answering machine on the third ring, and he turned on his most amiable sales voice.

"Hello, Mr. Shwiller. This is Martin Hightower. I'd like you to come over to my boat to change out my figurehead. Text me when you can at this number. I'm in kind of a hurry and am willing to pay a bonus for speedy work. Thanks."

Chapter Twenty-Eight

Jan. 25, Sunday, 10:00 a.m.

Today, Father Tomas was giving the sermon he'd been working on. He'd admitted to KO he was nervous about speaking in English before a crowd, so it seemed only right to be in the other man's corner for a change.

KO hadn't been much for church growing up, but now and then there'd be a potluck and his family would go for the meal. It was always a warm memory, not just the food but the company. He suspected his mother was embarrassed at the poorly disguised charity. When you have nothing, pride is all that's left.

Walking into St. Joseph's that morning felt both like coming home and visiting a foreign country because the more two things were alike, the more you noticed the differences. The rituals were strange to him, but he knew to stand when everyone else stood, kneel when they did, and pat his chest as the congregation recited their contrition. The Communion was different, the people going forward to receive it from the priest and not passing trays down the pew. He'd heard the cup held real wine so stayed where he was. No need to tempt Satan, especially in the Lord's house.

Finally, Father Tomas walked to the lectern to give his sermon. He was so small his robes made him look like a child wearing his father's clothes. He adjusted his glasses before looking down at his double-spaced notes typed in a large font.

"The sermon today is from the Gospel of John, chapter fifteen, verses twelve through seventeen, in which our Lord Jesus Christ commands that we love one another as he loves us, saying, 'Greater love hath no man than this, that a man lay down his life for his friends.'

"The world around us is short on love, much as a desert is short on water. The Garden of Eden is beyond our grasp, my friends. Those gates are shut forever, but we need not wait for the next life promised us in Heaven to know a godly paradise, not if we dare to do the hardest thing of all and love one another as our Lord has commanded us. As St. Paul tells us in his first letter to the Corinthians, love is not self-seeking. It takes joy in the truth and never fails."

KO shifted in the pew. The words that followed flowed into and over him like a pitcher pouring into an overfull cup. He knew God had just spoken to him through this small, pious man and felt a burden descend upon his shoulders.

When Father Tomas returned to his office that afternoon, he found an envelope taped to the door and KO's name on it. Turning it into his palm, two small poker chips, one green and one blue, spilled out with a folded note.

He limped into his office, sat down, and read the note, then his sermon. He wept, but while he wept, he prayed.

Chapter Twenty-Nine

Jan. 25, Sunday (cont.)

R uiz got the call while she was at her mother's house for a late lunch.

"Detective Ruiz? This is KO."

The man's voice was soft but clear. Sober. She sensed what was to come but didn't want to rush him. "Hello, KO. Is everything alright?"

"You remember how I said what I saw that night in the harbor was a vision from God? Well, today He spoke to me. I know what I gotta do. I'll take that drink and with God's help, no more after that. Guess I'll just have to find out if God's through with me once this is over."

"I don't think God gives up on anyone, even after they give up on Him," she said. Her mind whirled with questions. How to do this? Should Doc Stevens be there? How soon could they do it before KO changed his mind? "Where are you now, KO?"

"I'm still at the shelter. How soon can we do this? Now that I've decided, I want to do it as quick as we can."

"Let me call Sergeant Mankiller. Is this a good number? I can probably get back to you in an hour."

"I'll be here. Got no place else to go until this is finished."

"I'll call you back after I talk with him then." She tried to sound positive. "Hang in there, KO. I respect you for the sacrifice you're about to make."

"I believe you," he said. "Pray for me. Please."

"I never stopped."

***

197

Mankiller took the call as he was setting up his telescope. A meteor shower was expected around two a.m. and the skies were clear. The light wasn't the best at the edge of a large city, but the harbor in the center reduced the light pollution enough to see major phenomena. Mankiller sat on a low stool and made a few fine adjustments to bring the universe into focus.

The phone's ring took his eyes off the heavens, but he smiled when he saw Ruiz's number on the caller ID, and he hoped hot cocoa was involved. Maybe it was time to invite her over to look at the stars? There were policies against fraternization between supervisors and subordinates, but they hadn't crossed any red lines, yet. He wasn't sure how close they were, but maybe it was time to see if there was anything, well, worth a transfer for one of them.

"Maria Ruiz? To what do I owe the pleasure?"

"Uh, this is Detective Ruiz. Who are you and what did you do with Sergeant Mankiller?"

"Can't I be pleasant once in a while?"

"I don't know. It's kinda weirding me out."

"Sorry, I'll try to be grumpier. Uh, get off my lawn! How's that?"

"Pretty sure you don't have a lawn, *Jefe*, but it'll do." More seriously, she added, "KO just called. He's ready to take a drink whenever you say. I guess your dirty trick worked."

Mankiller sat down, his smile gone. Should he feel good or ashamed? "Good," he said at last. "Whenever, he said? Not tonight, I hope."

"The sooner, the better. I think Doc Stevens should be with us, don't you?"

Mankiller nodded as he looked up at the waiting stars. "Yes, I agree. I'll get with him first thing in the morning. Tell KO we'll plan on Tuesday night. That way Doc Stevens has time to prepare." He hesitated. "Think I should come along?"

"I dunno, *Jefe*. This is gonna be hard on the guy, even without an audience."

"You're right. I'm the bad cop. I think you and Stevens should be enough. This is just a scouting expedition. If you find something suspicious, we get a warrant and come back the next day."

"I'll call him back for Tuesday night."

"Deal. Thanks for your call."

"Thanks for letting me walk with him. I feel I owe it to him."

"Just let that thought warm you while you're freezing your butt off along the waterfront."

"Ah, there's the grumpy boss I know. It was nice while it lasted."

"Happy dragon hunting, Ruiz."

"Good night, *Jefe*."

The line went dead. Mankiller hung up. No hot cocoa this time.

He turned back to the telescope and his contemplation of the cold flecks of diamond that had been flickering long before he was born, that would continue to shine their cold, pure, impartial light long after he was gone.

Chapter Thirty

Jan. 26, Monday, 11:00 a.m.

Dr. Stevens was easily convinced to come along. Mankiller found him at his desk that morning, whistling softly as he shuffled papers.

"I hadn't considered it, but now it appears obvious. Not that I can hypnotize someone who's drunk, but his mind will be in a somewhat similar state. I can probably help him steer through his foggy memory, talk him through the time machine, so to speak."

"Glad to see you're so excited, Doc," Mankiller said. "Forecast calls for a real blizzard tomorrow night. Wear boots. I'll think kind thoughts of the three of you as you're stomping through the snow in the dark." He glanced out the window at the storm front already sending its first feelers around the northern edge of the sky. Turning back to the psychologist, he hesitated.

"Second thoughts?" asked Stevens.

Mankiller shook his head. "This is all we've got, Doc. No matter what comes of it, thanks. It'll make it a little easier when I have to face another family knowing we used every chance we had to catch this bastard. I owe you one."

"If this works, the case report I'll be able to write will more than make up for it, Sergeant. Thank you for giving me and KO this chance."

"You and KO? Huh. This *has* become personal for you, Doc."

"Just because I analyze people objectively doesn't mean I forget they're human. This is a damaged man who's trying to put his life back together. Whether his desire is caused by a drunken vision or a sign from God, we take courage where we can find it."

Mankiller frowned at the gathering clouds. "You don't think we're sending him back into the bottle?"

Stevens's eyebrows rose. "I thought you were the one pressing for the advantage, Sergeant."

"Was and am."

Stevens didn't look worried. "I understand something of the nature of addiction," he said. "Just think, if he can help us catch this killer and see how he can still make a difference, he'll think better of himself and that will make his battle with alcohol and life seem worthwhile. Once he believes he's worth saving, booze will be a little easier to resist."

Mankiller continued his contemplation of the sky before saying to himself as much as to the doctor, "Life's hard. A bottle's a comfortable refuge once you've moved in."

"And the only way out is by being drawn by something better."

Mankiller shrugged. "I guess we're all looking for a miracle, Doc. If you think there's a chance, I'll root for you ... and him."

"Ever the cynic?" Stevens smiled. "Even about a plan you helped put into motion?"

"Based on bitter experience, Doc. You're starting to sound like Ruiz."

The sun slowly disappeared behind a tendril of dark cloud as the detective left the other man to his paperwork. Psychology was something of a magical science to Mankiller, he'd readily admit, not that he didn't trust it. He'd grown up on folk stories about animal tricksters and shamans, remembering from an anthropology class that the word *shaman* originated with a Siberian tribe, meaning "One who sees in the dark." If ever there was a modern equivalent, it would be a psychologist like Stevens—a man who peered into the subconscious of the damaged people who found their way into the police station. Mankiller didn't envy him though, for there were monsters in the dark.

***

Gladys hadn't had a good run-in with Marty in a couple of days, so when she saw the note on her desk, she smiled.

She decided to go for the throat. Marty wouldn't fold, but it would be fun to knock that smirk off his face, even for a moment.

Lights ... camera ... action!

She stormed into Marty's office before he took his coat off. "Read this!" she demanded, shoving an interoffice memo into his still-gloved hand. "Mr. Bannon is requesting Wednesday off!"

"Gladys, you're here early."

"Did you even listen to what I said?"

"I did. And?" Marty didn't flinch.

"He's been with us less than a month, and he's asking for the middle of the week!"

Marty read the brief message. "Did he tell you why he wants it? Maybe there's been a death in the family or a medical appointment?"

"No! No explanation at all. I just found this on my desk when I came in."

"And it didn't occur to you to ask him before rushing into my office before I've even had a cup of coffee?"

"He's your good deed, Mr. Hightower, not mine. Besides, I've no authority to give him time away. You'll have to deal with it."

Gladys waited patiently, savoring his momentary loss of panache. *Gladys one, Marty zero.*

"Alright, Gladys," he said, off-balance from her early morning ambush. "Have him come see me when you can. I see no reason not to give him a day off without pay—unless it's for a medical appointment. It wouldn't cripple the firm if you had to make coffee for a day," he rebooted his neon smile, "unless you've forgotten how?"

Gladys scoffed, pondering how strong she could make it and still have him drink it. With KO gone, she could "forget" to ensure the men's room had enough toilet paper ...

***

When KO arrived, Marty was halfway into his morning paper. He looked up and noticed the ex-boxer had bags under his eyes. He waved KO toward a chair before holding up the note.

"Gladys gave me this when I came in this morning. What's going on? Doctor's appointment?"

"You could say so, Marty. It's something like that."

Marty felt his upper lip moisten at KO's evasiveness. What happened to the open book? Marty coughed, then he folded his hands on the desk. "I think I deserve a better answer than that, KO. Don't you?"

KO rubbed his hands over his trousers. "I know this is a good job, Mr. H—Marty. I couldn't ask for one better."

"You're not planning on leaving?'"

"Not at all, not if you're willing to keep me. It's the best job I've had outside the ring."

"Well then, you're talking in circles, KO. Be straight with me."

KO looked everywhere but at Marty. "I guess you deserve the truth, since you've been in my corner."

Marty sat straighter in his chair. "What are you telling me, KO?"

"It's about what the psychologist said."

Shit.

"Tuesday night I'm going down to the harbor with the police. I'm gonna get drunk, supervised, and see if I can go back to where I found the body."

Shit!

Marty picked up his coffee, turned his seat to the window, and took a long, bitter sip. He had a plan, and this was no time for half-measures.

He swiveled his chair back and faced the man who could send him to death row. "And what if I said I'd fire you if you did it? I don't want to be the bad guy, I hope you understand that, but how could I trust you again?"

KO stood. "I'd say you had the right to do that. I wouldn't blame you. Father Tomas as much as told me I'm sending myself straight to Hell for this, but ..." He looked down at his hands. "Thy will be done."

"Well ..." The finality in the man's voice told Marty his bluff had failed. *A bird in the hand*, he reminded himself. "Your devotion's admirable. KO." Marty stood and offered his hand. "It'll be a day off without pay. Come back *sober* on Thursday, and if you do that, the job will be here waiting for you."

"Thank you, Marty. If I ain't sober Thursday, you'll never see me again."

"Fair enough. But how's it going to work? Will you be leading a squad of police like a bloodhound?"

"The detective said it would just be her, the psychologist, and me. If I see something she thinks is worth investigating, they'll come back with a warrant."

"I see. You do know there's a *huge* storm heading our way?"

"I do, but this can't wait. It's tearing me up inside, Marty. I'm afraid if I wait too long, I'll lose my nerve."

"Strike while the iron's hot, right? Sounds like tomorrow night will be quite an adventure. I hope to see you here Thursday morning." *For both our sakes.*

Marty prided himself on being able to look three steps ahead when he played the market. KO was becoming more of a threat. Time to shorten the leash. "I really want you to stay straight, so how about this: I give you Wednesday off, and you promise you'll be sober from then on—just hold on a sec ..." He dashed off a note and handed it to KO. "I want you to give this note to Gladys. It says for her to get you a cell phone. The bill will be paid for by the company as long as you don't use it to call outside of the country. That way, if I need you for something outside business hours, I'll be able to get hold of you, at time and a half, of course. Sometimes I entertain high-end clients and I could use you to help and clean up after. That OK with you?"

KO took the note and not knowing what to say, nodded his thanks and left.

It took approximately three heartbeats before Gladys came through the door. "Mr. Hightower, how can you justify this expense! What would your father say?"

Marty didn't even try to smile. She wasn't worth the effort. "I don't know, Gladys. Why don't you ask him yourself? Why don't you ask him why I should continue to tolerate your efforts to block everything I've tried to do to help this man rehabilitate himself? Or better yet, why don't you ask my father why I'm acting in accordance with *his* wishes? Please tell me when you plan on having that conversation because I'd really like to be there."

If Gladys's dentures weren't top of the line, they would have cracked. She'd turned to go, bloody but unbowed, when Marty twisted the knife.

"By the way, please cancel all my calls for the rest of the morning. I've got to spend some time on the company portfolio."

His smirk was wasted on her back as she stormed out, knowing he had just consigned her the unpleasant task of calling some of their wealthy and demanding clients to tell them they would have to reschedule their calls. Rich people tended to be nice to those who handled their investments—not so much to their executive assistants.

Tormenting Gladys had let Marty forget his danger for a moment, but he had some serious thinking to do. Like a trade in the market, he had to consider the risk–benefit ratio of his next action on his own "portfolio."

He knew how to end this. There really was only one way.

It was just a matter of when.

Chapter Thirty-One

Jan. 26, cont.

Gladys stewed. She'd noted Marty jumping at the slightest annoyance. If they'd been playing cards, she'd have called his hand because she knew when someone was bluffing. It must have something to do with KO's sudden request for a day off. What about that would have put him on edge? And why did KO suddenly need a phone?

She'd lost this round, and she hated losing.

When she returned to her desk, she activated a company cell phone (breaking a fingernail in the process), issued it to KO, and updated the company phone roster while being as professional as she knew how. Though she reminded herself it wasn't his fault, KO was fortunate he didn't have eyes in the back of his head because the look she aimed at him as he left the reception area would have reminded him of the dragon he'd seen in the harbor.

She was confused by the day's events but knew that Marty, being Marty, would only be this nice to a minor employee if he thought it was to his benefit. The old fighter clearly had some sort of hold on him, but KO seemed too dim to know it. Marty had always known the old boxer was helping the police ... There had to be something to that.

KO came by with the mail just as Gladys finished the day's correspondence. She took a deep breath and activated some long unused facial muscles to raise an approximation of a smile. "I'm sorry about your loss, Mister Bannon."

"Loss, Miss Gladys? I don't know what you mean."

"Oh, perhaps I misunderstood? Mr. Hightower told me you'd had a death in the family and that was why you needed Wednesday off."

KO shook his head, puzzled. "There was a death, ma'am, but no one I knew. I'll be helping the police Tuesday night to try to find where I saw a woman murdered—begging your pardon. I know it's a horrible thing to hear. But that's why I won't be able to come in to work the next day. It's a one-time thing and I should be back on Thursday."

"Oh, I see. Well then, that's very noble of you. You should have said so in the first place. I won't bother you further."

Shortly after, Gladys picked up her cigarettes and headed to her smoking refuge to fume. If she were Sherlock Holmes, she might have called this a "three-pack problem." Taking in the relatively fresh air of the alley, she pondered this new information. She'd taken up smoking during her poker-playing days. It made her fit in with the guys, sure, but also hid her eyes. There was no bluff like a long, slow, and powerful drag to intimidate another player. Many a victory had come down to using the haze to her advantage. The rest she owed to patience. If you could wait, you could win.

Still, no one lived forever.

Gladys was thinking a lot about the future these days. She'd won a lot of poker hands thanks to tobacco, but her doctor told her the bill was coming due. Her ribs were showing more these days as she worked harder to breathe, and nighttime oxygen wasn't far away.

Gladys accepted her fate. She liked to think she'd face the Devil head-on just like she had everyone else, but she'd be damned if Marty took over his father's business before or after that happened.

The police. Clearly, Marty was worried about the involvement of the police. Well, she'd use whatever time she had left to make sure all his fears came true. She owed that much to Mr. Hightower Senior for his kindness. Then she could rest in peace.

KO was someone Marty kept an eye on. Marty was scared about something involving the police. Marty had always paid token kindnesses to keep on a good face, but this charitable mask was a whole new show. He'd been a selfish little brat even as a little kid. There was no way he'd change his stripes because of some bum his father had taken in.

And KO was helping in a murder investigation.

She thought of the intern again and that signature she'd tried to prove was fake.

Gladys finished her smoke with one slow, powerful drag, then headed back inside to get to work. Important work.

***

Marty hit redial on his cell. Didn't this man ever check his messages? This time he got a live voice.

"Shwiller, marine mechanic and custom woodwork."

Marty knew a customer could hear a smile through a phone, so his wattage was at maximum. "Mr. Shwiller, you're a hard man to get hold of—a sure sign of success."

"Yeah, I suppose. How can I help ya?"

"I have a custom figurehead I love but my wife hates. Changing it is cheaper than a divorce, so I'd like you to come by and swap it for something simple—the sooner, the better."

"Why the rush? You going someplace in this weather?"

Marty bit off the first words that came to mind. He wasn't used to tradesmen questioning him. "To be honest, I'm hoping for a romantic evening onboard later this week and I'd like to surprise her with the apology."

"Ah, well, you called at a good time. I'm caught up at the moment. Once spring gets here, I'll be swamped. I can come by later this afternoon to look at it and give you an estimate— of course, I can customize before I install it."

"You couldn't customize it later, after it's been installed? I'm in kind of a rush. If you're a married man, you'll understand."

"I'll have to take your word for it, Mr. Hightower. Sure, if you're in that big a hurry, but it'll cost you more. It's harder to work on once it's installed. If you just need the old one gone, I can come back later to install the replacement. That'll give you and the Missus time to agree on the design and let me work on it in my workshop and do a proper job."

"An excellent idea, Mister Shwiller. Yes, let's just get rid of the old one for now. What time can you come by?"

Once arrangements were made, Marty hung up and switched off the smile. It was approaching three. The markets would still be open for another hour, but he broke protocol this once, reaching for the French Brandy in his lower desk drawer. Gladys might notice the smell on his way out, but she could go to hell.

***

Gladys, meanwhile, spurred by the knowledge that the afterlife was closer than she'd like, was doing her research. Working backward from when KO had started at the firm, she found five possible murder cases he could be involved in, but one stood out: a murder along the waterfront. She'd handled enough calls from ship suppliers and the marina to know Marty kept the "company yacht" a couple of miles from where the woman's body had been found. This was interesting, though not conclusive.

She knew how to out-bluff a bluffer, but to do that you had to know what cards they were holding. He'd have to show his hand a little more before she could call her bet.

***

Shwiller was far from charming, but Marty appreciated a man who knew his business and arrived on time. When the mechanic unwrapped the figurehead and saw the design, he gave a low whistle of admiration. "Whoever did this was an artist. Shame you have to get rid of it."

"Yeah, well, the things we do for love, right?" Marty said, trying to mask his impatience. Smile and pay on time, he reminded himself, and you could disappear.

"How about I keep this and reduce the cost of installing the new figurehead by a thousand?"

"If it gets the job done sooner, it's a deal. Can you give me an invoice? The boat actually belongs to my company."

"Your company? So, it's not technically your boat? You got the right for me to work on it? I ain't doing this for free."

"I am the company," Marty said, irritated this man in greasy overalls would talk to him like that. "Here's my card."

"Nice card," Shwiller said after glancing at it before stuffing it into his wallet. "Well, since I'm getting the figurehead anyway, I'll take this with me today and submit an invoice to you to give your bookkeeper for the total job. I've got one that'll fit just fine. Once your company pays me, I'll do the design you choose and install it. That good for you?"

"Perfect."

Chapter Thirty-Two

Jan. 27, Tuesday, 7:00 p.m.

The good Scotch sparkled like amber in the dim lights of the harbor as Marty sat inside *Lamia*'s cabin, hidden from view. He listened to the wind scream like a beast over the water. It was his second glass of the evening. He was taking his drinking slow, letting it mull but not muddle his thoughts. He had to stay calm. He had to sit and not stew.

Anytime now. Anytime—or not at all.

Marty reminded himself that most people were stupid. And since stupid people didn't know how stupid they were, Marty was miles ahead.

Most of the cops Marty had met were bullies. At best, they thought he and they were the same, that because he had money and they had a sidearm they were in on a joke, one where money and power meant anything goes. Speeding tickets and parking fines had a tendency to vanish if Marty was friendly enough, especially after they'd seen his ID.

His next thought warranted another glass of Scotch. He poured it out slowly in the near dark and held it in front of him. He set the bottle of expensive brown liquid next to the black revolver. He'd had it a few years now: a .357 Colt Python. The salesman said it was the finest production handgun ever made, and Marty loved the feel of it in his hand. He'd never had to use it. Not yet. But good insurance was worth paying for.

But, what about a detective that bet on psychology and investigated dead nobodies? That might be the kind of narcissist who could cause problems money couldn't solve.

His hand shook with his next sip, and he blamed the wind for this nagging doubt. *Ghosts in the wind are nothing*, he told himself. *My hunters are human.* His boat looked empty. The storm was building. Even if they found *Lamia*, they'd only have time to mark her, and Marty would have until morning to tie up loose ends. He couldn't run—boats needed fuel and marinas. Credit cards left trails. No, he'd have to make sure there wasn't anything that would stand up in court. Or anyone.

***

The sun set behind the storm and a bitter, biting darkness hung over everything as Ruiz and Stevens arrived with KO at the harbor in an unmarked car.

Like God doesn't even like what we're doing, Ruiz contemplated. The gray of the evening grew darker with the arrival of night. She shook her head. *Snap out of it! You're starting to sound like your boss.*

KO was bundled up in what he called his "arabber clothes," and Ruiz was at what she'd come to think of as maximum penguin with her tactical vest and sidearm placed over her coat, in case they found a dragon interested in fighting back. Stevens wore a faded leather Air Force flight jacket with boots to match, the kind with inflatable bladders. She recalled another veteran friend calling them "Mickey Mouse" boots.

Ruiz parked them at an entrance to the harbor that KO remembered, one upstream from where the body was discovered. It was the best she could do with what they knew.

"Whadya think, Doc?" she asked, peering through the windshield. "Do you think this'll work with the storm? It might be too different."

"Actually, I think it's an advantage, Detective," Stevens said. "This is a journey of the mind, as much in KO's head as it will be along the waterfront. The snow will blur the details enough that he can add his own back in, sorta like a blank canvas. It will make the surroundings less of a distraction."

"Whatever you say, Doc. We only get one shot at this." Turning to the back seat, Ruiz said, "You ready, KO?"

KO had been reading over a folded note. Now he carefully creased it with two fingers and slipped it inside his coat before they climbed out of the car and into the cold. He shut his eyes once, and she let him alone in case he was praying. When he opened them a long minute later, he nodded.

"Yes, Detective. It's time."

Stevens pulled out a bottle of Four Roses and handed it over. "I got the one you requested, same as that night."

"What d'I owe you, Doc?"

"This one's on the house."

KO unscrewed the lid and peered down the bottle's neck like he was looking for a snake. Then he shut his eyes tight, raised the bottle, and sighed before swigging three swallows without stopping. Ruiz took the bottle as he nearly dropped it. He didn't cough or blanch, though his face twisted like he'd just had a drink of vinegar.

Probably got high capacity, thought Ruiz, weighing the bottle in hand. She noticed it was lighter already.

KO opened his eyes, stared at the bottle in her hands, then reached for it. Stevens held up his hand.

"Just one more for now, KO," he said. "We'll get you there slowly and help you control it. That way you can still walk and talk."

KO sighed, took another long, deep drink, then wiped his mouth with his coat sleeve. "Doc, if I could control it, I wouldn't have wound up like this," but he handed the bottle back. "You'll be my bartender. How's that?"

"A good plan," Stevens said. "Let's hold off for half-hour and see how far this takes you."

KO nodded. "Fair enough."

Ruiz shivered beneath her layers as the wind pinched her cheeks red. "Can we start walking? I need to get my blood moving or I'm going to freeze."

Stevens nodded. "Yes, we should get the blood moving along with the alcohol, and the rhythm of walking will help KO think."

They set out at a careful stroll, Ruiz and Stevens flanking KO. For the moment, his steps were steady. A block or so down, Stevens asked, "Do you remember anything new, KO?"

"I'm not sure."

"Try to associate what you remember with this place. Remember the fireworks? Lights in the sky, that splash ..."

KO nodded along with the doctor's rhythmic speech. "I was cold then, too," he thought out loud, "but I wanted to see the lights. I called Amy on my cell phone ..." He patted his coat pocket at the thought.

"What were you thinking then?"

"I was thinking ... if I froze to death, the police would find her from the number in the phone. She'd know she was finally free of me."

Ruiz nodded. As a beat cop, she'd discovered more than one homeless person frozen under a bridge or in an alley. Having a phone with a recent call in its memory helped deal with the aftermath.

The snow was getting serious now, falling fast and thicker by the minute. Even so, Stevens was all patience. "And where did you go next, KO?"

"Down," KO said, his steps moving forward with care. "Down, down, down to the water, to the lights, and to the boats. All those pretty boats. And the dragon ..."

Stevens gave his arm a squeeze. "If you're ready, we can walk down there together, alright, KO? You're not alone this time."

KO shuddered. His next step faltered and he slowed. "I think I need another drink, Doc."

"You're doing fine, KO. Let's pace ourselves. Take us to the water, to the boats ..."

KO shut his eyes. He nodded. "To the dragon, yes."

Squaring his shoulders, KO walked on, slowly but with heavy purpose. The snow fell in ever-thicker flurries, forcing Ruiz and Stevens to keep close to his side to steady and keep him in sight.

As they passed a steam grate, he stopped. "Fish," he said. "I smell fish." He looked around, then pointed. Ruiz and Stevens followed the finger to the window of a bar across the street. A violet flash through the falling snow caught their eye.

"It's ... COPEN!" gasped KO.

Ruiz peered at the bar's neon window sign. "Open?" she said, but then there was a blink from neon purple to green and she realized what he meant. The right half of the "O" flickered out. For just a second, there was a "C" before the "O" reappeared. "Well, I'll be ..." she laughed. "Why didn't we think of that?" A chill shot up her spine that had nothing to do with the wind. "KO, it's working!"

KO only nodded, lost in the haze somewhere between the present and New Year's night. His eyes were red; he wiped them.

She patted his arm, her eyes leaking too, before pulling her phone out and taking several shots showing the changes in the sign, then used her GPS to note their exact location. She'd have an interesting show-and-tell tomorrow morning.

"It wasn't dyslexia!" Stevens said. "You read better than we did, KO. I'm sorry I didn't take you at your word—your literal word."

KO raised his arms like a fighter who's just been declared the winner. "I didn't figure it out neither, Doc. But you believed in me," He closed his eyes and let the snow fall onto his upturned face. "But I really need that next drink now, Doc," He opened a hand. "Give it here, and I'll take you to the dragon."

Stevens hesitated. "This isn't a reward, KO, but yes, as your bartender, I think it's time."

He handed over the bottle but kept his hand out, reclaiming it as soon as KO took a swig.

"That should be enough for the rest of the night, I think," said Stevens.

KO shrugged, swaying slightly. Ruiz had only tried whiskey once, but that was enough. KO swallowed that last drink like it was water.

"You alright?" she asked.

"Wears like an old coat," he admitted. "But whatever you say, Doc. Whatever ..." His voice trailed off as he stumbled onward into the blinding whiteness while Ruiz and Stevens hurried after.

The avenue beside the docks was about fifty feet wide. They hugged the far side of the water to keep away from the tossing waves to their left. The night was noisy with the howling wind and the sound of water slapping boat hulls. The pleasure craft rose and fell, bumping and pushing up against the tires that lined the dock like racehorses in the starting gate, anxious to be set free. KO stopped at the sight of them, then pointed right to a warehouse wall.

"Here. I was here," he said. "I passed out and ... the fireworks, they woke me, yes! And I saw the lights there." He turned toward the line of boats. "I heard a splash. I walked to it." Saying this, he wavered forward, Stevens holding his breath as they came close to the edge of the pier. KO pointed down. "Here," he said, voice unsteady. "I saw her here."

KO stood looking into the water, his fists opening and closing, then raised his head and looked around slowly, scanning the boats in the dim light of the marina.

He started mumbling something that sounded like a chant, and Ruiz and Stevens leaned forward to hear.

"Here, dragon, dragon, dragon. Come out and play."

"Thatta boy, KO," Ruiz said. "You tell him." She turned on her flashlight and began scanning the boats. "He can't hide forever."

***

Marty peered over the edge of the cockpit's window. He froze as three dim figures approached out of the black-and-white nothingness and looked around. When the flashlight beam stabbed into the darkness toward him, he dropped beneath the window, hissing a curse. When it passed, he slowly raised his head again. They were still there, huddled together.

Go on, leave.

They didn't leave.

Go on ...

They didn't move.

Shit!

His heart pounding, Marty picked up the tumbler of Scotch. Three glasses already, but what the hell. It would do for his nerves, and he finished the tumbler in one go. Then he picked up the heavy revolver. The blackened metal made it invisible in the night. Six shots for three people. Well, he'd take them by surprise in the dark at close-range. He could do it. The weight of the pistol made him feel powerful. In control. He eased slowly to the side door and readied himself ...

He was a hunter in the dark, and the thought of the three of them dead at his feet gave him a rush.

He looked down the row and saw the lights on in the boat three down from his. Old Mr. Jenkins lived on his boat year-round. He was partly deaf, but even he would hear the gunshots and the old bastard probably had a gun of his own. KO and the psychologist would be unarmed, but the cop would be packing. He'd have to take them quickly before they could react or scatter in the dark and the storm. Mr. Jenkins was one variable too many. Marty shook his head to clear it and slowly lowered the barrel, putting the gun down but within reach. He wouldn't panic. Not this time.

Marty peered back out and at last, the trio started moving past him, the flashlight sweeping back and forth ahead of them, fading away into the blur of the falling snow.

He was safe. For now.

He reached down for the revolver and grasped it again. The heft of it in his hand felt as good as the burn of good whiskey. *I could have done it*, he told himself. *But I'd have to kill Jenkins, too. That would bring the cops too close to me.*

Drastic times called for drastic measures, but even with too much Scotch he knew he couldn't be sure he could pull it off. Cops shot back. He pulled out the small drawer under the driver's seat to drop the revolver out of sight, but nearby. No need to go that far.

Tonight.

***

KO stopped after another hundred yards. "It ain't here. We gone past it but I didn't see it."

Ruiz looked at Stevens. "Anything else in your bag of tricks, Doc?"

Stevens shook his head. "I think we've done rather well tonight, don't you? It's possible the dragon was a *Game of Thrones* poster, nothing more. We know the area now. We have a real place, thanks to KO. I vote we call it a night. Detective, is it okay if I come with you to drop him off?"

Ruiz nodded. She turned to KO and put her hand on his shoulder. "Thank you, KO. We're done. Let's take you home."

He shrugged. "You mean the shelter, don't you? I'm a long way from home ..."

"Let's get you back to a warm bed and a good night's sleep," she revised.

"I am cold, but I dunno if ... dunno if I can show my face." KO passed both hands over his cheeks and moaned. "You can put me in the drunk tank if you want. I've been there before, probably where I belong."

Ruiz knew better than to argue with someone drunk and only patted his shoulder. "The car's this way. Come along, you got this ..."

They walked back to the unmarked car and once inside with the heater at full blast, they made their cautious way back from the land of dragons.

Ruiz glanced back at KO in the rearview mirror. He was still awake, swaying slightly with the motion of the car and looking more miserable by the minute.

Can't have that. "Don't be hard on yourself, KO. The Devil's had more than one shot at you, and you're still standing. He'd only want you to give up now after you helped catch a killer."

KO didn't answer.

"We'll get you to the shelter, then Doc and I will talk about what we found. Tomorrow, we'll pick you up for a bit more discussion, but for now you deserve a good night's sleep."

"Do I?"

"You do," Stevens said. "We didn't see a dragon tonight, but you still had to face one, right? You walked into the storm and found the truth. That's what matters."

"We'll call you tomorrow," Ruiz said when they arrived at the shelter. "Count on it. Take care of yourself."

They walked him to the door, where Father Tomas waited to greet them and guide a weary dragon hunter to his bed.

Ruiz clenched her hands around the steering wheel as she drove slowly through the storm. "This better be worth it, Doc," she said.

Stevens nodded slowly. "I think it was."

"I only mean, it really, really better be."

***

KO followed the priest to his bed gratefully. "Thank you, Father, for taking me back. I don't deserve it."

Father Tomas tucked the old fighter into bed before answering. "I need your forgiveness, KO, for how I judged you, mistaking your courage for weakness. I will be in your corner for as long as you need me. Now, get some sleep and come by my office tomorrow. Your sobriety chip will be waiting for you."

Chapter Thirty-Three

Jan. 28, Wednesday, 10:00 a.m.

Marty had been jumpy all morning, and Gladys couldn't remember the last time she'd enjoyed herself so much at work. She only had a short time left, but she'd be damned if she didn't pull that little weed first.

"Everything all right, Mr. Hightower?" she asked, hovering in the doorway. It was clear Marty hadn't read the page of the newspaper he was looking at. He'd been staring at it for ten minutes.

"What?" He looked up at her question. "Fine. It's fine!" Marty snapped.

"It's just that you seem very preoccupied today."

"It's nothing. The market's a bit unsteady. You know, peace negotiations in the Middle East going badly—again."

She returned to her desk, trying to add up what she knew. Marty was sweating like a man with a pair of twos in Las Vegas. It had something to do with KO taking the day off to help the police on a murder investigation. She had nothing that would hold up in court, but she'd didn't need all the right cards to win the pot.

On her next smoke break, Gladys took along a steno pad and a fresh pen. Writing things down helped her think.

***

KO woke with a familiar headache and kept his eyes closed to keep away the morning light. He heard movement all around him. Soft voices. He was lying in a bed. Clean sheets. A hospital? It didn't smell like a hospital.

He opened his eyes ... and everything from the night before came rushing back. He looked down at the floor beside him, hoping for a bottle containing brown liquid. None. He lay back to gather his strength before facing another day. The thirst for another swallow of oblivion was as strong as ever. He wiped away a tear and swung his feet to the floor. Coffee and eggs would have to do.

***

Father Tomas's sermon had done so well that, somewhat to his regret, he'd been asked to give another in a week's time. He was hard at work on his battered word processor, trying to craft his love of God into a five-minute message.

Today, he'd tried American coffee for the first time, a coffee far milder than he remembered in Africa, where coffee was treated like a gift from God. Maybe the difference in flavor was a matter of culture. With the weather so harsh here, perhaps people wanted their flavors mild.

He moved the mouse on its pad and looked at the screen, maneuvering the little white arrow about as well as he could ice skate. Finally, it reached the data disk symbol, and he carefully clicked the left button and a save menu came up. He pecked a title, hit "enter," and slumped in his chair as he recalled the labors of Hercules.

"If I might borrow a phrase, my Lord," he murmured. "'It is finished.'" *Almost*, he corrected himself. Now to connect the printer and convert the glowing pixels into words he could hold in his hand. Hercules, he reminded himself, had twelve tasks.

He was sorting through the cables on his desk when a soft knock interrupted. The gentleness of the knock upon the cheap hollow door told him it was KO.

"Come in."

He stood when the old fighter entered and extended his hand after suppressing his first instinct to embrace him, remembering KO was a private person who recoiled at being touched. Perhaps that too was born of American culture.

"Good morning, KO. How are you feeling?"

KO's kept his eyes down. "A little hungover, Father, but not the worst I've had. I could probably go to work if they needed me."

"This was an ordeal, my son," Tomas reminded him gently. "You were wise to take the day off. They do not need to see you when you are at less than your best, even if it is for a good reason. No. A *noble* reason. Were you able to help the police?"

"Yeah ... I mean, yes, Father. I was able to find where I saw the body and a bar that was nearby. No dragon, though."

"There are dragons enough, not to worry," Tomas assured him. "That is excellent. Truly excellent. Are the police finished with you now?"

"I'm not sure. The detective said something about talking with me one more time, but things were getting pretty blurry by then. I think she said she'd call today. I hope I remembered it right so I can get this done. I need to be looking forward, not back."

As he spoke, Father Tomas rounded his desk and reached into the top drawer. "And I have something for you, as I promised." He held up a green poker chip. "If you still want it."

He offered it in his open palm, and KO reached out slowly and removed it, holding it in both hands.

"More than ever, Father," he said, staring at it. "Last night gave me a powerful thirst and the first thing I wanted this morning was a drink to dull the hangover. It's the same as it ever was."

KO returned the chip to his trousers pocket, where it belonged. "If I learned anything last night, it's that booze still has a hold on me." He sighed. "I've still got a long way to go."

Father Tomas laid his hand upon the other man's shoulder. "As do we all, my son. As do we all."

***

Marty sat at his desk watching the storm clouds grow darker as the snow returned in earnest. He'd always loved storms, the wilder the better, but then, he'd always loved chaos.

Studying his "personal portfolio," he could see his risks of getting caught getting higher all the time. The beam of light from the detective's flashlight sweeping over him had felt like an icepick to his heart. Maybe not weighting the second body before he'd dumped it wasn't such a good idea after all.

The cops weren't going to stop coming after him, but until now they'd had nothing to go on. Then KO just happened to be at the wrong place at the wrong time and tried to be a good citizen. Pathetic.

But KO was all they had. Without him, they'd be as lost as ever. No witness. Just the recorded ramblings of some drunk any good lawyer could tear apart without KO on the stand.

It was time to cut his losses. In this storm, the traces would be easy to hide.

Then Marty had a thought that made him sad.

The boat. He'd always been careful, but there was no way to be sure the cops wouldn't find something on it from his visitors over the years. The boat would have to go, too.

People would call him stupid for taking his boat out in a storm like this one promised to be, but lucky for him, stupid was still legal.

Chapter Thirty-Four

Jan. 28, 3:00 p.m.

R uiz found Mankiller at his desk when she brought him her report of the previous night's activities. The station was almost empty, the city partially locked down due to the snow. The building was heated at sixty-four degrees as a cost-saving measure, and Ruiz had on two sweaters and a dark-blue wool beret that was a little too big for her, covering her ears while her eyes peeked out below the rim.

"Ah, Inspector Penguin, I presume?" said Mankiller. "I deduce by your presence this morning that you invested in some proper all-weathers?"

"Don't look so smug, *Jefe*. A tropical girl needs all the help she can get when driving in the frozen north," Ruiz huffed.

"We'll get you a sheepskin cloak or something, maybe a horse named Bjorn."

"Yeah, well, I've got a horn full of hot mead waiting for me at my desk."

"Graduating from penguin to Valkyrie?" Ruiz scowled under her beret, and Mankiller thought of a grumpy mushroom.

"You've never made this many jokes in a row, *Jefe*. If you start calling me Brunhilda, I'm reporting you to Internal Affairs."

"I'd never dream of it," said Mankiller, who'd considered it for just a moment. He pointed at the report in her hand. "How'd your dragon hunt go? Catch the big one?"

"We figured out where his memory of COPEN came from. Doc Stevens thought it was his dyslexia giving him problems with an OPEN sign, and he was sorta right. We found a bar with a sign with a defective "O." The right side kept flickering on and off, so I can see how in the dark and very drunk it would be remembered as COPEN."

She pulled out her phone and showed him the images as the "O" changed into a "C," then the exact location on GPS where the bar was in relation to the marinas along the harbor.

Mankiller whistled a low note. "I'd never have figured that out on my own. That's the value of shoe leather over Google."

"Yes, *abuelo*, I get it," said Ruiz sweetly. "We whippersnappers need to put our iPhones down and pay more attention to your aged wisdom." She pulled the beret back a half inch as it started to slip. "But now I'm gonna put the internet to work for us. KO seemed to think the dragon couldn't have been more than a couple of blocks from the bar sign. Nothing in the photos we took matches, so I'm gonna do a recheck of all the boats in the next two marinas east of there for any names that may be dragon related."

"Why can't you just walk the piers again?"

"Because, *Jefe*, a lot of boat owners put their boats into dry dock for the winter. Moorings are hard to come by in the Inner Harbor, so they keep the lease. I'm more likely to get a hit this way."

"Care for another dose of aged wisdom?"

"Sure, Boss, what ya got?"

"We don't care what boats are *registered* in the marinas."

Ruiz slapped her forehead, causing the beret to slip over her eyes. She jerked it back up. "You're right! We just care about the ones that are there now."

"Get a couple of uniforms to help you, and get two views of every boat in the two marinas east of the bar with the funny sign, and have them ready for KO to go over when he comes in."

"I'll get right on it, but one other thing, Boss." She paused, serious now. "KO gave us everything we asked for." She turned to leave, then looked back. "I pray it wasn't too much."

She closed the door harder than necessary, and Mankiller's good mood was spoiled. He wouldn't say he prided himself on being a good cop, but he worked at being good.

But maybe this time he was the bad guy.

***

Shwiller lovingly laid out the carved figurehead on the worktable beside his drafting easel. She was part-mermaid, part-serpent. The look of avarice in her face was unsettling, and like any expert craftsman he wanted to study how the effect was created.

His mind pinged as he gazed at the macabre wooden figure. There was a list he'd sent that detective, yes. But she'd said nothing about mermaids. He paused. *Hell, they'll probably take it as evidence, and I won't see it again for years.*

But he wasn't a dishonest person. Shwiller pulled out a sketchbook, a soft-lead artist's pencil, and began trying to capture her cheekbones. To him, a face was built around a triad of chin, eyes, and cheekbones. If you got those three right, the rest fell into place.

"*Lamia*, eh?" he muttered as he worked. "One of Zeus's little ladies on the side ..."

In that story, Hera, always second fiddle to her lusty husband's latest obsession, had cursed the poor mortal with eternal insomnia. That might explain the look in her eyes.

"Cursed to never sleep," he went on, shading in the eyebrows just so. "I can sympathize." He frowned, wondering what the cops were investigating. Not that it was his business. Still, he couldn't help but wonder.

"Well, *Lamia*," he said at last, putting the finishing touches on the sketch and smiling at the likeness. "Maybe you can tell that detective what your troubled eyes have seen."

Chapter Thirty-Five

Jan. 28, Wednesday cont.

KO got a visit that morning, but not from whom he'd expected.

"Teddy?"

The big man was beaming in the front hallway of the shelter. "Get your coat, KO. You know what today is?"

KO hesitated and looked over at Father Tomas standing nearby, looking on with a satisfied grin.

"It's payday!" Teddy laughed. "Father Tomas told me you got paid today. Time to get a new pair of shoes!"

"Teddy—"

"Father Tomas told me everything."

"It's alright, my son," he said gently. "We're both in your corner. Shame is the Devil's tool. It has no place here."

KO hurried to get his coat. Payday. He'd mentioned to Teddy at the last AA meeting he'd wanted to buy a new pair of shoes if he made it that far. A small step, with many still before him, but on a bright winter morning the two friends bid Father Tomas goodbye and headed out to celebrate a milestone.

***

KO was silent during the bus ride, and it wasn't until they were at the department store when he asked, "Why aren't you mad at me, Teddy? I know how much it meant to you, to sponsor someone who didn't fail. "

"That's why I'm not mad," Teddy said. "I'm not gonna lie: I was upset when I heard what you were gonna do, especially after we'd talked about it. Father Tomas and I were praying something fierce for you."

"You were?"

"And you know what the Lord showed me? That you're a *fighter*, and you were fighting out in that storm for something so important you had to face the Devil himself. I worried for you, but I also worried for my pride. This morning I realized I'd put a burden on you on top of the one you already had, one I was supposed to help you carry. I hope you'll forgive me."

Teddy patted him on the shoulder. "I'm proud of you, my friend. It's like the Good Book says in Isaiah: we wait on the Lord, and we'll run and not grow weary, walk and not be faint. And speaking of walking"—Teddy handed him a box of black loafers—"it's time you had good shoes for the road."

***

KO arrived promptly at one at the police station for what he hoped was his final visit. He was striding in his new, freshly polished shoes and felt on top of the world. Shoes no one else had ever worn before. He hoped they'd carry him a long way.

"How you feeling, KO?" Ruiz asked as she sorted through photographs of boats, some sporting logos of snakes or bearded serpents. "Would you like some coffee?"

"Sure thing, Detective," he said. "Cop coffee is just what I need for this hangover. Though Lord willing, it's the last one I'll ever have."

"But for a good cause," Ruiz said and brought him a paper cup of steaming black caffeine. "Take it to go. Doc Stevens came in about ten minutes ago and you're the only person he's scheduled to see today. Once you're done with him, I have some pictures I'd like you to look at. Deal?"

"Whatever you say, Detective." He smiled. "Anything for free BPD coffee."

Ruiz laughed. "Now I know you've spent too much time here."

Doc Stevens was in a good mood, especially considering the gloomy weather report for the next forty-eight hours.

"How you feeling, KO?"

Sitting, KO hefted the steaming paper cup. "I'd gotten used to not waking up with a hangover, Doc. Between my headache and this stuff I think the Devil's been scared away. At least for now."

"That's good news."

KO sipped his coffee slowly, his smile fading, and Stevens waited for him to speak. Much of his job involved waiting for his clients to sort their thoughts.

"Was it worth it? I mean, was it worth me taking a drink again? I wanted a drink real bad this morning, and Lord help me, if there'd been a bottle on the bed beside me, I'd have emptied it."

"But there wasn't," Stevens said. "Because you had the strength to do what it takes to be in the right place at St. Roch's. That has to count for a lot, KO. But, yes, I believe your action has helped. It's possible the boat has sailed on. Boats are made to move, after all. But we've gone from the entire harbor to a couple of marinas to search. I think it's now just a matter of time before we sort out which boat it was and find the owner. Serial killers are hard to catch and there's no way I can tell you how many lives you might have saved last night— but even if it's only one, it's still worth it, don't you think?"

KO blinked as his vision blurred. "Yes, Doc, I do. Like the good shepherd going out to find the one lost lamb. You've sure put up with a lot of trouble from me."

Stevens nudged over a box of tissues. "Not at all. You've been a great help to us; I hope I've helped you in return. Next time you want a drink, remember what your life was like before and what it's like now. Stay with AA. It sounds like you have a powerful ally in Father Tomas and your sponsor. Don't be afraid to ask for help when you need it. You're worth it. I understand Detective Ruiz has some pictures she'd like you to review. Let me walk you back."

KO stood and stuck out his hand. "Sure thing, and thanks, Doc. For everything. For not giving up on me."

They shook hands, and the man who'd been knocked down by life walked out of the office with his head held high for the first time in a very long while.

When he reached Ruiz's desk, she pointed to the chair across from her. "We've only got twenty-five boats here, KO. Let me know if anything stands out."

The pictures were arranged sequentially by distance from the bar, and KO took about thirty seconds with each pair of photographs, but he shook his head each time. "I really don't remember the boat, Detective," he said. "Just the dragon."

Ruiz, ever the optimist, smiled back. "Once the weather lets up, we can go through the registry of all the boats currently in the two marinas, and we might call you back then. When we catch the guy, and I do mean *when*, we'll need you to testify in court. Will you be alright with that?"

"'Course, I will. I wouldn't leave something like this half-done. Anything else?

"Not for the moment, KO. Thank you for everything."

He stood. "Thanks for believing in me, Detective."

Ruiz remembered the look in his eyes as they'd watched Mankiller interview the mother. *Maybe it was worth it, after all.* She wondered what Father Tomas would say.

"What happens now?" she asked.

He smiled, a man at peace with his demons. "I'm going back to the office." He lifted his emptied paper cup. "Ain't no one there makes coffee as good as mine. Besides, I gotta stay busy. Keeps my mind off other things."

"Vaya con Dios, KO."

"Thank you, Detective." He turned to go. "I hope they'll be happy to see me."

***

Ruiz looked around at the mostly empty office. The department was going to skeleton staffing effective at five, but several of the detectives were taking personal time to hunker down at home before that took effect. She wasn't the only one reluctant to go out into the storm.

She went to Mankiller's office and was unsurprised to see him reading reports.

"*Jefe*, the world's coming to an end, can I have the rest of the day off?"

He looked up over his reading glasses. He tried not to be seen in them but didn't try to hide his specs once he was caught *in flagrante*. "Anything new on our dragon?" he asked.

"KO couldn't ID any of the boats, said he only remembered the dragon. I called the marina and the one next to it where KO thought it should be. They've all left and won't be back 'til next week ... like most sane people."

"We're cops, Ruiz. No one would accuse us of sanity."

"True, *Jefe*, but I don't think we're gonna get anything done until this storm blows over."

Mankiller closed the report file and stood, suddenly crisp and distant. "I think you're right. Go. Enjoy your cocoa."

"*Brr, Jefe*. You sure it's not warmer out there?"

"What? Oh ..." He looked at her again, the unspoken question heavy between them.

"Sorry. No. Maybe once the storm's passed you could come over and I could show you my telescope, but if I came over now, I might wind up stuck in your apartment a couple of days."

Ruiz didn't see any downside to that but was diplomatic enough not to say so. "*Bueno, Jefe.* Be safe. I'll see you once the Ice Age is over."

"Drive safe, Brunhilda. Say hello to Bjorn for me."

It took her forty minutes to make it to her apartment, a drive that usually took only twenty, but the flakes were already starting to come down large and wet, and the street prep wasn't fully deployed. She heard a ping on her phone while she was at a stoplight but waited until she got home and the cocoa was heating up before she checked it. She showed off her vocabulary of Puerto Rican *maldiciones* when she saw it was from Shwiller.

There was a picture of some strange carved creature that looked like an evil mermaid. The text read: "I just removed this figurehead for a plain one I'll install and customize later. This ain't no dragon, but I thought you might be interested. The boat belongs to a company, so it's probably not the one you're looking for. I'd rather not tell you who called me unless your witness can ID it, as my other customers might hear about it. Get back to me if he says yes. Enjoy the storm!"

Ruiz studied the figure. It didn't look much like a dragon to her, but then she wasn't drunk at midnight looking at it by the light of exploding fireworks, freezing, and scared out of her wits. It certainly looked evil, though.

Then she thought some more: Why would someone be so frantic to swap out their obviously expensive and intact figurehead just as a major storm was coming? No one would be taking their boat out now.

Yes, this was worth looking into, so she called KO's office number, hoping he might still be in.

"Hightower Securities, Gladys Prince speaking."

"Hello, Mrs. Prince, I'm Detective Ruiz, we've talked before. Could I speak with Mr. Bannon? It's rather urgent."

"Is this about the murder investigation he's been helping you with?"

Damn. I guess I should have expected he'd have to explain his absence, but still, when admin knows ... "I'm Sorry, ma'am, but I'm not at liberty to answer that question."

There was a long pause and Ruiz could just hear the woman's nails clicking as if she were pondering her next response.

"I tell you what, Detective. Mr. Bannon has gone home for the day, but he was issued a company phone yesterday. If you tell me how to get back in contact with you, I'll call him. He left to take a bus about thirty minutes ago, so he may not notice it until he reaches the shelter."

I don't think so, Ruiz said to herself. *Not today.* "I tell *you* what, Ms. Prince. You give me KO's number right now, or I'll have you charged with obstructing a police investigation. Now give me his cell, or the next cop you see will have a piece of paper with your name on it. Got it?"

Ruiz heard some wheezing on the other end for a moment before the voice croaked out, "Of course, Detective. Happy to help."

Chapter Thirty-Six

Jan. 28, Wednesday, 5.00 p.m.

Amy got the call from work at four thirty. The evening shift tech couldn't make it in. Was Amy available to pull a double, starting at six, at double pay? She wasn't about to say no to four days' pay in one night.

She didn't have time to make Taylor his supper before she'd have to leave for work. Given the streets, she'd have to set out half an hour early.

She'd just taken Taylor next door to Mrs. Henley and was out shoveling snow from around her car when the SUV pulled up to the curb and a large man got out. She squinted through the thickening snow and could just make out her father's boss beneath the coat as he pulled down his scarf. What was the name again?

"Mr. ... Hightower?"

He waved but didn't smile. "Amy Sellers, is that you?" he said. His voice was strained.

Amy's chest tightened ... *Dad*. "Yes. I was just about to head to work," she said. "Something wrong?"

"It's your father," Mr. Hightower said. "I felt I had to come in person. I didn't have your number ..."

"What is it? What's happened?"

"He collapsed at work. The doctors say it's a heart attack. I just got off the phone with Johns Hopkins. They're ... They're afraid he won't make it."

"I have to ... that is, I have work, I ..." Amy shook her head, at a loss for words. She thought of Taylor but, no, he'd be okay. "Jesus Christ ..." She looked up at the clouds, both in prayer and in fear of the weather, then looked down again at her car, a fifteen-year-old heap with bald tires. "That's in the city, so ..."

"Let me give you a lift, please. I've got four-wheel drive and all-weather tires. We'll make better time."

Amy clutched her purse. She hated owing anything to anybody, but, no, she wasn't going to let her pride get her stuck in a snowbank, not with one last chance to make things right with her father, not when he'd been trying ...

"Let's go," she said. "I'll call my boss on the way."

After she called in her emergency, apologizing for making a bad situation at work even worse, she accepted the coffee Marty offered her from the cup holder.

Funny, she thought after a few sips. *Coffee usually doesn't relax me like this.* Then she noticed drowsily that they weren't heading downtown. Her last thought before falling into a deep sleep was, *Who stops for coffee on the way to the ICU?*

Chapter Thirty-Seven

Jan. 28, Wednesday, 6:00 p.m.

KO had just made it back to the shelter when his phone pinged. He saw Ruiz on the caller ID and paused. Now what? He opened the message, and the leering face of the dragon emerged from his nightmares onto the screen in his hand and he had to stop himself from hurling into a wall.

✳ ✳ ✳

It took KO a moment to realize its position wasn't right. It lay on its side, maybe on a bench somewhere. Even so, there was no mistake. The meaning hit him next: the beast in his nightmare was real. Just like the flickering sign, just like the dead woman. It was all, all real.

The message with the image said Ruiz wanted to talk to him about what she'd sent. Good. They'd found his dragon. He was about to call her back when his phone rang.

"Hello, KO," said Marty.

"Marty. Are you alright?"

"Oh, I'm fine. Just fine. I gotta ask, are you alone? Can we talk for a minute?"

"Sure, anything."

"It's just I've got someone who wants to talk to you."

"What? Hello?" KO said, then another voice, a woman's voice. It sounded slurred, like the owner was dizzy or sleepy. It was also immediately familiar.

"Daddy? Daddy ... that you?"

"Amy!" KO gasped. Had Marty found Amy somewhere? "Baby, what's wrong? Where are you? What's happened?"

Marty's voice returned. Except it wasn't his voice. At least, not how KO thought of it. It was still selling cars, but there was something harsh about it, like a car dealer who sold drugs on the side. It said, "Listen carefully, you maggot. I've got your daughter. We're on my boat and I've got a gun. A gun that will make a huge hole in her chest if you're not here in one hour. Alone."

"What? Marty ... what are you doing?"

"Alone," Marty repeated. "I might be stuck on a boat, but if I see any flashing lights or even smell a cop, Amy's going down before I do. You got that?"

KO's chest pounded. "Marty, why are you doing this? What do you mean your boat? You have a ..." Then it dawned. "You have a boat," he said quietly, and the cold sank into the pit of his stomach. He didn't dare pull the phone away to look at the picture, but he realized why Detective Ruiz had sent it. "That was your boat I saw."

Marty's laugh was like a drop of ice water on the back of the neck. "That's right, little man. That's *my* boat. My boat, my big gun. *Your* daughter. I don't have to tell you it's not an empty threat, do I?"

"No ... no, you don't," KO said quietly.

"Good. Now get your ass down here."

"I will. I'm gonna. I'll do it all like you said. Just ... just don't hurt her—"

"You'd better. If you're slow, I'm running. But not before I punch a hole in her to clean up any *credible* witnesses—and don't get any ideas about being a hero again."

"But ... But, Marty, the storm ..."

"It's six. You've got 'til seven—that's one hour. You've got one hour, and not a minute more. So, get moving, you bum!"

The line went dead, and KO stared at the phone like it had just bitten him. One hour. Could he make it in an hour? On a good day it would take him twenty minutes to get to the harbor.

But today was anything but good.

Marty had Amy, but what about his grandson Taylor? He swallowed bile. *If he had Taylor, he'd have told me*, he thought. *I gotta believe he's safe, at least for now.*

KO tried to think logically. What could he do? He needed Father Tomas or Detective Ruiz or Teddy ... Teddy!

Teddy's apartment was on the way. Maybe he could get something more solid than spiritual guidance. KO looked at his watch. He'd already spent three minutes thinking.

Father Tomas would tell him to call the police, but that would only slow him down. He looked down the hallway at the door of the little priest's office, then turned toward the door and the harbor that lay beyond.

***

Teddy was surprised by KO's visit as the storm was reaching full force, and even more by his request, but he trusted the old prizefighter, knowing how long and hard KO had worked to earn his respect.

"Must be bad trouble to need something like that," Teddy said. "I just keep it as a reminder of how far I've gone from my old life. You sure you don't want me to come?"

"Sorry, Teddy. I know I could count on you, but this is something I gotta handle myself. I'll tell you all about it once it's over."

The big bear of a man hugged KO harder than anyone. "I'll be praying for you, KO."

"Thanks, I'll need all the prayers you can send my way." He touched the bulge in his coat pocket, "but this can't hurt."

And with that, the little man with the heavy burden disappeared into the blizzard, his footprints filled in with fresh snow almost as soon as he left them. He was no longer a drunken, washed-out boxer looking for a place to hole up with a bottle. He was KO Bannon. Father. Grandfather. Dragon slayer.

Chapter Thirty-Eight

Jan. 28, Wednesday (cont.)

After years on the street, KO knew how to "surf" the buildings in bad weather, moving quickly from the shelter of one to the next. Even so, the wind must have been nearly fifty miles per hour from the north, making him walk bent over. There was no traffic save the one snowplow he saw trundling down an adjacent street. He was walking through a city of over a million people, yet entirely on his own, invisible. In a way, that was how it had been for years.

As he trudged on, he couldn't help checking his watch every time he stopped to catch his breath. He had forty minutes ... twenty ... fifteen ... He remembered Marty's warning and kept going, pushing against the wind and the snow blasting in his face.

But Marty had lied before. What if this was all a trick? What if Amy was already dead? What if the last thing she'd ever known was her father wasn't there—again. Maybe it was all a way to frame KO for everything. What if everything he'd tried to save disappeared just like that? Father Tomas, Teddy, his life ... It would be nothing, and it would be his fault.

KO's feet slipped on slush, and he went down on one knee. Scrambling, he clutched at his pocket for his phone to make sure it was safe, his lifeline. He felt something else in his pocket and pulled out the aluminum cross Father Tomas had given him a lifetime ago.

He didn't want to think about what was waiting for him, but he couldn't stop; the memory of that dead woman in the water wouldn't leave him. It seemed to twist and change shape.

"Oh Lord, don't let me get there to see my Amy in the water. Please, Lord ..."

And what about Taylor? KO's vision blurred white as he pressed on. What if something had already happened to him? Marty could have done anything. He'd already done horrible things ... KO might have let him go on doing them. If he hadn't helped the police, his family would still be safe.

KO pushed on, clutching the cross and praying. He had to believe something greater than the police were on his side. There was no one out here but him, his fear, and God in the storm.

At last, he heard the lap of the waves hitting the boats and the lines creaking as they kept the floating vanities of the wealthy secure, and he smelled the harbor. Almost there ... He glanced at his watch and saw he had five minutes. It had to be enough.

He crunched on the thickening snow in his arabber boots as he hurried through the marina. He worried he wouldn't recognize the right boat. Every OPEN sign in the harbor was off. Everyone closed down on a night like this.

At first, KO saw only one boat with its cabin lights lit, then a second one further down the slip. He squinted. No dragons ... but the first one seemed right. He walked around to the lowered gangplank and found his nightmare waiting for him.

Marty was inside in the cockpit/saloon, sitting down across from the entrance, face blurred by the melting snow on the window, but KO could still make out his smile—that salesman smile.

As he approached, KO saw Marty held a very big revolver in his right hand, pointed toward the floor. He sidestepped across the narrow gangplank to the door, flinching as the wood creaked underfoot, but Marty didn't look up, holding the gun steady—pointed down.

KO tried to see through the windows for Amy, but furniture blocked his view. Finding the door unlocked, he stepped into the dragon's lair.

***

The warmth of the cabin was a welcome relief after the bite of the wind, and KO felt the blood surge to his face. He tightened his fists, preparing for the fight of his life.

Marty didn't get up, but his smile didn't change. "Hello, KO, welcome to *Lamia*," he said. "After passing by all those times, I think it's time you had a look inside." He pointed at something with the gun, and KO stepped forward slowly.

There was Amy, lying tied and gagged on the floor at Marty's feet. Her back was turned toward KO and she wasn't moving. Not at all. KO hurried forward.

"Back!" Marty barked, and he waggled the gun with a warning.

KO froze. Marty glanced down at Amy, then up at the ex-boxer's frozen face. The fake smile turned into a sly grin.

"Right there's fine," he said. "Don't worry, she's alive. I'm a salesman and I've kept my end of the deal. You keep yours?"

"I'm alone. Swear to God."

"Good." Marty gave a nod and glanced at KO's fists. "But this is a negotiation table, not the ring. Drop your hands."

KO forced his hands open and down. "Amy ..." he groaned.

"You're being very impolite," said Marty. "You just barged right in. What do you think? Nice place, isn't it? I had her made custom."

"Nice," KO said stiffly, not wanting to do anything to lose the attention of the gun or the man holding it.

"Your girl, she didn't seem very impressed, though now I think on it, it's hard to talk after an unhealthy dose of Valium, not to mention the gag." He shrugged. "I guess I got carried away."

"If you hurt her ..."

"You'll what?" Marty sneered. "Call the cops?" Now he turned the gun on KO just out of reach in front of the ex-boxer's face. "I don't think so."

"Look, she doesn't know anything. She never talks to me," KO pleaded. "Just ... let her go, Marty. You want me. Without me, the cops don't have a case."

"That's right, KO. They don't, which is why you're here. I'm glad we're on the same page." He shrugged. "Alright, KO. You win. Untie her and she can go. I got you. That's all I need."

Marty backed away to the far side of the cabin. KO watched the distance between Marty and Amy grow. And he watched the gun. A bullet could cover the distance before he could blink. He had to get Amy out of here. Then it didn't matter where the bullet went. He inched forward.

"Amy ...?" Now that he was close enough, he could see she was breathing. How had Marty known where to find her?

Then he remembered. The letter. Marty had offered to mail the letter, and KO had just written her address on it and handed it over.

Marty wagged the gun at him. "Hurry up, or I might change my mind."

KO undid her gag, then the cords behind her back. He gasped in relief when she moaned. He tried to wake her, gently shaking her shoulder. "Amy? Amy, sweetheart, you OK?"

She blinked her glazed eyes. "Daddy? Where ...? That man, he said ..." she fumbled for her pockets, "said we were going to the hospital, said you had a heart attack, that you weren't gonna make it."

KO helped her up, putting himself between her and Marty. Maybe he'd just shoot them anyway, he thought. But KO was going to give her every chance to get away.

"I'm here, sweetheart. I'm fine."

"Where are we?"

"It's gonna be okay, sweetheart. See, I'm okay. But I'm gonna get you out of here."

"But how did I even get here ...? I ..."

KO saw her eyes shift to something over his shoulder. He didn't have time to think before the heavy barrel struck his head.

***

KO came to and felt the rumble of the engines as the boat rocked over the chopping waves. Amy was standing at the wheel with Marty behind her, his gun pointed at her as he gave her directions for steering the boat. KO tried to stand but found his hands tied behind him. Probably the same cords he'd taken off Amy. He'd made it easier for Marty to move them from her to him.

He couldn't feel his hands.

***

Three slips down from *Lamia*, Marty's neighbor, Old Man Jenkins (Sergeant Major, retired), was sipping black tea augmented with a double shot of Irish whiskey and a teaspoon of honey when he noticed his neighbor's boat pulling away from the dock.

The old soldier had always enjoyed a good storm if he wasn't out in it, and he shook his head as *Lamia* slid past him. That stuck-up rich kid who never said hello was next to some woman. What kind of fool went out into a storm like this, much less risking someone else's life? From what Jenkins had seen of the boy's handling of the boat in the harbor, he doubted Mr. Fancy Pants was enough of a sailor to handle his craft under these conditions.

He considered calling the Coast Guard so they could turn the fool around, then said to hell with it. Maybe this would teach him a lesson ... if he survived.

Jenkins raised his grog and muttered, "May you have fair winds and following seas," but only for the lady's sake.

Chapter Thirty-Nine

Jan. 28, Wednesday (cont.)

I t had been at least a half-hour since she'd sent the picture, but KO hadn't gotten back to her. It was just a hunch, Ruiz told herself, but it was her hunch. She looked out the window at the worsening storm, shivered, and got ready to go out, just in case.

KO should have called by now, she thought as she exchanged her fuzzy slippers for Uggs. *What could be keeping him?*

She looked at the image the boat mechanic had sent her and had a thought.

Shwiller answered on the third ring.

"Yes, Detective, was your witness able to ID the image?"

"He's not answering the phone, and I don't feel like playing twenty questions while there's a killer out there."

"What? Jeez, you didn't tell me this was about a murder! You said you were with Robbery/Homicide, so I figured someone was switching registrations or something to help smuggle drugs. Those are the kinds of people you don't want to piss off if you don't have to."

"It was strictly need to know. Sorry."

"Okay, right. What do you need from me?"

"Is the figurehead you texted me from a boat in the Del Mar Marina?"

"Yes."

"Then I need to know what company it belongs to."

"Easy enough. Hightower Securities."

"Say that again?"

"Hightower Securities. The man who called me was a Marty or Martin or something."

"*Madre de Dios!* What's the slip number?"

"Number fifteen, halfway up the pier on the right side."

Ruiz hung up without thanking him and sat down hard as the implications of what she'd heard sank in.

KO's boss. He'd been playing them all along!

Dio!

He'd been using KO to keep them informed on the investigation. Her shock was soon replaced with anger.

He's had his fun. Now it's my turn.

*****

When the phone rang again, Gladys saw it was from the same rude detective. She almost didn't answer it, but maybe they could trace her by her phone and know she was still in the building? Maybe they could tap into the building's security cameras?

She gritted her teeth and answered with no pretense at politeness. "Yes, Detective? Any other threats you forgot to mention?"

"Ms. Prince. I'm sorry I had to get terse with you. I have just one final question before we find you a safe way home."

"What do you mean, Detective?" Gladys suddenly felt more cooperative.

"I need the current location, or home address, of one Martin, or Marty, Hightower Junior."

A pleasant surprise! Although the talk of safety had Gladys wondering. She'd always heard that all good things came to those who waited, and for once, it appeared to be true.

"I don't know where he is now," she answered, "but I could pull up the address for you, Detective."

"Thank you, Ms. Prince," Ruiz said once the address had been confirmed. "I'd recommend you lay low."

"You ... think he might attack me?" Gladys's steel wool voice was a little less sure of itself now.

"If he thinks you're the one who turned him in, most definitely. We can send an escort to get you home if you like. In fact, I'd recommend it."

"It really is serious?"

"We have cases we suspect he was involved in going back at least three years," Ruiz explained. "He must be able to put on a good face. Do you think he'd suspect your help in this?"

Gladys swore like the old poker player she was, and Ruiz wished the call was recorded for future study.

***

I hope he resists, Ruiz thought as she hung up, then felt ashamed. She'd have to remember that the next time she went to confession.

She called Mankiller next.

"We got our man."

"Come again?"

"I said, we know who Romeo is. Now we just gotta bring him in."

"We know? You know. So why haven't you told me yet?"

Ruiz wished she could laugh. "It's KO's boss, Martin Hightower—Junior. He somehow learned KO was a witness and hired him. He must have pumped KO for information on the investigation. The boat mechanic I found got a call from Hightower to replace his figurehead just before we went dragon hunting. That's why we didn't find it."

"Goddam! Good work, Ruiz. Do we have an address for Junior?"

"We do," said Ruiz, and told him.

"Right answer!" He wrote it down and read it back to her. "I'll send our duty detectives out to grab him right after I call the night judge to get us a warrant. I reckon we'll want to tear his place apart, but a rich kid like him can afford a lot of lawyers. We don't want anything thrown out on a technicality. Give the on-duty team a heads-up while I get the warrant issued." Mankiller looked out the window. "Tell them to dress warm."

"Anything else?"

"Make sure our witness is safe. With the legal team Hightower can throw together, we'll need to bury the jury in evidence, and he's our star attraction."

"Got it. You want me to send a cruiser out to the shelter?"

"Good idea, at least until Hightower is in custody, but call ahead so KO doesn't freak out. Won't hurt to give that little priest a heads-up as well, so he can reassure his flock."

"On it, *Jefe*. I wish I could be there when they collar the bastard."

"Well, like the great philosopher Mick Jagger once said, 'You can't always get what you want.' I'll call the arrest team as soon as the warrant is ready and call you back when they have the perp in custody."

"Thanks, *Jefe*."

"No, thanks to you. Your shoe leather led to the mechanic, and the mechanic led us to him. This is your collar, whether you're there at his arrest or not. We'll talk again soon."

***

Mankiller always had a deep appreciation for the night judge. Few men chose a shift in the dark hours. The wheels of justice usually turned slowly, but when a judge had nothing else to do and a serial killer was on the loose, a valid warrant could take just fifteen minutes.

Bailey was once again the night detective, and he and his partner, Kelly, had the faxed warrant within fifteen minutes and were on the road.

The streets were clear, but even in a department SUV with all-weathers and four-wheel drive, it took them thirty minutes to arrive at the condo. After no answer to their knock, the super let them in when they showed their badges. Nothing. Well, nothing but a custom gun case for a very large revolver. An empty case.

Mankiller smiled when he saw who was calling, but the smile quickly faded once he heard what Bailey had and hadn't found.

"Get with vehicle registration. We need to put out a description of his car."

"What do you want me to do?"

"Stick around the apartment for now. Maybe he's stuck somewhere and will come dragging in later. I'd rather you be there to greet him."

"Got it, Sergeant. At least I'll be warm."

"I can see why you and Ruiz get along so well. You've got a similar outlook on life."

***

Ruiz's throat tightened when she got no answer on KO's phone after her third try.

Could be the storm, she told herself. Could be ... No, her gut had been right so far tonight. She called the shelter, pacing as the phone rang and quickening her turns as someone finally picked up.

"Father Tomas, how may I help?"

"Father, it's Detective Ruiz. Have you seen KO?"

"I'm afraid not since breakfast."

"He didn't say he had somewhere to be?"

259

"No, and I'm worried about that. He wasn't at dinner, nor the AA meeting after. He hasn't missed a meeting since he first came here. I assumed he was caught up in the storm. Is everything alright?"

Ruiz winced. The man was already worried, and she was about to make his night worse.

"He may be in danger, Father. I wish I had more time to explain, but it's about the murderer we've been looking for. I think he knows what KO saw and wants to kill him to keep him from testifying."

"How is that possible?!"

"I don't have time to explain. There'll be a couple of uniformed police officers there soon to protect you and everyone in the shelter. Please ask around to see if anyone has seen KO and if so, tell the officers and have them call me right away. We all want to keep him safe. I wouldn't mind if you said a few prayers for me as well."

"I will do as you ask, Detective, but do not be afraid for us. I have faced men far more dangerous than this in my own country. Go with God, my child."

"Thank you, Father."

Hanging up, Ruiz pondered the situation. Her gut told her time was running out before something awful happened. She had to do something. But what?

If the suspect knew about KO, he knew police were searching for him, but this suspect was rich and had always been rich. Rich men, especially rich young men, thought laws happened to other people. A "fine," for example, was just a longer word for "fee." This whole thing would be a game ... Maybe even getting caught was too, if he thought his lawyers could save him.

There were only two things his fancy lawyer could give them a hard time about: first, the eyewitness. KO was a known drunk. His altercation with the frat boys could be cast into something far more sinister than a good deed. And he was black. Yes, a "good" lawyer—Ruiz inwardly sneered at the term—would be sure to argue for a carefully selected jury—one that would surely believe KO was the most likely suspect. If they couldn't manage the race angle, there was always the middle-class mind to take advantage of, the one that said money was virtue and thus the poor were always guilty of being poor. The lawyer would argue KO's attempt to cast suspicion on rich Mr. Hightower was an attempt to escape prosecution.

So that left the second thing they needed to prove this: the boat. No matter how carefully the perp scrubbed, there must be something on the boat that would tie it to at least one of the victims, and therefore to him.

If she were in his shoes, what would she do?

It hit her like a kick to the gut. Sink the boat! Either with KO onboard or already dead and his body dumped.

But KO was a fighter. The killer would need some way to force KO to come to him. But what ...? Her stomach turned. Sometimes getting into a perp's mind made her physically sick.

She called Mankiller and got a busy signal. When voicemail picked up, she said, "*Jefe.* I'm heading for the boat. I think that's the most likely place for Hightower to go. He's probably got KO or has something to make KO come to him. We need to send a patrol car to KO's listed next of kin. He has a daughter and a grandson. You can get her address from KO's arrest record for the fight. She bailed him out, Amy something. That's the only thing that would make KO do what Hightower wants." She swallowed. *Something else? Anything else ...?*

"Call me as soon as you can."

She put on her puffy coat, then after adjusting the Velcro, her tactical vest with her 'go-to-war' equipment, and headed out the door.

"Well, *Jefe*," she muttered, "time to see if those *maldita* all-weather tires are really worth the cash."

Chapter Forty

Jan. 28 Wednesday (cont.)

Marty was only five feet away from KO as the man focused on navigating the harbor in almost whiteout conditions, giving Amy directions in a calm, measured voice. On his boat he was more than a king; he was a captain, a title with power any despot could only yearn for. Everything was under control now, and he was in no hurry for this to end. He'd never had two playmates at once and he was going to make the most of it.

He looked back and saw KO's eyes were open. "How's the head, my friend? I reckon it hurts, but nothing you haven't had before, right?"

"It hurts, Marty. Is that what you want to hear? Yeah, it's like a jackhammer at the back of my head. Let me show you."

"That's the thanks I get for a boat ride? Well, I guess you should be a little cranky, after all, as it's only one way." He pointed to two red gasoline cans at the back of the saloon. "If anyone should be angry, it should be me. I'm gonna have to sink this wonderful boat and splash around in the dingy until the Coast Guard rescues me. I can practically quote the lecture they're going to give me for going out in this storm." He sighed. "There'll probably be a fine, too, for ignoring their small craft warning. Ah well, a price I'm willing to pay to tie up a couple of loose ends."

He pointed to a heavy chain coiled beside his feet.

"A human body floats better in seawater. Did you know that? But it doesn't take much weight to keep it down, at least until it starts to fall apart. By the time bits of you and your daughter start popping up, you'll be nothing but fish bait."

Beside him, Amy watched the gun move back and forth as Marty lectured KO. She was small like her father, five feet four and 130 pounds. She'd never get the gun away from him, at least not by herself.

A channel marker suddenly loomed straight ahead, and Amy jerked the boat to the left without thinking.

"Right, turn it right!" Marty yelled, and the boat swayed as she jerked it back the other way.

KO had been a street fighter before he became a boxer, and he knew a few tricks not allowed by the Marquis of Queensbury, even with his hands bound behind his back. When the boat swerved hard to the right, he swept Marty's legs out from under him and yelled, "The gun, Amy, grab the gun!"

Marty hit the deck hard and saw stars as the gun loosened from his right hand. He felt the woman's hands on his arm and instinctively tightened his grip while grabbing her hair with his left hand. She twisted around and bit down hard, catching his thumb in her incisors. Marty screamed in fury and pain.

Now KO was up and landed a hard kick in Marty's right side, satisfied with the give of a snapping rib. Marty grunted as the pain of breathing stopped his scream.

Marty jerked Amy by the hair to free his hand from her mouth. The pain in his side from pulling her across his body nearly made him pass out. Then he felt his gun hand slammed to the deck as KO stomped hard with his leather shoes on his wrist. The gun slid free and across the floorboards.

With no one at the controls, the boat continued to turn right in a wide, slow circle. KO kicked the gun away to the far side of the cabin, then the boat slammed into the channel marker and KO went flying forward, stumbling over Marty to hit face first into the control panel. He tumbled halfway down the stairs to the forward cabin.

He lay dazed, his head downstairs, his feet up, and heard as though from a far way the battle between Amy and Marty as Marty tried to roll over and crawl toward the gun.

Amy used her fingernails, her teeth, her knees and elbows—all to rain as much damage on Marty as possible.

KO's head swam as he tried to get his feet under him. Suddenly, he was back in the ring ... the end of the eighth round, Sugar Ray barely breaking a sweat. KO's corner man had slit the swollen skin around his eyes to drain the bruising so he could see and stuffed cotton up both nostrils to stop the bleeding. He felt tired, so tired. His head might weigh a hundred pounds. Hadn't he fought long enough?

Then he heard Amy scream, and he was back on the boat ...

And he answered the bell.

***

He slid down the rest of the way to the cabin, then flipped over. Bringing his knees to his chest, he slipped his hands over his feet and finally had his hands in front. Better. He charged up the stairs as he worked the cord with his teeth, using his gold-crowned canine to good effect; he felt it give as he reached the top.

Amy and Marty were still on the floor, Amy on Marty's back as Marty splayed his fingers reaching for the gun barely a foot away. Suddenly, he twisted and elbowed her full in the face. Her head snapped back and her body went limp. KO flipped her out of the way as Marty reached the gun and rolled over.

The gun came up as Marty turned to his left, trying to protect his broken ribs on the right. KO grabbed the hand and wrenched it to the left with all his strength. Something in the wrist gave way and Marty found the breath to scream again.

The gun dropped and KO kicked it away again.

Marty was down, but not done, his right foot coming up to launch KO across the cockpit, slamming him into the entry door. He staggered to his feet and spotted his gun on the deck beside his opponent. He had a good fifty pounds on him and was going to use every bit of it.

KO saw the gun to his left but knew he wouldn't have time to pick it up before Marty was on him. Marty and KO stared at one another when the old fighter began to laugh.

"What's so damned funny?" Marty said. "Booze finally rot your brain?"

"I was just thinking, Marty. I came here to fight a dragon, and all I find is a spoiled rich white boy. Nothing to it. I've whipped your kind before."

KO dodged a haymaker, then reached into his pocket.

Though he was right-handed, he slipped the brass knuckles on his left hand as Marty's hands found his throat, leaving Marty's ribs exposed.

KO's vision blurred as he slammed the ridge of the brass knuckles into the damaged rib cage. Marty's grip loosened, but KO wasn't finished, working his way down the man's right side. After three more blows, Marty was on his knees, face gray with pain.

KO shifted the knuckles to his right hand, ready to tenderize the big man's face, when Marty grabbed him at the knees and flipped him onto the floor before diving for the gun.

KO knew how to take a fall, but Marty's weight across his legs left him unable to move and he heard the hammer cock as his opponent rolled over onto his side, the barrel aimed at his face. They were lying five feet apart, both panting in pain and exertion, and KO thought the black hole at the end of the barrel was the biggest he'd ever seen.

A one-way tunnel to oblivion.

Chapter Forty-One

Jan. 28, Wednesday cont.

Mankiller saw the voicemail from Ruiz and swore when he heard she was going to the boat alone. He called the station and told them to send a patrol car to the marina to give Ruiz backup, then got in his car and drove like he was in the Olympic bobsled trials.

They arrived at the marina together. Mankiller had the license plate number and description of Marty's SUV, and it was easily picked out in the marina parking lot as there were only two cars there. The second one was a beat-up, formerly red pickup truck with an Eighty-Second Airborne and Welsh dragon sticker on the back window.

"Backup's on the way, Ruiz," Mankiller said once they'd stepped out. "Wait for them here and guide them down to the boat."

"To hell with that, Sergeant. My case, my collar. You can wait here and guide the backup if you want. I'm going to the boat. Romeo's going down, today, and I'm gonna be the one who makes it happen."

Her face told Mankiller this wasn't up for discussion. Ruiz was an avenging angel with flaming sword unsheathed. No one told an angel to back off, not even a police sergeant.

"Right," he said. "Plan C. We go down together. I'll call the responding officers, let them know where we're going, and they follow when they can."

Ruiz nodded once, hard. "Good plan. Let's go."

They moved cautiously into the wall of blustering snow, lest they walk right up on their quarry before seeing him—or fall off the dock into the freezing water. Luckily the fresh snowfall offered good traction, even if the crunching made it impossible to move silently.

They crept past the rocking white outlines of snow-covered boats until they'd reached *Lamia*'s slip, holding nothing but a black patch of rolling water.

"Shit," Mankiller hissed. "Ruiz, call the station and have them patch you into the Harbor Patrol. We need eyes out there, now!"

He turned to peer into the storm to see if any running lights were visible when he noticed the lights on in a boat three slips down. Ruiz was talking to the Harbor Patrol dispatcher, giving a description of the boat and the situation, so he tapped her on the shoulder, pointed to the other boat, pointed to himself, and moved out.

The boat was named *Death From Above* and was about forty-five feet long. Mankiller stomped on the gangplank, and a figure inside the cockpit waved him in.

The occupant was a short, fat man with gray whiskers. He held a corgi that was more spherical than cylindrical, and the detective wondered if the dog could still walk. Mankiller showed his badge, "Sergeant Mankiller, Robbery/Homicide. We're looking for the man who owns *Lamia*, three slips down from you. The boat's gone. Did you see when it left?"

"Retired Sergeant Major Jenkins, Sergeant. Pleased to meet you. Yeah, the damn fool left about thirty minutes ago. I saw a woman at the wheel with him beside her, like he was teaching her how to steer a boat, which is the craziest thing I could think of in this storm. They were creeping along, can't have gone far."

"Any idea where they might be heading?"

The old soldier snorted. "Ain't but two directions, Sergeant, either out to the Chesapeake Bay, or upriver and they was headed for the Bay." He lowered his voice. "Anything you care to tell me?"

"Sorry, Sergeant Major, no can do." He added, using their shared military experience, "OPSEC. You understand."

Jenkins nodded sagely with an expression somewhere between the Buddha and Santa Claus. "Operational Security. Got it. My lips are sealed."

"Thank you, Sergeant Major. You'll read about it in the papers in a day or so." *Though the headline is still uncertain*, he mused.

When he rejoined her, Ruiz was about to end her call. He gestured for her to pass it over. Mankiller shared what Santa had just told him, adding that there was at least one hostage, a woman, on board.

"Right, Sergeant," the dispatcher said. "We'll have a boat pick you up at the dock in about ten minutes. The weather's too risky to put a chopper up, but we can send out a drone. That's the best we can do."

"Then that's the best you can do," Mankiller replied. "Give the Coast Guard a heads-up as well." He turned to Ruiz. "You got a description of the boat?"

"Yeah, boat's named *Lamia*," she said. "Tell them we'll call right back. Give me the phone back when you're done here and I'll get the details from the mechanic."

After a brief conversation with Shwiller, Ruiz forwarded the information: "Be on the lookout for a forty-two-foot Grand Banks Classic Trawler, white with blue trim, named *Lamia*."

Once the call was made, there was nothing to do but wait for their ride. Ruiz gave Mankiller a side eye and considered the boat of the retired Jenkins.

"That was a lot of information from that witness, *Jefe*, and in about two minutes, max."

Mankiller shrugged. "What did you expect? I'm a people person, remember?"

Soon lights blazed out of the snowfall. The harbor craft arrived, twenty-five feet long with a single cabin and cockpit. The three cops on board looked as miserable as Ruiz felt, but once Mankiller told them the situation their faces hardened. They were as much cops as anyone on the force; they just spent their days in boats instead of patrol cars.

"Let's head out in their last known direction," said the sergeant in charge. "Hopefully our little bird will see something to give us a more direct heading."

"I don't know the water like you do, Sergeant," said Mankiller. "We're gonna have to rely on your knowledge and instincts. Where's the closest place someone could go to kill two people and dump their bodies without being seen?"

"We also suspect he's planning on sinking his boat to cover up any evidence," Ruiz added. "So he won't go too far out so he can be picked up quickly."

The boat's sergeant turned to his helmsman. "Straight out to the bay—but keep it half-speed," he instructed, then he turned back to Mankiller, who was frowning at the last order. "Any faster and we might not see them in time and sail right past," he explained.

"What about radar?" Ruiz asked.

"Radar will keep us from colliding with them, but we can't assume it's the only boat out there, no matter how crazy."

The third member of the crew, Officer Thompson, carried an impressive case in one hand. As they set out, he stepped out onto the front of the boat and set it down. Already the prow was rolling heavily in three-foot waves—waves which only grew higher as they traveled further from the shore. Firm on his sea legs despite the storm, the man unpacked and launched a drone with the cool expertise of a falconer. When he retreated to the cabin with the emptied case, he leaned over a monitor as the flying robot disappeared into the wind and snow.

The helmsman's caution paid off about ten minutes later as they came upon the recently rammed channel marker.

"We must be on the right path," he said, pointing it out as they passed. "I travel this route almost every day. Those scrape marks and paint weren't there yesterday. Our perp had to have gone this way and gotten careless."

"Maybe he was watching the hostages," Mankiller concluded.

"Good eyes, Ferguson," said the sergeant. "Kick it up to three-quarters speed."

They squinted into the storm, trying to see their quarry before it saw them. They all jumped when the drone pilot cried out, "Got 'em! Less than two miles ahead!"

The sergeant looked at the screen. The drone was flying a circle about fifty feet above the boat. After a moment's calculation, the sergeant turned to the helmsman to give a slight course correction and then the order: "Full speed ahead! The boat's drifting out of control and a man is holding a gun. He hasn't seen the drone yet, but he could any time."

He turned back to the drone operator. "Call your bird home, then radio the Coast Guard for assistance. It looks like we're gonna need it."

Chapter Forty-Two

Jan. 28, Wednesday cont.

The gun wavered back and forth with the rocking of the boat, the movement reminding KO of a cobra preparing to strike.

"Brass knuckles, KO? Really? I'm disappointed in you," Marty wheezed, his left hand trying to stabilize his right hand.

"You're half again as big as I am," KO answered. "Just wanted to even the odds."

"Doesn't matter in the end though, does it, drunk? You were a loser in the ring and you're a loser now. I just want you to know that before you die." He waved the gun toward Amy's collapsed form on the floor on the far side of the cockpit. "And before she dies."

***

Amy lay there motionless, playing possum, her eyes open a slit looking for the slightest chance to trip or kick the man with the gun. If he would just come a little closer ...

Her right shoulder shielded her chest from Marty's view, but she knew her father could see her hand. As he glanced at her, she tapped her right forefinger slowly against her heart three times, telling him he wasn't facing this monster all alone.

Marty said, "Well, this has been fun, but all good things ... You know the rest," pointing the gun at KO's chest.

"Wrap your daughter's legs from her feet to her knees in that chain. Now."

KO bent over, picked up one of two heavy chains. Each one must have been about eight feet long and weigh thirty pounds. KO was a fair swimmer but he knew he'd sink to the bottom of the bay in seconds with this wrapped around him.

He turned his back to Marty ... then ducked and spun hard to his left, swinging the chain for the gun hand like a batter swinging for the fences.

Slowed by the pain in his ribs, Marty fired the gun as the iron chain bludgeoned his fist. The revolver went flying as the window behind KO shattered from the shot.

KO had been too small for football in high school but knew from his ring experience to get low and drive with his legs. He rammed his left shoulder hard into Marty's ribcage and staggered the big man backward through the cockpit door and outside along the rail. Marty clung to his attacker, trying to squeeze the breath out of him as he slipped on the snow-covered deck, then fell—back and over the side, taking KO with him.

***

"Shot fired!" the sergeant called just as the dim form of *Lamia* took shape ahead of them.

"Bring us alongside!" Mankiller ordered, then gave a command he'd never issued before: "Prepare to board!"

On *Lamia*'s deck, a young woman was hauling on a rope as they drew closer. On the other end, KO hung onto a lifesaver ring for all he was worth.

"That's our witness!" Mankiller told the harbor sergeant.

"Pull up to the far side!" the sergeant ordered the helmsman. "We don't want to suck him into the prop."

KO was ten feet from the swimming platform at the back of the boat when he suddenly went under and a gasping Marty popped up, holding KO around the chest, pinning his arms to his side. KO got his face up for one quick gulp before he and Marty disappeared beneath the water.

Ruiz's track coach would have been impressed with her standing long jump. She was first onto the boat, rushing to the far side with her gun drawn in one continuous movement.

Bubbles and froth marked the site of the battle, but neither combatant surfaced. Ruiz thrust the gun into Mankiller's hands as he caught up.

"Hold this," she said, then fumbled with her tactical vest before ripping it off and leaping out into the dark, cold water of the Chesapeake Bay.

Ruiz landed beside the circle of bubbles, nearly overcome by the shock of the water before taking a deep breath and diving beneath the froth. The brackish water stung her eyes as she squinted and saw dim, struggling forms beneath her. She grabbed at the first within reach and began hauling it up.

She surfaced with a limp KO clutched in one hand and snatched the ring with the other.

"Pull, *pendejos*, pull!" she cried.

Mankiller hauled them to the side and around to the swimming platform just as Marty emerged from beneath it with a roar, grabbing Ruiz from behind in a chokehold. She jerked her head back into his nose—and they went under.

Mankiller yanked KO onto the platform, looking back in time to see Ruiz resurface alone. Five feet away, the water broke, and Marty made for her again. Mankiller pulled his gun ...

Shit! Snow and spray filled his vision as the deck rocked, threatening to hurl him into the water alongside them. He couldn't shoot, or he might hit Ruiz.

He cursed as he ground his teeth, desperate for an opening.

Ruiz trod water, waiting for Marty's advance like she had all the time in the world. "Surrender, Mr. Hightower!" she gasped. "'S over!"

His face a mask of pain and rage, he said nothing as he drew nearer. At arm's length, he reached to grab Ruiz.

The Mace she fired flew into his snarling face.

He choked as the burning vapor burst into his mouth and eyes, thrashed at the silky water wrapping around his throat, and Ruiz saw the panic in the eyes of Martin Hightower as, this time, Death came for *him*, his mouth wrenched in a final, silent scream as he disappeared behind the bubbling froth and was pulled beneath the cold, dark waves.

Mankiller holstered his gun and grabbed the ring. "Ruiz!" he cried as he threw it to her.

She dropped the Mace and thrust her right arm through the ring, locking her right hand with her left. She began shivering uncontrollably as the near-freezing water sucked her small body's heat out into the dark, hungry cold of the Chesapeake Bay. She couldn't feel her arms or legs anymore, and it took all her willpower to hang on until she was dragged alongside the platform.

She couldn't let go and take Mankiller's hand when he offered it to her, afraid she'd sink and never rise again. He grabbed her arm, and she was hauled roughly to land on the deck like a prize fish, soaked and shivering.

Ruiz tried to stand but almost staggered off the platform, so Mankiller threw her over his shoulder and carried her into the cockpit and down to the cabin below. Once there, he tore off her wet outer clothes and threw her into the bed, covering her in all the blankets there.

Her lips were blue, her stare confused, classic signs of hypothermia. Worse yet, Mankiller noticed she'd stopped shivering.

"Get KO down here!" he ordered to anyone who might hear.

Together, the Harbor Police Sergeant and Mankiller jostled a stripped-down KO next to Ruiz beneath the blankets together, but even with the cabin heaters blasting they were increasingly unresponsive.

Mankiller turned to the woman who'd guided KO down. "You his daughter?"

"I am."

"He needs you right now. Needs your body heat." He nodded toward the bed. "They both do."

"Gotcha." She nodded, shed her jacket, and slipped between the two human popsicles, wrapping an arm around each. "You getting us home?"

"All of us," Mankiller promised, then hurried up to the deck where the drone pilot, Thompson, waited.

"Any sign of our perp?" the harbor police sergeant asked his man as he joined Mankiller in the saloon/cockpit.

"Nothing. The Mace probably made him swallow some seawater and finished him."

"Too bad," Mankiller said. "I'd like to have questioned him to clear out some cold cases, but I'm not sorry he's dead. Can one of your men drive this boat back to the harbor, Sergeant? This is a floating crime scene, so we'll need to limit further contamination as much as possible. And radio ahead to have two ambulances ready when we get back."

"Can do, Detective. You gonna stay on board or come back with me?"

"I'm staying here. Time to put my army survival training to use."

"Right. Thompson, you got the helm. Get them to the dock nearest Johns Hopkins as soon as I get off!"

A Coast Guard boat arrived as *Lamia* took off at full speed for the harbor. After a brief conversation between them and Harbor Patrol, a rescue swimmer went over the side with an underwater searchlight.

Mankiller didn't look back as the pleasure boat churned the water, a phrase from the gospels coming to mind, "Let the dead bury the dead," he murmured, his focus on the living.

He went down to check on the two swimmers. KO was shivering enough to shake Amy with him, but Ruiz was unmoving, her breathing shallow. Mankiller took her pulse from her neck when he couldn't find it in her wrist.

Forty-five. Bad.

He rushed up to the galley and filled the largest pot he could, trying not to spill the water from the tap in the rocking boat as it fought its way to the harbor.

"Tell the Harbor Patrol boat to go ahead of us with the siren on and the lights flashing!" he ordered Thompson at the helm. "We've got to make some time! And tell the ambulances to have heated blankets!"

"Will do, Sergeant."

At the stovetop, he heated the water short of boiling, then stopped the sink before pouring the water into it. Grabbing a handful of towels from a drawer, he plunged them into the water, soaking up as much water as he could, then rushed back below decks.

"How you holding up, Amy?" he asked. She nodded, shivering herself as he wrapped a towel around Ruiz's neck, then around each hand to the elbow. He put the last around KO's neck. The ex-boxer was shivering but alert, his larger body size protecting him better from the cold than Ruiz's slender frame.

Mankiller remembered the hands and feet were where arteries ended and veins began, so the quickest way to get warmed blood back into the body's core was to warm those areas. The hot towels on the neck would warm the blood going directly to the brain and stimulate breathing.

It was all he could do. Now it was up to the men at the helms to get them to help in time. The brutal north wind hurled them back into the harbor as night joined the snow in covering the city.

Chapter Forty-Three

Jan. 28, Wednesday, cont.

Mankiller made to climb into the back of the ambulance with Ruiz, but the paramedic took one look at her and said, "Get out! I'm gonna need all the room I can get."

"No problem," Mankiller said. He jumped into the passenger seat up front as the ambulance accelerated into the dark, snowy night, lights flashing, as fast as the driver dared.

At the ER, Ruiz and KO were promptly swarmed by people in white coats armed with pointy things.

"I can't get their body temperatures to read on my thermometer!" a red-haired male intern cried.

"Their temps are too low for a clinical thermometer," a senior female doctor said. "Get the two from the lab they use for the water baths—*now!*"

The young man sped away.

"What's going on?" Mankiller said. "Do you people know what you're doing?"

"You, *out!*" the lady doctor ordered. "Or I'll give you a shot of Haldol and knock you out!"

Mankiller knew when he was outranked, and he trudged wearily to the waiting area, his night far from over. Better let the lieutenant know some Very Important People in Baltimore society were about to have one of their own accused posthumously of being a serial killer. Better the lieutenant tell the mayor before the press got wind of this.

***

Amy's temperature was accessible on a normal thermometer and registered a frigid but tolerable ninety-five. She was wrapped in heated blankets with a shiny foil covering.

KO's temperature read ninety-two, necessitating a special rubber blanket filled with circulating hot water and an IV with heated fluid.

Ruiz's temp was ninety. Her lack of shivering and low responsiveness also earned her a rubber blanket and a heated IV. The red-haired intern was about to insert a catheter to irrigate the bladder with warm water when he felt a strong grip through his hospital scrubs in a place that got his immediate attention.

"You ain't shoving that thing where I think you want to shove it, *muchacho*," Ruiz croaked. "Or you're gonna have a life-changing experience."

Later in the medical record, the intern noted, "Catheter deferred, per patient request."

***

Maybe justice was blind, but campaign donors were not, and the chief needed to keep the mayor in the loop for the inevitable calls he'd get from the people who invested in politicians. Mankiller was glad he wasn't the one who'd have to call the top of the food chain.

He'd just gotten off the phone with his lieutenant when the Harbor Patrol sergeant called. The Coast Guard located Marty's remains before it got too dark to call off the search. Someone from the team would have to attend the autopsy, if only to confirm the identity. Mankiller looked back through the entrance to the treatment area, then phoned the ME's office, leaving word that he'd represent the department. "Fingerprint the body and send a copy to Forensics ASAP so they can do a sweep of the boat tonight," he ordered before hanging up.

He wouldn't mind the sight of that bastard lying on one of the same tables his victims had been placed on. Moments like that reaffirmed his faith in justice.

While waiting for someone in the treatment area to update him, Mankiller called the leader of the forensic team who would board the boat. "We have a ton of circumstantial evidence, but since our perp can't confess, we need something concrete to tie him to the murders so we can give the families closure," he instructed. *And protect the department from any lawsuits his wealthy father might want to throw at us to protect his son's name.*

Finally, the senior doctor came out and glared at him, then motioned to follow her back in, where he saw a pale Ruiz under the rubber blanket with tubes circulating warm water.

"How you doing, Ruiz?"

Her eyes fluttered open. She nodded toward the rubber blanket over her. "I gotta get me one of these, *Jefe*." Then her eyes closed, and her face sagged in sleep. He looked at her and marveled how such a small woman could be so tough.

The doctor herded him toward the exit. "She'll be fine, Sergeant. We'll move her and Mr. Bannon upstairs to the ICU in about an hour. They were lucky, especially your detective. She could have died from cardiac arrest." Then the doctor added grudgingly, "You did a good job keeping her alive in the field before she got here. Just don't try to run my ER again and we'll get along fine."

"But what about—"

"We have your number and will call you if anything changes. Visiting hours start at nine."

"Right, Doc. Thanks. For everything. Sorry about the unorthodox, uh ..."

"Don't mention it, Detective. I've seen worse. At least we haven't had to drag you out ... yet."

Mankiller nodded and beat a strategic retreat.

Chapter Forty-Four

Jan. 29, Thursday, 10:00 a.m.

R uiz and KO were assigned adjoining rooms, or what Ruiz called "VIP suites." Their body temperatures had recovered, but being that cold for that long was known to cause irregular heartbeats for a couple of days as the body chemistry sorted itself out, and they were kept an additional night as a precaution.

Mankiller went straight to the morgue the next morning. The sight of Marty's body on a slab made even the jovial Dr. Hamera a little happier than usual. There were still plenty of predators out there, but the streets of Baltimore would be a little safer tonight.

In his book, that counted as a win.

From there, he went to the hospital to share the good news.

"Ruiz, if it were in my power, I'd name you the founding member of the Puerto Rican Polar Bear Club," he said. "I hope you have your acceptance speech ready."

"What was it Sherman said? 'If nominated, I will not run; if elected, I will not serve'? If it's up to me, *Jefe*, from now on my only experience with ice will be in a frosted glass with a paper umbrella, thank you very much."

"It should have been me that jumped in."

"Bullshit, *Jefe*. You'd have tried to use your strength, and he'd have killed you. I knew he was stronger than me, so I used my lifeguard training. Plus, I couldn't have hauled you aboard the way you did me. It was the right call. Besides," she said with a wink. "I didn't want to share the collar. He was my first case as a detective, and I'd be damned if I'd let you take the credit." She sighed. "I hate to admit it, but you were right. It was worth putting KO through all this. We got our man."

He shook his head. "We got lucky. The perp could have killed KO and his daughter, sunk the boat, and we'd be hard-pressed to prove anything. You were right to doubt me. I was being the big bad wolfhound."

"So sometimes we sheepdogs get it right?"

"Don't push your luck," he said, grinning, "but yeah. I think I need a ..."

"Don't dare say poodle!"

Mankiller's phone rang before he could answer, and Ruiz started to drift off while he talked, just enjoying being warm and ... well, warm.

His grin when he hung up made her notice the small lines around his eyes. *He should smile more*, she considered.

She wanted to drift off just like this when he shook her gently.

"We got him, Ruiz. You got him."

"What? 'Course I did. You think I'd jump into a frozen ocean and *not* get him?"

"Yeah, there's that, but I mean forensics found something on his boat. A print from one of our floaters. The one KO saw."

Ruiz bolted upright. "Damn! *Jefe*, I got a huge favor to ask."

Mankiller almost said, "Anything," but his sanity returned in time. "What is it?"

"Okay, two actually. First, I want to be the one to tell KO. You owe it to me."

He nodded. "You're right, I do. After what I put the two of you through in the interrogation room, that's only fair. What's the second thing?"

"When we're off-duty, call me Maria."

He made a show of looking at his watch. "Agreed ... Maria."

Chapter Forty-Five

Jan. 29, cont.

Mankiller wheeled a grinning Maria Esperanza Ruiz into KO's room, only to find there was barely space for another visitor. Father Tomas, Teddy, and Amy were all sitting around KO's bed. There was even a big shiny teddy bear balloon, from Teddy, of course, with "GET WELL SOON!" emblazoned across its chest in big red letters.

"All these smiles," Ruiz said, adding her own to the collection, "there's gotta be chocolate here somewhere."

"Uh-oh, cops are here," Teddy said. "We're busted!"

Mankiller turned to KO. "We found some brass knuckles on the deck," he said and pretended not to notice Teddy's wince. "In this case, no one's going to say anything," Mankiller added. "In fact, I'm glad you had them. But just a friendly warning, you could be arrested for carrying them. I'll give them back to you once the investigation is complete. From what I saw at the morgue, you made good use of them."

"I'm sorry, Detective," Father Tomas said. "KO borrowed them from me." He smiled as all heads turned toward him. "Confession can sometimes become ... confrontational."

A long silence followed before Mankiller found his voice again. "Right. Sure, Father. How you doing, KO?" he asked, sticking out his hand. "You took a hell of a beating, but you didn't give up."

KO looked up at the detective and noticed his face was no longer hard. He took his hand. "Well, good thing I got a lot of experience getting my ass whipped," he said.

Mankiller squeezed the old fighter's hand once before letting go. "Yeah, but you also learned how to get back up." He looked at Amy, Teddy, and Father Tomas sitting around the bed. "Looks like you got back up to stay this time."

"We'll make sure of that," Amy said.

"I have some good news to share," Ruiz said, locking her eyes on KO. "They found fingerprints on Marty's boat that match those of the murdered woman you saw in the water. You did it, KO. He'll never kill again."

"Praise God," Father Tomas said.

"Amen," said Amy. "I'm proud of you, Dad. You came. For. Me," she added, tapping him on the nose three times.

KO focused with all his might, engraving Amy's words and her look of pride into his heart.

Chapter Forty-Six

Jan. 30, Friday

After lengthy negotiations with her family, Ruiz convinced them to limit the delegation to sign her out to one brother and sister on the condition they bring her straight to her mother's house.

Mankiller sat in his office and looked out the window as the sun finally returned. Between the investigation and the weather, his cupboard was getting pretty bare, and he had some comp time coming his way. As he waited for the clock to reach noon, he decided to write out a shopping list.

Looking into his desk for some lined paper, he saw his old Saint Christopher in a tray. He pulled it out, hefted it, and slowly put it back on. *I guess you're a traveler until you're where you belong.*

He looked at his list with a nagging feeling he was forgetting something. After some thought, he added, "cocoa."

Chapter Forty-Seven

May 2, Saturday morning

KO only returned to Hightower Securities to turn in his badge and collect his final paycheck. Gladys seemed genuinely sorry to see him go and retired soon after, her final task complete. The following month, she moved to a senior community on the edge of Las Vegas, only to discover they no longer allowed smoking in the casinos. She learned how to bluff while chewing (nicotine) gum.

A nurse in the ICU learned of KO's former fame as a prizefighter. One phone call led to another, and soon he was leading boxing for fitness classes at the local Y, teaching two classes a day, five days a week. It took a few months of regular food and exercise, but within the year his Y instructor polo shirts fitted him well.

***

"Breakfast is ready," Amy called. "Come get it while it's hot!"

"Yes, Mommy," Taylor said, scampering in from the living room, his small eyes shining at the sight of a table laden with pancakes, syrup, and bacon.

After a rapid but heartfelt grace, the family settled down for the feast before them.

"Pass the pancakes, please, Grandpa," said Taylor.

KO did as he was asked, his heart full. He felt like a king, restored at last to his rightful place. A place where he was needed.

The place where he needed to be.

The end

Afterword

Arabbers

These fresh fruit and vegetable vendors, once common sights in most major cities along the East Coast, are now only found in Baltimore, and they proudly fight to preserve this ancient African American tradition of horse-drawn cart vendors serving their own communities. When we began this project, we feared that they had become extinct, but a recent article, dated June 2021 (see link below), documents how they served their community during the COVID crisis, allowing people with limited transportation and means to supplement their diet with healthy, locally sourced food.

"The Baltimore tradition of arabbers (pronounced A-rabbers) dates back shortly after the city's founding in 1729, and today's closely knit group of arabbers is the last of the door-to-door food merchants in urban America.

"James Chase is a third-generation arabber who manages and runs the Fremont Avenue stables in west Baltimore's Sandtown Winchester neighborhood. He is president of the Arabber Preservation Society, the undisputed leader of the arabbers, and can be considered a national hero for what he and his arabbers did during the height of the COVID-19 crisis."

https://afro.com/securingthebag-arabbers-fill-food-void-in-baltimore/
(Article used here with permission.)

State-Dependent Learning

Co-author Bradley Harper first learned of this condition in medical school, and it is a well-documented, though unreliable, phenomenon in which a person must return to a similar level of alcohol or drug that was in their system when the memory was encoded to recall it. I say unreliable as there is no guarantee that returning to the prior physiologic state will allow the memory to be retrieved, but the idea has lingered for decades as a foundation for a story.

For more information, please refer to the link below.

https://counselorssoapbox.com/2012/10/15/what-is-state-dependent-learning-memory-problems/

Emergency Treatment of Hypothermia

While a medical student, Brad helped resuscitate two boys who had fallen through the ice on a pond. When they first arrived, their body temperatures were too low to register on the clinical thermometers in the ER, and Brad was dispatched to retrieve two thermometers from the lab. Within two hours, they were wondering how much trouble they were in with their parents, after being told not to walk on the ice the day before, and the clinical staff knew they'd recover just fine (at least while under *their* care!).

Mankiller

Our Cherokee detective is named in honor of Wilma Mankiller, the first elected female Principal Chief of the Cherokee Nation of Oklahoma. During her tenure, she spearheaded the tribe's economic development and established a robust health service, which has recently provided the tribal community exemplary support during the COVID pandemic. Her lifelong commitment to serving and protecting her tribe was recognized after her death in 2010 by the Presidential Medal of Freedom, our nation's highest honor bestowed upon civilians.

Those interested in learning more about her are referred to her autobiography, *Mankiller: A Chief and Her People.*

For her example to all of us who come after, we say, "*wado.*" Thank you.

Thanks
for reading

Thank you for purchasing and reading this book. We hope you enjoyed it.

Remember *Fifty Shades of Grey*? 'Twas good ol' word of mouth that spread the word for that. It's *you*, the *readers*, who are the lifeblood of publishing. Honest reviews encourage readers to check out and buy books, and sales enable writers to write the stories you read ... Simple!

So, if you did enjoy the story, please consider letting others know, won't you? A brief review—even just a line or two—& rating on the site from which you bought the book, e.g., Amazon, and/or Goodreads can mean so much to authors and independent publishers.

About the Authors

Bradley Harper

When an Army Pathologist retires, naturally he goes back to school to get degrees in writing ...

Bradley Harper is a retired US Army Colonel and pathologist with extensive experience in autopsies and forensic investigation. Along with clinical experience, he had four commands, and is the only non-Italian to ever receive the Knights of Malta award for his support of the Italian Army. A lifelong fan of Sherlock Holmes, upon retirement he received his associate degree in creative writing from Full Sail University, to help him write his first book *A Knife in the Fog* that he'd always wanted to read. A life-long fan of Sherlock Holmes, he did intensive research for his debut novel, which involved a young Doctor Conan Doyle in the hunt for Jack the Ripper, including a trip to London's East End with noted Jack the Ripper historian Richard Jones.

A Knife in the Fog was published in October 2018 and was a finalist for a 2019 Edgar Award by the Mystery Writers of America for Best First Novel by an American Author and is a Recommended Read by the Arthur Conan Doyle Estate.

Knife went on to win Killer Nashville's 2019 Silver Falchion as Best Mystery. The audio book, narrated by former Royal Shakespearean actor Matthew Lloyd Davies, won Audiofile Magazine's 2019 Earphone award for Best Mystery and Suspense. The book is also available in Japan via Hayakawa Publishing.

Brad's second novel, *Queen's Gambit*, involving a fictional assassination attempt on Queen Victoria, won Killer Nashville's 2020 Silver Falchion Award twice, once for Best Suspense and again as Book of the Year.

In October 2022, Brad received his master's degree in creative writing from Napier University in Edinburgh, Scotland. His animation, *Dark Tryst*, won Best Super Short Film at the Paris Film Festival in January 2023, and Best Experimental Film at a festival in Bali.

Find out more about Brad's projects and check out his newsletter at bharperauthor.com.

BIBLIOGRAPHY:
- *A Knife in the Fog*, Seventh Street Books, 2018
- *Queen's Gambit*, Seventh Street Books, 2019
- *Dark Tryst* (animation), released in January 2023

Lydia Galehouse

Lydia Galehouse is an American currently living in Japan, where she edits homework, drinks green tea, and cooks fancy curry. She's been writing stories since she could write, but finally got around to doing so professionally when her friend Brad Harper had an excellent idea for a plot.

Lydia can be contacted c/o Papillon du Père Publishing

Also Available from
Papillon du Père Publishing

13 by 11

Thirteen short stories by
eleven award-winning and up-and-coming authors

"*13 by 11* excels in strong images and depictions that provide much food for thought."

– D. Donovan, senior reviewer *Midwest Book Review*

Features 4 entries by Bradley Harper, including

Dark Tryst
(text version of his graphic novel and award-winning short film)

Dark Tryst II

Yoyo Man

13 by 11

Part ONE encounters life both within and outside of the earthly realm. Stories by Vincent Czyz and Derek McFadden ask readers to consider the ties that bind and define us in our earthly existence, with tragic, yet hopeful, tales of loss and love.

Part TWO visits characters at different stages of life: childhood, early adulthood, and parenthood. Jeffrey Kahrs's charming vignette journeys back to a childhood incident and its effects—both immediate and lasting—on family dynamics, while Caroline Scott introduces us to two teens embarking on adulthood while coping with the pressure of their pasts. Erol Engin warns us how the first child—and Steve Jobs—can change a marriage, leading to competition and vicarious coping, shall we say.

Be careful what you wish for in **part THREE**, where enticing temptation meets delicious pleasure, but at what cost? Your life? Your soul? Bradley Harper's dark, tantalizing poems wrap around Lilla Glass's unfurling tale of hunter and prey ... and hunter, before Harper spins a whodunit, with a dash of whimsy and perhaps time travel, if the detective's client is to be believed.

Part FOUR transports readers to other spaces. Harriet James shows the futility of resisting the spark of attraction in a charged love-across-the-divides spec-fiction story. Carla Rehse whisks us off to outer space, where we find two partners, divided in a way we could never imagine, fleeing from a Church determined to part them. Will Knight's dialogue-driven diary tale looks for smiles as it touches on hope vs. reality, even as we wonder what the space of that reality is.

The anthology concludes in **part FIVE** by considering loss. Bradley Harper's short passage here is a true story of loss of life, while Greg Gerke brings the collection to a close on a pensive note as he describes a gradual loss of self, finding that travel does not necessarily enrich the soul.

Enjoy this delightful mix of award-winning and up-and-coming authors. Together, they blend literary, historical, speculative, mystery, and romantic fiction with a dash of light sci-fi thrown in ... with stories all centering on connection to others—in life, in death, in school, in families, in space, in cyberspace. Even in France.

"Readers seeking a literary anthology filled with satisfying revelations and unexpected forays into other worlds will find *13 by 11* a uniformly powerful collection where each piece shines. Another plus is that one can start anyplace in the book to choose a standout piece...there is no linear progression to stories, allowing for reader flexibility."

– D. Donovan, senior reviewer *Midwest Book Review*

- Vincent Czyz received the 2016 Eric Hoffer Award for Best in Small Press for *Adrift in a Vanishing City*.

- Erol Engin's *The Sea Monkeys* won the Page Seventeen Short Story Contest in 2012.

- Lilla Glass earned a Silver Honorable Mention in the Writers of the Future Winter 2021 Quarter competition for her short story *Best Spuds*.

- Bradley Harper's debut, *A Knife in the Fog*, was a finalist for a 2019 Edgar Award by the Mystery Writers of America for Best First Novel by an American Author and won Killer Nashville's 2019 Silver Falchion as Best Mystery. The sequel, *Queen's Gambit*, won Killer Nashville's 2020 Silver Falchion Award twice—for both Best Suspense and Book of the Year.

- Derek McFadden's *What Death Taught Terrence* was a 2021 Next Generation Indie Book Award Finalist and a Silver Medal winner at the 2021 Wishing Shelf Book Awards.

The Bells of Christmas Series

Bradley Harper et al.

"Christmas Joy!"

"A wonderful collection of 8 Christmas stories in one book... Feel good stories that warm the heart."

"The Bells of Christmas II is a beautiful selection of short Christmas stories."

– Amazon 5-star reviews -

Features 3 entries by Bradley Harper

The Bells of Christmas, A Winter Candle,
and *What Santa Has Taught Me*
(essay on Brad's experiences as a real-life Santa Claus)

The Bells of Christmas II

"Roll up, roll up, folks! Hear ye, read ye ... these eight stupefying stories we have for you upon this year's yuletide. Come one, come all for tidings of Christmas hope! Savor these dainty dramas and delight in delicious darkness fantastical, with all sure to enchant readers aplenty this holiday season!

"Come, good gentlefolk, as we alight gently on December 24th, the last sleep before Christmas! In Bradley Harper's *The Bells of Christmas*, the midnight carols have echoed off into the night as Julius slumbers beneath his bleak blanket, nestled in the bowels of the homeless shelter. A visitor will arrive to make his Christmas wish come true in a most unexpected way...

"Beware, have a care! For Derek McFadden is back among the ghosts in *The Last Christmas Gift*, in which Travis is on the edge of despair while on a most unexpected boat ride. Look yonder, good gentlefolk, for there, just boarding... surely not Pops, his beloved grandfather departed these twenty years hence...?

"Now, light ye all *A Winter Candle* as we partake of Bradley Harper's telling of Ben, newly retired from the military. What is an old soldier to do when he feels his family is lost to him? Why, folks, become a Santa Claus, of course! But who is it that detects the faintest flicker of hope in his heart? I tell you, someone up North is watching...

"But lo! Not all these gifts within are fiction. Oh, no, good folks! For within, there sit true-life encounters too. Hear Bradley Harper recount fact stranger than fiction! Hear ye what he's learned in *What Santa Has Taught Me*, an essay of experiences as a real-life Santa Claus.

"Good people, come close... let me whisper this to ye... Who among us didn't love Christmases when we were all but wee wildlings? Ah, then relive the magic of your childhood in Maria O'Rourke's *Calling Us Home* as she lovingly recalls the magic of Irish Christmases of yore, where enchantment and excitement were magic unto themselves!

"Will Knight's *The Bear's Last Word (on the Matter)* fairly hales at the heartstrings in this final pull of Christmas crackers for one lad's special childhood friend at the "Bears Cares Home." With one last Christmas together, are their adventures truly concluded?

"And now, I ask you all, fair folk: dare you encounter the bitter-sweetness of *The Sugar Plum Redux*? Lilla Glass gifts us a fantastical fae, a tenebrous telling of The Nutcracker from a very different point of view...

"Ah, but all good things... Yet still one last journey, fair folk, where we must ask ourselves if Gus is not the hero in his own story, then who can it be? Andy, the 'real' and righteous writer? Or perhaps Daphne, the nonconformist neighbor? Before we reach journey's end, Erol Engin will show us how even the most selfish and insecure can provide a Christmas miracle in *A Tintoretto of the Soul*.

"Bless you, one and all, for your forbearance! Click ye yonder 'buy now' button and may your generous soul bequeath donations desired by that most worthy and hearty of hospitals, St Jude! For, above all, 'tis surely the season for children. For who among us deserves magic more than they?"

Award-winning authors **Bradley Harper**, **Derek McFadden**, and **Erol Engin** lead this seasonal collection of magical storytelling, with 100% of profits from sales going to St. Jude Children's Research Hospital.

The Bells of Christmas II features Bradley Harper's flash-fiction story and his essay previously published in *The Bells of Christmas.*

100% *of profits*
made on the sales of this book go to
St. Jude Children's Research Hospital.

St. Jude Children's
Research Hospital
Finding cures. Saving children.

Mystery, adventure, and romance
from **Shea Adams**

Monica Wade, Private Investigator, Mystery Series

"I was hooked from the first page. Kept me wanting more."
– Amazon 5-star review –

1. The Ashbee Cove Murders
2. The Perfect Stranger
3. The Art of Murder: The Shadowman
4. Who Killed Rosemary Bud?

The Monica Wade, PI, Mystery Series features a strong female MC who takes the lead in dealing with danger, thugs, and murderers.

With its blend of adventure, mystery, and romance, the series is written to display warmth and wit so readers will enjoy spending time with the prime characters, Monica Wade and her best friend, the flamboyant Andy Weston.

Reminiscent of classic TV shows like *Hart to Hart*, *Remington Steele*, and *Moonlighting*.

Book 1
The Ashbee Cove Murders

A young father sits in the wheelhouse, going over maps of Ashbee Cove Lake. A young mother prepares dinner in the galley. Two young children run around their luxury yacht, playing Pirates of the Caribbean.

Shots fired from a handgun... A knife piercing innocent flesh...

Before dawn the next day, this family will be dead.

Why is the police force at Ashbee Cove so reluctant to talk?

Is it because of its sloppy investigation? Or is it something to do with an ancient Celtic cross discovered in the lake?

Enlisting the help of the town's coroner, Trevor Bowen, private detective Monica Wade sets out to find the link between the murders and the cross. But there is interest in her investigation: Irish mobsters are increasingly intent on acquiring the priceless artifact...

Book 2
The Perfect Stranger

"Well, isn't this just peachy! Now I'm involved with a couple of smugglers. Anything else I need to know?"

Is it fate or simply good fortune when Monica Wade meets Rick Dalton on the beach near her Malibu home?

When she agrees to join this intriguing stranger on a boat trip with his old friend Dutch Hammer, it's a decision that sets in motion a precarious chain of events. For Dutch has crossed his old boss, and now the cartel is hunting the three of them.

Monica must find herself again—find the resolve she'd all but lost—if she's to save all their lives as they set sail for Alaska... not entirely sure of what awaits them there.

Book 3
The Art of Murder: The Shadowman

Lies, shadows, and secrets. But who is really chasing whom?

Having returned from Alaska, following the events in *The Perfect Stranger*, a restless Monica Wade decides to move to the charming Township of Brooke, Oregon. Her best friend Andy Weston agrees to move with her, and they settle into their new homes and make new friends.

But Monica is forced to put retirement plans on hold when she needs to chase down a "shadowman" that has emerged to taunt and threaten her. But who is really chasing whom? And should Monica let Andy and the recently arrived Rick Dalton help?

One way or another, Monica will have to revise the rules of the Shadowman's game before there is another murder—her own...

Book 4
Who Killed Rosemary Bud?
The Haunting at Rosebud Manor

For eighty years they've asked, "Who Killed Rosemary Bud?"

St. Casis, California, 1942

The gala is almost underway at Rosebud Manor, the mansion perched atop the rocky cliffs over the Pacific Ocean. This yearly event brings the movers and shakers from all over the country, from both the entertainment world and the ever-changing world of politics. The gala is a fundraiser of sorts, with donations going to help underprivileged children around the globe.

But it will be the last gala of its kind at Rosebud Manor... The host, Miss Rosemary Bud, of the Bud Shipping Company, has fallen to her death. Or was she pushed...?

In the last entry in this cozy mystery & romance series, Monica Wade takes on a case of ghastly and ghostly complexity!

"Brings the series to a riveting close."

Cover design

PAPILLON DU PÈRE
PUBLISHING

www.papillon-du-pere.com

@PapillonPere

Copyediting

Jay Allchin
@ the Editing-Store.com

www.editing-store.com

Printed in the USA
CPSIA information can be obtained
at www.ICGtesting.com
JSHW011050300723
45626JS00001B/1